❦❧

Set in the Pacific Northwest around the turn of the twentieth century, this story of a prodigal, and the family who loved her, will feed your soul and warm your heart. I didn't want to stop reading.

 —MARION DUCKWORTH, author of *Naked on God's Doorstep*

Jen Hren,
Get your kleenex
ready. Merry Christmas!
Aunt Sharon

Jen,
Hope you enjoy the story!
God bless you!
Linda Reinhardt :·

REALITY FICTION™
Faith Meets Imagination

Like a Bird WANDERS

BOOK ONE
The McLeod Family Saga

Sharon Bernash Smith / Rosanne Croft / Linda Reinhardt

*A story so powerful,
it took three authors to tell it.*

OAKTARA

WATERFORD, VIRGINIA

Like a Bird Wanders

Published in the U.S. by:
OakTara Publishers
P.O. Box 8
Waterford, VA 20197

Visit OakTara at
www.oaktara.com

REALITY FICTION™ *Faith Meets Imagination* is a registered trademark of
Sharon Bernash Smith.

"What Do You Say to a King" (pp. 213-215) was first published by
Clubhouse Jr., Focus on the Family, December, 2006.

Cover design by David LaPlaca/debest design co.
Cover image, bird © iStockphoto.com/Oleg Prikhodko
Author photos: Sharon Bernash Smith, © 2008 Will Smith; Rosanne
Croft, © 2008 Bill Burns; Linda Reinhardt, © 2008 Katrina Baxter.

Scripture is taken from The King James Version of the Bible.

ISBN: 978-1-60290-145-2

DEDICATED TO

All who long for a prodigal's homecoming: May your wait be a hopeful expectation for the working of God's grace.
    —SHARON BERNASH SMITH (writing as Eva Jo McLeod Ehlers)

Those dear ones who leave and think they cannot return. Come back. You are loved!
    —ROSANNE CROFT (writing as Grace Rose McLeod)

To those you love who are lost. May their eyes be turned back to the incredible love Jesus has for them.
    —LINDA REINHARDT (writing as Nettie Louise McLeod)

Acknowledgments

I want to thank all who have encouraged me to continue my writing pursuits...those who believed, even when I doubted myself...especially Carrole Rude. Thank you, Linda, and Rosanne, for being strong women of God. Without you, and your determination to finish this book with me, the McLeod family's story would not have been told. Just like Eva Jo, Gracie, and Nettie, we are bound by the love of Jesus, truly sisters in His name. I'm a better person and writer because of our time together.

Thanks to Oregon Christian Writers for the many training workshops and conferences. All you do reflects the Lord. And thank you, Betty, for your commitment to excellence in everything you do. Having you for a friend blesses me.

Thank you, Focus on the Family, for first publishing the Christmas story from this book, "What Do You Say to a King?," in December, 2006, within *Clubhouse Jr.* magazine. It was a dream-come-true.

A huge thank you, OakTara, for taking a chance on the "new kids." Your faith to lend a much-needed hand is humbling.

Most of all, thank You, Lord, for the ability to serve you through the written word. May Your truth flow through the pages of Reality Fiction™ always. I am your grateful daughter.—SHARON BERNASH SMITH

Early encouragement was all I needed to pursue my dream to write. I thank my father, Tom Black, for filling the house with mountains of books. I also thank my Mom, Monica Mark Black, who wrote stories of her own, while raising five children. We can always talk about books together.

What a rare privilege to bond with two women like Sharon Bernash Smith and Linda Reinhardt, true sisters who are jewels among jewels. We found out what blood, sweat, and tears were all about! Thanks for bringing out the best in me and for being so much fun.

Thanks to my husband, Ray, who long ago asked me about my dream in life. Being a get-it-done guy, he held me accountable to use my gifts. My beloved daughter, Caeli, is a constant source of inspiration and joy to me. Thank you for believing in me, Caeli.

I would like to thank friends in my critique groups: Stanley Baldwin, Jeanne St. John Taylor, Barbara Martin, Lise Buell, Betty Ritchie, and Helen Haidle. Oregon Christian Writers was such a help to me. I went home from seminars uplifted.

Thank you, Ramona Tucker, Jeff Nesbit, and everyone at OakTara. You gave wings to our feet and slew the giant of publishing for us. Most of all, you loved our story.

Jesus is the heart of this story, and I thank Him for the grace that covers all sin and love that is unconditional. May He bless those who read this book. May His beloved lost children be drawn back to Him, and His redeeming love for them.—ROSANNE CROFT

I'd like to thank my best friend, my husband, Ben Reinhardt, for supporting me with a faith that says, "If you hear God telling you to do it, then do it." No matter how hard life gets, you continually point me to follow this dream to write that God has put in my heart. My sweet daughter, Sarrah, thank you for letting "Mommy" have writers' group time and for the time we spend creating stories together. Thank you, Sharon Bernash Smith and Rosanne Croft, for including me in this project. I love the memories that come from working together creating "a year in the life of the McLeod family." We began creating a story about three sisters and somewhere during the process bonded as sisters ourselves. You're two beautiful women of God, and I've gleaned so much wisdom from the two of you.

Speaking of sisters, I need to thank the "Sister Bluethreads" of my life, Brenda Connors and Lorinda Cheek, who are true prayer warriors. Thank you to my sister bluethreads' Bible study and the prayer team at Living Hope church.

Thanks to my parents, Cal and Margaret, for reading my stories when I was young. Your enjoyment spurred me to write another story, poem, or song. Also, thank you for having one-on-one time with Sarrah so I could go to writers group. Thank you to my sister, Wanda Krause, who continually cheers me on. My brothers, Wayne and Gary, and their wives, Julie and Karen, thank you for encouraging me toward my goals.

Also, thank you, Chris White, Kim Ferris, Lise Buell, and all of those who prayed for this project and gave their input. Thank you, Katrina Baxter, for taking my photo.

Thank you, OakTara, for allowing us this opportunity and the work that you have put into making our dream and call come to fruition.

Most of all, thank You God, for the many gifts you have given to me, for blessing my life with the knowledge of how much you love me. Thank You for filling my heart and mind full of stories I'm compelled to tell and for blessing me with those mentioned above. May you bless them and those who read this story incredibly.—LINDA REINHARDT

❦

Like a bird wandereth from her nest
so is a man who wandereth from his home.

—PROVERBS 27:8 KJV

One

She was dying. No doctor's diagnosis or tool of medicine had revealed it, but she knew the Master would be taking her home soon. Total comfort and peace surrounded the thought. Yet a nagging in her spirit told her there was something left undone.

Grace Rose McFarlane knew that after seventy years of walking with the Lord, there was no mistaking this urging that came from above. She smiled at His persistence; for even after all this time, the ways God manifested Himself in the daily workings of earthly life were amazing.

Grace's hand trembled as she sat her coffee cup onto the oil-cloth table. Ignoring the small stain gathering underneath, she admired the large, hand-thrown mug. Covered with dazzling gold stars, celebrated on rich cobalt, it was an early Christmas gift from Julia.

"Ahhh." Instantly she knew. The "nagging" had to do with her great granddaughter. She reached for the letter she'd received several weeks before Julia had arrived from college for Christmas break.

Grace winced at the urgent throbbing up and down her left side. She found it difficult to hold the paper steady while reading again the details of Julia's campus life.

December 7, 1966
Dear Gran,
Guess what? I'm going to be staying with you during Christmas break. I know you don't need anyone there, but I miss you. Know what else I've been missing??? Your cinnamon rolls...can we make

some? I've got a tad bit of school left before I'm all yours. Maybe we can go Christmas shopping in Portland, just you and me. Or is it you and I? Now that I'm a college freshman, I should know that, right?

There's gobs to share...hardly know where to begin, but here goes. Remember how Grandpa Shep would take me fishing on the Lewis River? (He'd even wade into the water to unravel my hook.) Well, I have a boyfriend who took me steel head fishing on the Willamette River, just yesterday. His name is Michael Hanson. Most guys are after one thing, but not him! He really respects me, Gran. I think I could be serious about him.

Twenty-seven makes him an older student, but only because he's had to work his way through college. We met at the Mill Race, feeding the ducks and geese one day after cutting classes for fresh air. We had this instant connection thing going on, talking for hours before walking to Del Haus for ice cream. He's amazing!

Don't tell Mom this stuff, okay? She talks too much, but you listen to me about everything. Last night, I went to a party with Michael...we had a blast dancing to the Beatles. (You've heard of them...they're those long-haired guys from England.) Anyway, even though there was a lot of beer and drugs, you'd be proud to know I handled myself well. We stayed late talking about the revolting things going on in Viet Nam. There's a huge anti-war rally next month and Michael's asked me to march with him. He's that kind of man...always standing up for the underdog.

Actually, there are a lot of protesters on campus, and you wouldn't believe how they're treated by police. I mean, the cops have GUNS while the students have peace signs. That's not fair! Tomorrow I'm going to a sit-in...it's the only way to get through to the Establishment. Why should the politicians be sending young men to die in Vietnam when they don't even have the right to vote? War hawks! Please don't worry about me, Gran. My chances of getting arrested are slim. I'll be okay with Michael. Anyway, we're just standing for our rights...I'm sure you'd do the same if you were me. You're always saying how I remind you of yourself at this age.

I was sweating getting back in the dorm so far past curfew. I had to skip classes to sleep in. I'm seriously thinking of taking a lighter load next semester. We'll see.

Some people from here are heading to southern California to attend a multi-state, anti-war demonstration. Michael says I'm going with him, and believe me, I'm ready. He says I'll love the warm ocean there, and thinks I'll look great in a bikini...don't tell Mom! I'm picturing the two of us in sunny California, walking, talking, just being a couple together. There are lots of other girls who'd love to be me with Michael. He's that magnetic, Gran.

Even though Michael and I only met recently, it's like we've known each other forever. He just gets me. Has that ever happened to you? When I told him I wanted him to meet my family, he hinted I was part of HIS family. It's like that here...one big "family." He thinks our connection to the Chinook Indians is cool...asked lots of questions about Winnowett and Little Dove, when I mentioned them. He believes Indians need to be included in the Civil Rights Movement. Honestly, he's so deep. You can tell from what I'm sharing what kind of a person he is, right?

I'm looking forward to seeing you at Christmas. Being in Eugene is exciting, but I do miss home. I write Mom too, but she's absolutely so judgmental when she writes back. I'm not a child, and certainly not her little girl.

You've always been there for me, Gran...so understanding and all. I know you hoped I'd attend that small Christian college in Seattle, but I think now you can see that the U of O is perfect for me. Remember, not a word to Mom about my life here. I can't bear one more lecture. Come on...this is 1966...we're out of the dark ages.

Love and peace to you,
Julia

P.S. Don't change the sheets or anything. I'll do all the work. Remember, just you and me. I'll bring Michael's picture. He looks like a movie star...especially his eyes.

P.S.S. When I told Michael my middle name was Rose (after you), he nicknamed me "Rosebud." Isn't he romantic?!

Grace finished reading Julia's letter and clutched it to her pounding chest, small beads of perspiration glistening on her forehead.

"Oh my girl." She sighed, tears falling silently. Her mind raced backward in time to the memory of her own youthful sojourn. No, *youthful sojourn* sounded too pleasant. *Near fatal sin* rang truer.

"Lord, is history repeating itself? Please, not my Julia."

She spent precious energy fixing some food, reasoning it might make her feel better. Exhausted, she sat back down, bowing her head in thanks before eating her daily breakfast of oatmeal, lightly sweetened with honey gathered from Basket Flats.

"A simple meal for a simple gal," she'd said often enough.

"My, my, August, I'm sure I've bored people with that one." Her ancient companion meowed in response. "After all, who cares what an old woman has to eat...or say, for that matter."

Taking a small bite, she found the meal tasteless, and eating sapped waning strength. She pushed away from the table, using it for support while she stooped to stroke the cat maintaining his chairside vigil. Wherever Grace rested, there he sat. Lately that had been mostly on the sofa or the bed. She also picked up Julia's letter.

Grace hadn't felt well for over a week, daily getting weaker. At first she shrugged it off as the onset of winter flu...it was going around church. With such a small sanctuary, when someone from Yacolt Evangelical Church sneezed, the entire congregation was exposed. No, this weakness was more than the common cold. Even though she didn't trust the medical community much, she wasn't above seeking a physician, but now she reasoned, with complete abandon, that her "time" had come. Several years before, she'd suffered a serious heart attack, and believed that the damage done then was the cause of this decline now.

She had said nothing because family and friends would question her sanity if she confessed to not wanting treatment. Yet the sisters must have noticed something because she was sure it was their concern that placed Julia at Grace's for the last couple of nights.

"Just like when she was little, Augustus. Well, almost. Then her feet hit the floor before the rooster's crow."

Petting the cat one last time, she left the breakfast things for later. Headed down the hall to her bedroom, using the walls for support, Grace prayed with every labored step.

"Oh my Lord, help me, give me strength to complete whatever it is you want...I'm needing to rest."

Never had this hallway been so long. She paused at Julia's door, but heard nothing. When at last she'd made it to her bed, infirmity kept her from getting on her knees. The Lord wouldn't care. Pulling a quilt from the footbed, she eased down, relishing the comfort. Exhausted and wet with sweat, she closed her eyes.

"Lord, forgive me for not going to Your Word this morning. I'm…just…so…weak. I know you have a message, Father," she whispered." I'll just wait right here for you to speak. Right…here…."

⮜❧⮞

She was young, replete in the expectancy of youth, on a strangely familiar path, palm trees dotting the pleasant landscape. Continuing, she lifted her head when someone waving appeared near a bend.

Julia?

But how could this be since Grace seemed to be Julia's age? She waved in return. Walking towards one another they met with a warm embrace, though no words passed between them. Julia apparently did not notice the restored state of Grace's presence as the journey resumed. Compelled to speak, nothing came forth regardless of how many times she tried. Something extremely important needed to be shared, a warning of impending great and lasting harm that had to do with Julia.

Now the road began to change, their path narrowing with every step. Treacherous dank canyons, deep in darkness, appeared on either side. Danger stalked them and evil consumed the air, choking Grace's effort to breathe. She glanced at Julia, who seemed oblivious to it.

Grace tried getting her attention; she must flee! But Julia broke loose, casually nodding as she went.

Suddenly a huge lion appeared from thin air, hunched down between them, ready to spring. He looked directly at Grace, his mouth opened in a silent roar, while his shaggy head swung back and forth between her and Julia. She could feel his caustic breath, see the saliva dripping from gigantic fangs. Horror rose, choking out life, filling her lungs with the rancidness of the beast. She'd lost sight of Julia. Where was Julia?

A voice, strong with truth, echoed off the canyon walls. "The devil is a roaring lion, roaming the earth, seeking whom he may devour."

Again she tried to scream a warning, her mouth opening and closing with the exertion, while Julia walked onward to the distance.

Lord Jesus! Lord Jesus! her mind called out His name....

Grace jerked awake with the name of Jesus on her lips, damp hair clinging to her forehead and cheeks. The pounding inside her chest now filled the room until her head spun.

Lord, help me understand this dream.

She pushed to sit upright a bit, mopped her forehead with a corner of the quilt, then reached for the water glass beside the bed. She steadied it with two hands before taking a long hard sip. Her heart slowed some, though the ache in her left shoulder remained. "Julia needs help, I know it."

Exhausted but determined, she opened the drawer on the side table to remove a pad and pen. Grace would not let Julia make the same mistake she had, could not let her fall into the pit of deception that had threatened her life so long ago.

No energy...no time. Every written word became a monumental struggle. She managed six. Panting, she leaned for the phone, dragged it onto the bed, and dialed. Her entire body shook in response.

Misty images floated dreamlike in her mind...warm ocean breakers crashing onto dangerous shores, a maniacal face laughing from dark shadows, the plaintive wail of a newborn....

"Grace? Grace, I can't hear you. Are you there?"

"I'm here, Eva Jo. I...need you...now."

"What is it, Sister? You're sick. I'm calling Doc Brady."

"No. Eva Jo, listen. Get...the...letters." Pressure crushed down, each syllable forcibly spoken through sheer willpower.

"The letters, Grace? Every one?"

"Yes...Julia...needs to know...the truth. All of it. And...leave the locket."

"Gracie, don't you worry, Nettie and I will do whatever you want. We're on our way. We love you, Sister. We love you, Gracie."

"I...love...you," came out a faint whisper.

Her lips parted, making an effort to speak to the Heavenly presence filling the room. Resplendent color overflowed every square inch, penetrating minute fibers of Grace's being, even her closed lids. Fragmented rays, brilliant with opulence, bounced off each other, then mingled into jeweled shapes like the inside of a kaleidoscope. She opened her eyes, tried to raise her head. Too heavy. She so desired to reach out and touch the scarred hand extended to her, one chiseled perfectly like fine marble, emanating with the fullness of life. Peace pulsed in gentle undulations from the most exquisite being she'd ever encountered, while a fragrance, light as air, flowed sweetly to Grace's last repose.

"Jesus. I knew you'd come." Her eyes blinked several times, fluttering like autumn's last leaf...drifting...drifting... "I...love You...Jesus." A slow, final sigh imitated the familiar breath of the morning breeze delicately rocking the windchime outside her window. No sign of struggle remained—only the graceful reflection of peace, her soul now resting in the youth of eternity.

"Eva Jo, she's gone." Nettie choked out a sob. "Oh, my sweet, sweet Grace."

She shifted closer, laying her head on Grace's still chest. Nothing. She reached up to stroke her face, then the snow-white braid resting on the pillow. Lifting her sister's left hand, she pressed it firmly to her lips in a lingering kiss. She performed the exact ritual to the right one, inhaling the lavender scent, a reminder still, of their mother.

Eva Jo sat on the other side. "My Grace, I love you. You'll always be my sister, always. We'll do exactly what you've asked. Nettie, quick, let's pray before waking Julia. Then we'll straighten the bed like Sister would want."

"As sad as I am, I'm thinking our next reunion will be our eternal one, right, Eva Jo?"

"Amen and amen."

They ignored the incessant ringing of the phone in order to perform this last loving deed for the middle sister. In their preparations, they found the letter from Julia. Now understanding Grace's desperation, they'd work out the details of her last request later. God was in their midst.

Grace's note to Julia went unnoticed by Nettie and Eva Jo when it drifted to the floor to disappear under the bed.

Something interrupted Julia's sleep and she reached her arms overhead, stretching as far as she could. Punching a fresh spot in the feather pillow, she rolled over, ignoring morning's invitation. This ancient bed was still the ultimate in comfort, and Julia relished the idea of lingering under its covers forever...at least through Christmas break.

Tests were finished, books closed; time meant nothing. Oh yeah, except for one small thing. Where was she? Stuck in the thriving nothingness of Yacolt, Washington. Far, far away from any thing remotely resembling her new life. Frustrated, she wondered why she'd let herself be talked into staying at her great-grandmother's for the entire holiday. After all, there were parties, parties, and more parties she would have attended, in Eugene. And of course she'd miss the candlelight peace vigil on Christmas Eve.

"I love you, Gran, but this is not what I had in mind. Hmm...Julia Rose Gustin, the nursemaid? I think not."

Her mind skipped to Michael and she smiled. Thinking of Michael always made her smile. His presence gave her a new wonderment about life that sent shivers down her spine. This yearning could overwhelm her senses (and her morals) if she'd let it. Did he even know the power he had over her?

"I hope not," she said aloud. But deep down she wanted him to know everything about her.

A groan escaped her lips after glancing at the clock. Seven. Seven?

Too early. Snuggling further down, she intended to sleep until noon. The jangling of the phone caused her to groan again…one…two…three rings.

"Gran, pick up the phone," she muttered between clenched teeth. …four…five…

"Maybe I should answer. Gran might have gone somewhere." Julia threw back the covers, shoved her feet into slippers, then sprinted towards the door. It became a mission to reach the phone before its shrill ringing stopped. Whoever it was must know it takes Gran forever to answer. Man, it was cold.

"Hello!" Julia shouted, breathing hard. "Hello?" Nothing but dial tone. She swore, slamming it down, forgetting where she was.

Retrieving August, the cat who'd meandered to her side, she heard muffled sounds coming from Gran's room.

Gran was probably talking to herself again. Well, maybe praying. No, she heard two voices. She saw the bedroom door ajar. Touching it open a few more inches, she dropped the cat.

Her great-aunts were sitting on the bed, one on either side of Gran. "Gran?"

Julia's frantic cry startled Nettie and Eva Jo. Both looked up in unison.

"Julia. Julia, your Gran's with the Lord now. Come." Eva Jo reached for her.

"No, you're wrong." Julia clutched at her pajamas with one hand, raising the other in protest. "You're wrong, because we're…we're going Christmas shopping. Together…today."

"Julia." Eva Jo rose from the bed, stepping towards her great-niece. "Julia, Grace is home."

"Together. Today," Julia repeated. "We're going to Portland…to the Lloyd Center." The palms of each hand went to her eyes, pushing hard against the tears. "Then to the tea room at Meier and Frank downtown." She stumbled, making her way to the bed. Bending over, she said, "Gran, Gran, wake up. I need you, wake up!" Sitting, she touched Grace's face, gently caressing each cheek with a finger, then bent to kiss her cooling brow tenderly.

Julia put one cheek on Grace's and whispered, "Gran, I love you. I love you all the stars." She looked up at the sisters. "That's what we always say to each other."

"I remember," answered Nettie and Eva Jo together.

Eva Jo walked to Julia's side and handed her a handkerchief. "Julia, Grace loved you with all her heart. And you know what, my girl?"

"What?" Julia sobbed, obediently blowing her nose.

"Now she lives among the stars."

"But I'm not ready to let her go."

Now Nettie was beside Eva Jo. "We're not either, Julia girl, we're not either."

Julia stood, submitting to be embraced. She felt guilty and ashamed at her selfish impatience earlier. She went back to the bed, easing next to the first person she remembered loving unconditionally.

"I'll just lay here for a little while, okay?"

Eva Jo spoke. "Honey, you stay as long as you need. We'll call your mama." As the aunts tuned to leave, Nettie spotted a white sheet of paper just under the bed. She walked back to retrieve it, stiffly bending over. Her face turned pale at the contents, and hesitated briefly before handing it to Julia. "It's for you."

Sitting up, Julia took the note. "What's this?"

"Your grandmother's last words to you."

She took the paper, unfolding it curiously. It was Gran's writing all right, though shaky and weak. She stared at the cryptic message, unable to process its meaning.

"I don't get it."

She looked up for answers from her great-aunts, but they'd left. Sobbing again, she stood to her feet, the note falling back to the floor. Anguish filled Julia as she took one last look at her Granny Grace before blowing a good-bye kiss.

"All the stars, Gran, all the stars."

She shut the door gently, almost forgetting the note. Going back in was difficult, but she didn't glance at her Gran, just picked up the crumpled paper, stretching it open. What did it mean anyway?

Julia, the lion will destroy you.

Julia managed to get her lean frame up the last steps of the creaky ladder by grabbing both sides and pulling hard. When her body cleared the stingy space, Grace's musty attic closed in, cobwebs clinging to her long auburn hair like stale cotton candy. Brushing them aside, she reached into a jeans pocket for a leather band, then deftly formed a ponytail. A small mouse crossed just inches in front of her. She didn't flinch but laughed out loud, remembering it was Gran who had taught her that in the McLeod's lineage of pioneer-spirited women, any fear of God's creatures, great or small, was simply not tolerated.

"That definitely skipped my mother, bless her. She's afraid of anything that moves."

Only the dust bunnies were listening, and they were plentiful. Wondering how long it had been since anyone had mustered up the courage to venture into this memory vault, Julia recalled loving it as a child, never tiring of the hours spent pretending with her siblings or any of the multitude of cousins. Great-Gran had made time for them all, each believing they were her "special" one.

Dodging several baskets hanging from rusted ceiling hooks and stacks of boxes on splintered floors, Julia noticed a trail in the dust leading to where a small trunk rested.

"Mmm, curiouser and curiouser."

This was something unique, maybe a child's. Obviously, someone had meant it to be noticed. But who had moved it to this spot and who was the finder supposed to be? She couldn't imagine Gran climbing up those steep stairs. Yet...? Her feisty great-grandmother had shocked them all when she insisted on going for a horseback ride to celebrate her eightieth birthday. Said if she fell off and died from a broken neck, she wanted that fact engraved on her tombstone.

"Oh Gran, I love you."

Still not over the shock of Grace's death, Julia struggled most with the cryptic note left for her. Surely the aunts knew the content, yet neither had mentioned it since. With all the funeral preparations, there hadn't been time to talk with either of them. Now it was the day before

Christmas Eve, and because they were old, she thought it best if she kept her thoughts to herself and helped the best she could. Even though she still dreamed of college parties, Julia knew her place was here.

Julia imagined that Gran probably had more "stuff" than anybody in Yacolt, or all of Southwest Washington for that matter. Her attention returned to the mysterious container, comparatively sparse with dust. She gently blew and watched shafts of light magnify the suspended particles like tiny dancing angels. Angels! That's what she'd believed inhabited those myriads of dusty streaks until she was nearly nine. She'd believed Jack Frost was real until then too. Both Grace's influences.

A single tear landed on the cleared spot, despite making a decision before the funeral that, being the mature college student, she would not cry publicly. A "woman" needs to have control, be "in" control, she was reminded often. Now, in this place of sweet reveries, all her defenses vanished.

When she'd first left home, she hadn't felt like a woman at all, more like the country mouse visiting the city. U of O's campus, with dozens of brick buildings and acres of rolling ground, seemed a hundred times larger than Yacolt, Washington. She was one girl from the sticks, the outback, the boondocks. At first she imagined they probably still smelled horse sweat on her. Convinced she was the poster-child for outsiders, she never admitted to family how homesickness consumed her daily.

After several weeks, Julia's confidence grew when she'd made some friends. Boys especially wanted her opinions, even her advice. Tall, with copper-colored hair cascading down her athletic back, she was noticed in any crowd. She was unaffected by this natural beauty, but men thought her attractive, women found her unassuming.

A strong leader in her home church, she'd drifted from anything overtly Christian on the vast campus. Although there was a small Sunday service, those mornings became the only time to catch up on sleep lost from late homework vigils kept nightly. Especially after she'd met Michael.

Michael. She'd shared a little about him in a couple of letters to Granny Grace. But she'd yet to find words that described exactly what he was capable of doing to her heart. It was magical. Others saw him the same way: a leader, natural-born, and charismatic. When Michael Hanson entered a room, everyone noticed. With chiseled good looks, women of all ages found him charming. Each time he called her "Rosebud," she felt the magnetism of him growing stronger. What he saw in her, she couldn't figure out. They were worlds apart in nearly everything, especially in matters of faith. "Religion is the opiate of the people," he proclaimed. Though her conscience protested in the beginning, she made a decision to keep silent about her own beliefs.

Soon they were a "couple," something new for her. Oh, she'd gone steady in high school with Emmit Anderson, but that had lasted two months. This was something bigger. She liked how other coeds envied her being a noticeable part of Michael's life, his inner family circle.

It was all about finding your own way. Right? Right! She couldn't explain with any clarity to family that she considered her new life at the university a million miles from life in Yacolt. Her roles had switched. Now she was the outsider at home. Isn't that what leaving the nest was all about? She was definitely an adult now, and they'd have to accept it.

That was exactly how she wanted it, except lately Julia had been pressed by a powerful conviction at the back of her mind...relentless like northwest winter rains, pushing until it invaded even her sleep. It created difficulties she couldn't ignore. At times it was impossible to sit still. Even her studies were affected. Often when awakening from a haunting dream, she'd hear, *"Come home."* Once she'd asked her roommate if she'd heard anything.

"Just you, snoring," had been the curt reply.

Now during Gran's death and funeral, the same soul stirring remained an even edgier companion, causing a restlessness she couldn't explain.

Pushing those thoughts aside brought her attentions back to the mystery vessel. As a child she'd been extremely adventuresome, always fantasizing about lost treasure and wonderful secrets contained in murky bottles long set out to sea. That same tingling excitement took over now as she fingered the latch on the trunk before her. Had Gran hidden a lot of money inside? Jewelry perhaps. She laughed out loud again, because one of Grannie Grace's favorite sayings was that her children and grandchildren were all the precious jewels she'd ever want or need. Besides she'd add, "My true treasure is in Heaven with the Lord." Then what was inside?

"Well stupid, open the trunk."

Her fingers trembled as she turned the key in the hourglass lock. It didn't budge at first, and she was afraid it might break if forced. Exhaling when it lightly clicked, she pushed the squeaky lid open, her eyes resting on the "treasure."

"Bummer. No money."

Lifting a blank envelope from the top of old papers, she saw they were tied with a piece of soft yellow ribbon wrapped around dried lavender. Was it her imagination, or did it still have a hint of delicate fragrance?

The envelope revealed a lone sheet of paper inside. Removing it, she was stunned to see her name on a printed, unsigned note. No clue as to the writer.

> **Dear Julia,**
> **May you find what you need in the letters contained herein. There is truth for the seeker.**

"'Herein'? Who talks like that? Who says ' herein'?"

Laying the envelope and the clueless note aside, she proceeded cautiously to explore the stack of letters. Untying the knotted ribbon, she hoped they wouldn't fall apart in her hand. The first page looked like a journal. It was signed, *Nettie.*

"Aunt Nettie wrote this," she whispered.

She flipped through a few more and saw they were all letters from Gran's sisters, prayer journals too. But where in the world had she been to have received so many? Wait—Gran's handwriting revealed that for every three or four letters from Aunt Eva Jo and Aunt Nettie, she had written one in response.

"Wonder why she kept her own letters as well…gee, my Grandmother…a woman of mystery."

Julia glanced around the attic for better light and reading comfort.

This find was just too good to pass up. She imagined some deep, dark secret hidden in their upstanding Christian family. Her skin tingled with the possibility. She laughed. "Not a chance."

After tossing a pile of musty clothing off an old rocker, she dragged it over to a paned window in the peak of the roof. She leafed through the top stack of letters, all in chronological order, even a faded telegram. She couldn't tell if they were always like this, or if someone had arranged them recently. Julia picked up the first yellowed sheet gingerly, with a sense of…what was it? Wonder? Curiosity? Both, she decided.

PRAYER JOURNAL
NETTIE

December 26, 1901
My Lord Jesus,

I pray for mercy on my family. Christmas was a nightmare. It's as though a dark cloud covers our house. Gracie is gone!

Is this what death feels like? Right now, my heart doesn't know the difference, and I have no idea how to survive.

There's a hole in my life that only Gracie can fill. I bump into where she should be, all day long. Instead of her welcoming smile, there's only empty space. No more Grace. No more silly comments or encouraging words. She might be gone, but I can't forget, not for a second…no matter what Papa says.

I don't know if it will be dishonoring to him, Lord, but as soon as there's a word on Gracie's whereabouts, I plan on writing a letter or two. Maybe she'll change her mind and come back home. Then she'll reconcile with Mama and Papa, and we can be a family again.

Gracie is obviously on everyone's mind, though hardly a word was spoken at dinner today. I didn't know what else to talk about. Papa and Mama seem like strangers to me. Their silence was screaming around in my mind.

Lord, please bring forgiveness to my parent's hearts. I pray to be able to forgive them and Gracie. I love them all. Anger is welling up within me. Tomorrow I'm going to Eva Jo's and talk over this whole matter some more.

I love you Lord,
Your daughter,
Nettie

Directly under the first letter, Julia found a telegram.

DEAR FAMILY STOP GETTING MARRIED STOP HIS NAME IS JAKE HUDSON STOP TOOK TRAIN TO LOS ANGELES STOP PLEASE WRITE STOP ADDRESS WILL BE 100 E TEMPLE STREET STOP I'M WELL STOP GRACE

January 5, 1902
Gracie Darling,

Thank God we know where you've gone. Hearing you're well brings relief, though your departure has left a huge hole in our lives. Christmas lacked greatly because of your absence, our celebration saddened by Mama's continual crying, and unending questions from Will and Percy. Reading your words eases my mind, but Papa made a declaration and now refuses to discuss anything to do with your leaving. This of course, makes it even harder for our mama.

Nettie and I have had our discussions alone together, so as not to add to the clamor, but she says Papa's anger is felt even in his silence. I'm not sharing these things for the laying on of guilt, but if you are grown enough to leave home, then I believe your shoulders are big enough to carry the consequences, hard though they be.

I want to write as often as possible, because my heart would break with the effort not to, but I too feel burdened as to the way you left us. But more than the way, Gracie, I'm wondering about the why.

I heard some news in town today that promises to make it easier to communicate. We're getting a telephone! Well, not we, as in our house, but the post-office will have one soon. What a marvelous invention. Now, I'm not sure if this is absolutely true or not, but Mr. Miner, the post-master, said he believed we'd be able to talk all the way to California. Can you believe it? Well, I'm sure you can, now that you're in such a big place. I'm sure our ways seem very "small town" now.

Although I'll be thrilled to talk with you, the memory of your voice lingers slow in my mind, your laughter a sweet calling to dearer times. I'm watching out the window, seeing how the winter mist clings to everything. That's how it is with my memory. Wandering as it chooses, I can't remember not remembering you close. Early recollections have you in the middle.

When Nettie said your name for the first time, your face lit up, bright as day. After you ran to tell Mama, your joy remained with me.

Odd things trigger it. Like the clean scent of Lulu after a full bathing by the kitchen fire. I don't think you and I had a bath apart until we were maybe five and eight. I recall the glowing of your fair skin after getting scrubbed with Grandma's lye soap— nothing like the store-bought we can get today.

I'm wondering what teases your memories, little sister. Do you ever walk by a church and hear our favorite hymn? Are there children in the street that remind you of Willie and Percy? Maybe you've seen some girl with wild, tousled hair racing in a field on horseback, and remembered me. Have you ever walked by a sweet shop and pictured our Nettie baking in Mama's kitchen?

When you left, some of me came up missing. But I take great comfort in knowing that wherever you go, and forever how long, God goes with you. I pray you'll hear His voice in the midst of city clamor.

Can you hear my heart's cry? Come home, come home, little sister. Come back to the one who loves you so.

Love, your big sister,

Eva Jo

Two

Julia grabbed a tissue from her pocket, blowing her nose loudly.

My Gran ran away from home. She shook her head, finding these writings of Great-Aunt Eva Jo and Nettie's heartbreaking. She tried picturing them when they all were young, not hard to do since the box contained a picture of them, sitting prim and proper together in a portrait. It was easy picking out Grace…Julia being told "they favored one another." Funny, she'd never noticed the look in those eyes before. Peering into Gran's young face, she saw for the first time restlessness, and something more. Rebellion.

The three older McLeod siblings were known as "the sisters." Inseparable growing up, they were often described as "a threesome to be reckoned with."

Eva Jo, the oldest, a "tomboy" from birth, was found often with Papa, either in the fields, or trudging the woods on his weekly hunting excursions. At twelve she was as tall as her mama and could outshoot any teen boy in the valley. Preferring to ride bareback (in a pair of Big Jim's old work pants), many a clucking tongue spoke of the "unladylike wildness in that oldest McLeod girl." Either singing or whistling some happy tune, she was often chastised: "Eva Jo, whistling girls and cackling hens always come to no good end."

Ignoring them all, she grew up to be a strong, fun-loving (albeit opinionated) woman of faith, ready for life at the beginning of the twentieth century.

Grace Rose McLeod was born serious, or so family lore recalled. Able to read before age five, she spent hours hidden away, devouring whatever written word she could find. Starting with *A*, Gracie had memorized a Bible verse for every letter of the alphabet by age six, although she was too shy to recite for anyone but family. Completely different in personalities and temperament, the first two children of Louise and Clement James, better known as "Big Jim" McLeod, were close in affections, if not habits. They played together earnestly, making secret "caverns" in giant haystacks, or pretended to be sweeping birds of prey inside the barn on rainy days.

When Louise began their schooling, each was eager and willing to learn, though reading did not hold the same wonder for Eva Jo as Grace. Physically stretched to the limit athletically, Gracie would come to Louise in tears, unable to keep up with Eva Jo. She'd held secret thoughts of not "measuring up" in her father's eyes.

Big Jim McLeod bragged openly about the many accomplishments of his oldest offspring. It wasn't that he didn't love them both equally, but clearly Grace preferred the inside of the house to the outdoors, where he reigned supreme on a daily basis. It didn't matter that his firstborn son had died at birth...he had Eva Jo.

The youngest of the McLeod's daughters came into the world early, but bent on survival. Tiny as a doll, she spent her household debut nestled in a shoe box on the open oven door to maintain a viable body temperature. Annette Louise became "Nettie" that day because Grace couldn't say "Annette." It was love at first sight for Eva Jo and Grace, though they were toddlers. Nettie's first smile was for them, instantly extending the McLeod duo into the threesome forever termed "the sisters."

Nettie remained small for her age but was never held back by lack of stature. She was strongly loyal to the older sisters and Mama, quickly becoming her shadow in the kitchen. Famous for feather-light biscuits, and griddlecakes that melted in the mouth, it was Nettie who baked family birthday cakes and Sunday desserts for after church dinners. She could sing from the day of her first word at eight months, prompting Eva Jo and Gracie to teach her every song they learned from the family hymnal.

Being the youngest didn't stop her from becoming the teacher when playing school. After the boys were born, she was delighted to have two more students on the McLeods' school roster. Percy was still eating from a high chair when he was inducted into her classroom. "Percy, please don't scratch the chalkboard with your fingernails," she would scold.

Later family archives showed her standing with a dozen children in front of the Good Hope School, where grades one through eight were taught by "Miss" McLeod, age sixteen, in one room.

Julia sat rocking for a few minutes. So many contemplations running together in her mind. *Do you ever really know people? Are there secrets in every family? Not mine...couldn't be. They were the "perfect" family. Strong, Bible believing. "Lovers of the Word and each other. Simple people, simply loving God."* Those were Grace's very words, spoken repeatedly and with vigor. She flipped the photograph and saw on the back in handwriting that matched great-aunt Eva Jo's. *Gracie darling.* This copy must have been sent to Gran.

Knowing this puzzle could take some time, she placed the mysterious letters on the floor and went downstairs. Her mother was gone, probably taking more things to the Goodwill. The others had left hours ago. It had been fun, not sad, going through all the many memories her great-grandmother left behind. Never having known her Mom's mother, Bonnie, since she'd died when Julia was small, Grannie Grace had been both grandmas rolled into one cherished role.

Julia shoved some cheese, left-over chicken, and two apples into a paper bag before heading back to the attic. She stopped by the phone, grabbed a pad and pencil, and scratched a note in large letters. *DO NOT DISTURB!* Placing it on the bottom step, weighted down with a tuna can, she climbed back to her spot by the window, noticing storm clouds low and threatening. She'd need more light soon, but thought the suspended bulb overhead would suffice.

She picked up the next letter.

Dear Nettie and Eva Jo,

You've not written a word to me since I left. I know you are angry, but try to understand. Eloping with Jake was so exciting! I thought you, Sisters, would empathize far better than Mama or Papa. Jake says we'll come back to visit in a year. By that time, the rail tracks should connect to Yacolt. That's what Jake was working on when we met.

He was in Washington State to build a railroad for small towns like Yacolt in order to link the Main Line south to Portland. Now he works for his father, who is the boss of the entire Southern Line here in California. Jake was only in Yacolt a short time, supervising the land grading for the P.V. & Y Railroad. I'm sure you've heard that they've already finished ten miles of it!

Do you remember when Aunt Frieda broke her arm back in November? Uncle Robert was anxious to get someone who knew how to make her biscuits, so I went to help. I made a little money and escaped my work on the farm. One foggy morning, Jacob Hudson came in for breakfast with two older men. Jake wore a red cravat, a gray suit, and the shiniest boots in our two-horse town.

He and Uncle Robert spoke, and I could tell it was about me. I served Jake's table that morning, though I'd been assigned to washing plates and putting biscuits into the oven. My hair was limp and damp from dishwashing, and flour from baking hung all about me, but Jake couldn't take his eyes off me. I admit that I thought him to be the most handsome man I'd ever seen. Especially in Yacolt, Washington.

While the other men slopped down biscuits and gravy, Jake ate like a well-mannered gentleman. As they were leaving, he smiled and told me he'd enjoyed every bite of the biscuits, then dropped a huge gratuity on the table. That wasn't all he left.

He slipped me a note. It said: *Meet me tonight at the oak tree by the schoolhouse, seven o'clock. Entranced by you, Jacob E. Hudson.*

It was all so intriguing, Sisters. Still, my heart wavered. I wasn't sure it was proper to meet him. Or even if I should dare.

But that evening, I made an excuse that I'd forgotten to round up Mattie, that old stubborn cow. Of course she was in her stall, but I knew you were all too busy to look yourselves. Papa murmured something about responsibility. I answered, "Yes, Sir," and slipped out. I hated "cow" duty, even though I'd been doing it since Eva Jo left home. You probably never knew how much.

Walking in shadows so no town busybody would see me, I approached the tree. At first I didn't see him.

As ebony colored as the keys on Mama's piano, his horse nearly blended with its rider. Jake wore a black cape and hat; his riding boots covered half his legs. Shivers of fear struck me, even though I recognized him. But only for a moment did apprehension remain. He removed his hat with a bow and smiled at me mischievously. My spine tingled with anticipation as he extended a gloved hand towards me. I was trembling. I did not understand this new sensation.

We sat on the back steps of the schoolhouse, out of sight. Oh, how we talked, Sisters! He said he was twenty-seven and would soon be a Railroad Baron like his father. "How could I stay in a town like this?" he wondered. "There's a whole world waiting to be seen." Then he told me about San Francisco and Los Angeles, which means "City of Angels," in Spanish.

I shared all about myself, and before I knew it, a pale winter's moon appeared. Like Cinderella, I had run out of time. He offered me a ride home on horseback. I told him I could run—I feared hoofbeats might be heard from the house. But he swept me onto the saddle and rode to a spot near the front gate. How gallant. He dismounted first, reaching up to help me down. His hands around my waist were warm in the cold. I was glad he wasn't able to see my blushing cheeks.

We walked hand in hand into the barn, laughing softly at Mattie chewing her cud in pure contentment. Our breath formed wisps of translucent vapor in the mist of moonlight pushing through the shadows. Once more he reached for me, enclosing my body within his cape. He kissed me. His kiss was like a man kisses, with passion and fervor. Not like Joey Haswell, the boy who grabs all the girls behind the outhouse in the schoolyard. Time stood still, and I knew I was in love. Nothing would stop me from seeing him again.

Please try to understand the intoxication between us. We have done nothing wrong. How I wish you could meet him. His eyes are mahogany, his hair jet black. Taller than Papa, Jake's clothing is from a tailor here in Los Angeles. Mine are going to be sewn by a dressmaker...I'll send you remnants, if you want. I'll be choosing my whole trousseau, Jake says. That's something modern—the groom providing the trousseau!

Sometimes I regret keeping my love a secret from you, though I'm sure you've heard gossip about him from Aunt Etta. I'd guess she's spreading bad things about Jake's behavior heard sorely through rumors from Portland. Her self-importance goes beyond reason. Don't believe a word of it. Jake is a perfect gentleman.

I've made my explanations, but I will write again soon.

Love, Gracie

January 1902
Dear Gracie,

Eva Jo brought a letter from you today. With tears in her eyes, she said I wouldn't like it. She was right. I did want to read it, though, so despite the cold I went to my favorite spot by the river after chores.

Sadness came over my whole being as your words jumped off the page, piercing my heart.

Forgive me, but you are completely unaware of what your leaving has done to us at home. Do you even care? I am amazed at your flippant attitude

How many late nights did we spend curled up together in one of Mama's quilts talking about our dreams of the future? Not once did you mention any grand desires of traveling away from here. The "Gracie" you let me know doesn't even resemble the "Gracie" in your letter. I don't know you at all.

Who are you really, Sister? I am young, so maybe that's why you had trouble sharing with me. But what about Eva Jo? You left her completely in the dark. She would have been an encourager in making things right. I cannot understand this.

You probably don't care, but I made you a very special gift and could hardly wait to give it you on Christmas morning. I woke up bursting with excitement. Hoping I was the first one to rise, I wanted to put my presents under the tree, stir the fire, and have coffee brewing for everyone. I crept down the stairs carefully, so as not to wake a soul. I was disappointed, though, because I heard voices from the kitchen. Curious to know who had gotten up before me, I continued on.

Stopped in my tracks just outside the door, I heard Mama and Papa in the middle of a heated conversation with someone. I leaned closer.

"Gracie is gone."

Right then my heart quit beating, while a watermelon-sized lump filled my throat. All breath left, and I stood, gasping for air.

Suddenly the door swung open with force enough to whack me to the floor.

First, Mama's face appeared, then Papa's, with Sheriff Willoughby, peering over their shoulders. I was caught eavesdropping, red-handed.

"Nettie, get up." I'd never heard Papa's voice so cold.

Mama gently lifted me and held me close. She knew, as always, what I needed. I looked into her face and saw the most terrible sadness. Then I understood what I'd heard was true. You were gone. I didn't know a person could have so many tears.

Mama said she noticed you were missing while making nightly rounds to tuck us all in. She panicked when she saw you were nowhere in the house. Where could you be? What could have happened? Papa went to the neighbors...all of them, pounding on doors, determined to find you. Finally, he ended up in town at the hotel. He found some answers there but was hard-pressed to believe what he'd heard.

The night manager said he was sure it was you that left with a man all dressed in black. Papa, said "no," he was mistaken.

But when he went back this morning, there was a telegram waiting, the one you sent from Portland on your way to California.

Why couldn't you have the wedding here, where Eva Jo and I could be your bridesmaids? You absolutely ruined Christmas, Gracie.

Our entire day was miserable. Eva Jo, Ephraim, Lulu, and the boys came over in the late morning. Soon after, though, we gave up pretending to celebrate.

Eva Jo and I took a long walk together, holding tightly onto each other—I didn't want to ever let her go. Words didn't have to be spoken; we were sharing the same loss. Togetherness was what we needed.

Winter dampness had us chilled to the bone before we slowly made our way back to the house. We lingered just outside the gate. Going inside meant having to face the reality and emptiness of your being gone. Worst of all, we'd have to look at the sorrow on our mama's face. You see, Grace, at dinner, Papa said something horrible to the entire family.

"Gracie is no longer my daughter. From this day forward, she is dead to this house." He was on his feet, red in the face with anger.

"Noooo!" Percy, screamed, jumping up so quickly, his chair fell over. He ran to his room, wailing the entire way.

When Mama stood to go after him, Papa ordered her to stay

right where she was. Slowly she sat back down, covering her face. But she couldn't hide the tears.

"But Papa," Willie cried, "Gracie is still my sister. Right, Papa?"

Now Papa's face turned white as snow. He put a hand to his chest before falling back into the chair. "Willie, leave the table."

"But Papa, I love my Gracie."

"Go!"

One by one, we all got up, leaving Papa alone.

Before Eva Jo left, she put her arms around me and pulled me close. With a sad smile she kissed my forehead, then whispered a prayer for God to keep you under the shelter of His wings, and to please bring you back safe.

That prayer gave me strength to go on. And so I did, grateful when Christmas finally dragged to its miserable end. Exhausted, I cried myself into a merciful sleep without my Gracie. I'm still praying for strength. You will forever be my beloved sister.

Nettie

Prayer Journal
Nettie

Lord,

I can't even begin to express my pain! Gracie is gone. My heart is broken and from what I see, I don't believe it can ever be healed. I need comfort that only You can bring, Lord. Only You.

Is she well, Jesus? I pray that You would be her hiding place, and she would take shelter under Your wings, like Eva Jo prayed. Please keep her from the terrors at night, be her shield and buckler. May Your Spirit comfort my family.

Your daughter,
Nettie

January 1902

Dear Eva Jo and Nettie,

Well, finally you've written. Let me just say up front that I don't care what Papa thinks of me. It doesn't matter that I'm not his daughter, because soon enough I'll be Jacob Hudson's wife. Papa's iron-fisted ways don't intimidate me at all, even though his temper will last a long season. Mama, loyal as she is, will take his side completely. But don't you two be angry. Regardless of Papa's proclamation, I haven't really dropped off the earth. I knew no one would guess where I'd actually gone. I found it fun leaving without anyone knowing. My first real adventure after all.

How can our old-fashioned parents begin to understand the reasons for my leaving? I have to be with the man I love. At least the three of us can continue to write.

I do think of you often, picturing your tea-time. I miss that sisterly ritual, but I know you will share my letters. Just think of me...at the table beside you, and I'll pretend we're laughing together. Nettie's warm hugs and our pleasant dreaming times are missed with fondness, regardless of her anger towards me. And of course, I look forward to all of Eva Jo's wild stories. Even now I long for Lulu's baby softness and gentle touches. We three have been so close throughout our childhood, that in spite of the riches around me, my thoughts stray homeward.

Not that I'm sorry for leaving, of course, but Jake seems unable to understand how much my family means to me. I've made a great sacrifice to be with him. I'm not despairing, mind you, because I'm more than confident he'll come around soon.

Exciting news! We've set a date for our wedding—February 14, at a well-to-do friend's house and garden. Very romantic choice, don't you think? It would make me the happiest woman in the world if my sisters could be here for the ceremony and stand up for me like we've always planned. Wouldn't Will and Percy look sweet out of their overalls and into fancy dress-up things? I'm sure, given the circumstances, you won't be here, so I shall have to make the most of it anyway.

Jake's father rents a large house to us. It has gingerbread-laden eaves and is the loveliest shade of rose with a spacious front porch wrapped around. He's hired a cook for us, Mrs. Flossie White, as well as a maid. I'm saved any work at all.

Jake and I live in separate quarters until we are married, just so you know. He goes to the office all day. Most evenings he spends at a Gentlemen's Club downtown. I manage to keep busy with arranging all that has to get done before the wedding.

I feel excitingly special to see people's heads turn when they see Jake and I together. He teases me often about my auburn hair, claiming that's the reason for all the attention. But I believe it's really because Emory Hudson, his father, is a man of high influence in this city. Yesterday, we finally met.

I've never imagined a home so grand. I'm sure I've not even seen pictures of one. Well, perhaps in books about European castles. The front door is twice as tall as Jacob, and leaded windows grace both sides. Above, ornate stained glass depicts lush gardens with playful nymphs, wearing gauze. A butler, attired in black, met us at the door. Once inside, I felt small in comparison to the opulence. Huge stairways wound down on either side of a royal balcony while electric lights illuminated the walls flowing with crushed velvet, the color of succulent grapes.

Another manservant ushered us into a library stacked to the ceiling with bookshelves. Even if someone pressed me for a count of the contents, I couldn't come close to an accurate tally.

To think Jake grew up here. I found it difficult imagining a small child wandering the cavernous rooms of such a place. This didn't feel like a home.

Mr. Hudson took my hand earnestly when introduced, but there was no warmth in his gaze. He spent most of the time talking with Jake. Well, I should say talking at him, because he treats his son rather like a child instead of an adult. I was not sure what to say to him when his attentions turned to me, so mostly I went on about how much I liked California. He listened with polished politeness and all, but I'm not comfortable in his imposing presence. There was something about the way he looked me over.... Our visit ended with an abrupt dismissal after a messenger delivered a telegram.

While at the mansion I learned more about my future husband. His full name is Jacob Emory Ortega Hudson. "Emory," after his father. "Ortega" was his mother's maiden name, though he's mentioned her name but once. Perhaps because she abandoned the family when he was barely older than a toddler.

While showing me a place to wash up before leaving, one of the younger maids, eager to share gossip, whispered that Mrs. Hudson had gone up to San Francisco and never returned.

"Is she still alive?" I asked the maid.

"No one knows, Miss."

"Well, she must be, since Mr. Hudson has never remarried."

"Mr. Hudson has no need for a wife, if you get what I'm saying."

"I'm sorry," I said, "I don't understand..."

"You see—" she looked around nervously—"Mr. Hudson has lots of women in his life. They...well...keep him entertained." She looked at me knowingly from over a shoulder.

My face blushed hot. "Well, Mrs. Hudson is surely forgotten around here now."

"Oh, don't be so sure about that, Miss. Don't be sure about that at all."

Then she was gone.

No wonder I felt the way I did. I hope I won't have to spend much time with Jake's father. I'm grateful my future husband is nothing like him.

What the maid meant about Jake's mother, I'm not sure. That has truly left me puzzled. I must question him.

After leaving, Jake was sullen. Not his future bride, nor the California sunshine could brighten his mood. Strange that, even in the warmth of the day, a chill swept over me as the footman took our coach down the long driveway to the street. Must have been a cool breeze from the ocean.

I remain optimistically yours,
Grace

P.S. I'm waiting for your letters.

PRAYER JOURNAL
NETTIE

My Father in Heaven,

We just received a letter from Gracie. But instead of bringing joy, it's brought more anger and bitterness.

I'll never trust her again. Not that she cares. She doesn't even sound like the sister I've known and loved. She's a stranger. What happened to her, Lord? She's given up all of us for one man...a man of darkness.

Earlier in the week, I overheard Willie and Percy conversing while they sat on the cellar steps, worrying about a "Black Rider."

"Willie, do you think he'll come back for us?" Percy asked.

"I don't know, but I've been practicing running and hiding. He won't be able to find me! I can hide and not make a sound for a long time. I can even run faster than his big black horse," Willie bragged.

"I don't think I could hide from him, Willie, and you run faster than me. If he catches me, will you tell Papa?" Percy was sniffing.

Silence.

"If I did the Black Rider said he'd get me right out of my bed." Willie's words were spoken so softly I could barely hear them.

Now Percy was wailing. "He'll kill us!"

"Boys," I interrupted. Both of them jumped at one. "I think this Black Rider nonsense has gone far enough. Willie, you're too big to scare Percy like this."

"You heard us?" Willie asked.

"Yes, I did. It's okay to play make-believe. But you've gone too far this time." I sat down on the step above and put my arms around them.

"We aren't playing," wide-eyed Percy said. He shook like a leaf. "Now the Black Rider is going to come and get me, just like he got Gracie,"

Willie began to sniffle.

"Boys, the Black Rider didn't get Gracie. She left."

"Uh uh." They shook their heads. "We saw her on his horse Christmas Eve. He knows where we live."

"What? What do you mean?"

"We can't say anything else, because when we were playing by the oak tree, we saw Gracie kiss the Black Rider. She caught us watching so we ran. But...but..."

"But what?"

"But he jumped on his horse and chased us. I ducked behind a bush, only he found me, then Will. He pulled us hard up on his horse. Our tummies hurt afterward, but we couldn't tell Mama 'cause he said he'd come and steal us away while we were sleeping, " Percy couldn't stop talking.

"Yeah, so we can't tell you anything about him," Willie agreed.

What a horrible man. Who would scare little boys like that?

"Well, the Black Rider is afraid of Papa and Mama. He won't come into the house when they are there."

"He got Gracie."

"No, you're wrong, Gracie chose to go with him. She's going to marry him. Go play, and stop worrying."

They rubbed their eyes, trying to be brave. I gave them one more hug, then shooed them off to the barn. I was furious. *Black Rider!* What kind of man could this be?

Lord, is anyone who I think they are? Whom can I trust? Gracie and Eva Jo have been everything to me. Maybe Eva Jo isn't really who I see. I'm confused. How do I know whom to believe?

For sure, Lord, I know I can believe in You. You are truth.

Help me, Father. I don't know how to go on. Do I need to tell Mama and Papa about the dark side of Jake Hudson he's shown to the boys? I've got to talk this over with Eva Jo.

Please perfect that which concerns me today.

I love You, Lord.

In Jesus' name, amen.

Nettie

January, 1902
Dear Gracie,

Hope this letter finds you well. We are healthy enough, yet still suffer from your absence. I'm wanting to talk face to face despite the fact your distance remains. There are many questions left unanswered, my mind ever in quandary.

Disturbing details have come to light, Grace, and I need some answers. Willie and Percy have been frightened out of their wits by a man they called the "Black Rider." It seems your Mr. Hudson imposed a dramatic impression of what he was capable of doing to them if they dared tell they saw the two of you meeting in the shadows. Papa was overtaken with outrage when he heard about it and left the house for hours, Mama not having a clue as to his whereabouts. The next morning at breakfast Nettie said his eyes were hollow and looked like he'd been spent with tears. Perhaps you could shed some light onto this? I believe Mama and Papa deserve to know more. What kind of man would want to frighten two small children?

Despite the drama, life goes on and so do we. The sameness of the days seem unremarkable, yet I'm incredibly blessed by the things that make them that way. You know...sunrise, chores, the lives of my children, Ephraim's love...all of it. It's the ribbon that day after day, the Lord weaves in and out, back and forth, until our days are finished. I'm believing that right now I'm living behind the loom, not able to see much but strange patterns, like shadows under the trees. But some day, when He's ready, He'll take my hand and walk me to the front and I'll see the total picture of what my life was all about. I want it to show love and beauty, but I'm curious as to how the hurts will look. Will that ribbon be purple? Maybe black. Can it ever be made into a thing of beauty? Perhaps my tears will be shown as a river. I wonder what color the love will be.

I was sharing these very same thoughts with Mama the other day, and she brought out this poem I'm sending. Actually it's a hymn, one of Mama's favorites. She and the author exchanged letters for years after Mama wrote to her about how much she loved the lyrics.

Children of yesterday, Heirs of tomorrow
What are you weaving?
Labor and sorrow?
Look to your looms again
Faster and faster
Fly the great shuttles
Prepared by the Master;
Room for it—Room!
Children of yesterday,
Heirs of tomorrow,
Lighten the labor and sweeten the sorrow,

Now, while the shuttles fly
Faster and faster,
Up and be at it,
At work with the Master;
He stands at your loom,
Room for Him—
Room!
Children of yesterday,
Heirs of tomorrow,
Look at your fabric
Of labor and sorrow,
Seamy and dark
With despair and disaster,
Turn it, and—lo,
The design of the Master!
The Lord's at the loom;
Room for Him—
Room!

—MARY ARTEMESIA LATHBURY

Well, enough of my rambling, Sister. Chores are waiting...will finish soon.

Two days later:

I want to share the latest tomfoolery of your two nephews...Pete and Repeat. I caught them red-handed into mischief behind the barn today. It was their wild laughter that brought me to the spot in the first place. The closer I got, the easier it was to figure out what they were up to, since then I could hear the calves as well.

Those two boys were whooping it up so loud, they never heard me coming. David John was "helping" his little brother onto the back of a protesting calf, trying to keep it in place with a firm grip on its halter. Once up, Lucas held on for dear life. That steer took off running as soon as David let loose of him. Lucas' hat fell off right before he did.

"You all right, Lukey?" The big brother asked.

Lucas went silent, gasping like a fish out of water.

I ran as quick as the muck would allow. By the time I reached him, Lucas was bawling like the calf he'd been riding.

I sent David to the house, protesting as he went, and tried to pick Lucas up, which was difficult since he was slippery as the day he was born. Try as I might, I couldn't get him standing. Next thing I know I'm lying right beside him. I looked at him and he looked at me through mud-laden eyelashes. Gently, I scraped his face...him now resembling some unfamiliar creature.

"Mama, you looka funny."

"Well, mister man," I said. "you looka funnier." I threw my head back, laughing myself to tears. "Mama," he says again, "you smell funny too."

By that time, I was on my feet with him in tow. We laughed our way to the house, which I'm sure eased David's disobedient mind. They both looked pitiful, especially when the mud began to dry.

I stripped those two, scrubbing like they were Monday's wash, but two days later, I'm still smelling cow muck when I bend to kiss them. Maybe I should have been more angry, what with the terrible mess they made, and the fact they put themselves and the calf in harm's way. But I couldn't bring myself to much disturbance, because all I could think about was when you and I did the same thing. Only it was much harder for you and I to get on a steer's back with dresses and bloomers. Mama made us bath in the barn we smelled so bad. It was backbreaking work hauling water down there. I recall you spilled as much as was fetched, which meant more work for me. But still I laughed.

I carry the guilt to this day, knowing your trouble was my fault. And that wasn't the last time you were drawn into one of my grand adventure schemes. You never told on me, and I felt guilty about that too. What a loyal sister you were...are. Not just a sister, but my most special friend. Even when Ida Mae Vanduzen started coming to church and we became fast pals, you were still number one. I've heard it said that twins have a special bonding, but I don't see how anyone could have loved a sister more than I loved you. I'm positive Nettie feels the same.

We "sisters" are not the same with two, minus you. When we're together, your absence is felt, even when nothing is said. Last week Nettie rode over carrying her famous blueberry muffins, wrapped in a flour sack for warmth keeping. (Their sweetness proceeded her, they were that fragrant.) Making tea in Grandma's pot suddenly brought me to tears. At first I didn't realize why. Since Nettie began weeping buckets at the same time, we knew the tears were for you. The three of us have shared tea-time together since children. Pretend or real, tea, sweets, and the sisters belong together. Our ritual was incomplete...pleasant enough after drying our eyes, but incomplete nonetheless.

We wrote a poem for you. Sure hope I'm not boring you with so many home stories. I'm going to have trouble stuffing all of this into one envelope.

Sisters

Sisters three, different yet still the same
Laughing, playing, sharing all, including our last name.
The McLeod girls, they say, have mastered the secrets of life
They lean on each other and God, together easing strife.
If ever you see but one, just wait a second or more
And sure as the sun rises,
two others will come through the door.
Loving each other day after day, growing but never apart
The three became one in spirit, in life, and especially in heart.
Now two wait without patience for the third one's returning
Their hearts full of sorrow with tears wrought in yearning.

Our sentiments are dramatic and laughable, but we really can't help it.

All my love,
Your Eva Jo

January 20, 1902
Dear Gracie...

I'm trapped! It's snowed for five days unending. This morning Ephraim had to climb out an upstairs window and slide down the roof so he could feed stock. The front door was frozen shut...solid, as were all the downstairs windows. It took some time to get to the barn, and by then the beef cows bellowed for hay, while our faithful milker bawled like a newborn, so laden was she. Ephraim said good thing he tied a rope from house to barn, or I might be a widow with fatherless children. So fierce is the storm with cold, ice-cream could make itself.

Even though we've plenty of provisions, and are comfortable in our log home, I'll be questioning my sanity come any more of this weather. I was born for the out-of-doors, and my spirit longs for God's natureful bounty. Though it might appear I'm not grateful, my children and husband are His blessings for sure. It's just that we've been close together for a spell longer than I can appreciate. Of course, there's the same household chores, yet I sorely miss my outside duties...especially feeding the animals.

It may sound strange, but I've named most of the chickens. Are you laughing? It gives me pleasure to check their well-being daily, and the eggs are a gift. (Of course they're not laying during these dark days.) I don't know if you knew that even though I've hunted game since no bigger than a grasshopper, I never could kill a cackler...ever. Papa used to scold me fierce for this, but after watching them grow from fluff yellow, I couldn't make myself put an ax to even one.

Mama had Grandma's touch for wringing necks, but that made my legs wobbly. I talk to all those girls. Sweet as can be they answer back...God's my witness to that, Sister. But Ephraim says it's my singing that causes them to lay more than any other chickens in the valley. That might not be true, but the eggs they give me are bigger than all the neighbors. Probably you're wiping tears from your eyes with all the laughing. Even so, we believe my singing is productive.

It's not just the chickens that benefit. Last time Miss Trixie calved, she set some kind of record for birthing time. Surely you remember? Bet you never knew the reason? I'm right sure on this fact...it's because I sang.

When I found her, she was down by the creek, huffing big. I realized she was holding back (maybe remembering the fact her last calf was half grown BEFORE it was born). I thought she'd die with the effort of it. People think cattle are dumb, but my Guernsey prize remembers things. Anyway, I was in a bit of panic before I heard a small command in my head.

Sing!

Not one to question that voice, I opened my mouth and sang every last word of "Amazing Grace"...twice. It was purely remarkable when that little brown cow laid her head in the tall grass, relaxing her entire focused body. When I finished, she stood up, shook vibrantly. Dropped the shiniest newborn heifer I've ever seen! A sound of pure contentment came from mama when her baby stood. I waited until she nursed some, before heading back to the house. The Lord put a new song in my heart, so absolute was the experience.

Back to now! I've cleaned, baked (more than is healthy), and read near all our books to the children. I'm caught up on the mending, until there's not a sharp needle left. Maybe I should have learned to knit, even though it's punishment for my soul.

What I'm thinking now is: God must want me to learn something. Patience? Contentment? Unselfishness? I'm ashamed, even as I write, for I've not been any of these things. Whining comes from an ungrateful heart. I've a mind to stop writing, but I will continue, so as to not waste this paper.

Two days later

Sweet sounds this morning...dripping. Things are thawing! Thudding chunks of icy snow are slipping off the roof, reminding me of thunder. (Only Lulu seems not to notice. At six months she can sleep through anything. What a fine-natured baby she's turned out to be.)

We can open the doors and David won't be risking his life to feed our animals, even though we'll have mud to our knees. The boys are begging to put on boots and play in the barn during morning chores. I need to go and tend them.

After bed

All the energy those children vented today truly wore them out. It's barely past seven and they're snuggled down like bugs in a rug. Mercy, I can't wait for better weather.

I'm curious with wondering, Gracie. I've read about California weather but still can't imagine all the sunshine you're having on a daily basis. Does it give you pleasure?

My mind knows how far away you are, but my heart refuses to accept it.

Your sister, Eva Jo

January, 1902
Dear Gracie,

I'm sending a quick note with Eva Jo's letter. Oh how I wish for some of your sunshine, because this cold and snow stopped being fun three days ago. There's nothing new left to read, and Will and Percy are driving each other...and me...crazy. At least they've stopped talking about the Black Rider.

My mind is trying to imagine what life in California is like. Do you actually swim in the ocean there? I read in a book once that oranges grow there in the winter. Is that true? We each had an orange in our Christmas stocking. Papa gave yours to Aunt Etta.

It's been nearly a month since you left me...us. I'm still very confused. Eva Jo and I pray for you whenever we get together, asking God to help us move forward without you. We also cry a lot. I do love you.

Your little sister,
Nettie

PRAYER JOURNAL
EVA JO

January 20, 1902
Lord,

The fierceness of this storm reminds me of Your mighty power. Safe and protected in our little home, I'm surrounded by Your love. I ask You, Lord, to keep my sister from harm. My heart is a constant ache of sorrow with her gone. Could I have kept her here if I had known of the hidden places in her heart? I've always been happy and content in our little valley. Why wasn't Gracie? Please comfort Mama and pour Your healing over Papa's anger. I've never seen their faith so stretched. Bring them peace as they put together the pieces of Gracie's departure.

Grace is young, Lord, unwise in the ways of the world. And who is this Jake Hudson? I barely remember him at the post office when I mailed a letter back in December. Tall, dark, and handsome for sure, but his heart could have no honor, else he'd have courted in the proper manner. I can't help thinking that when Willie and Percy called him the Black Rider, it more than describes what he was wearing.

So many questions for You, Lord. Please give me faith to stand and believe that You have all this in control. I feel like some dark cloud has fallen over our lives.

Ephraim loves Grace and the boys miss their Auntie. I'm remembering that "Auntie" was one of David's first words. Gracie could get him to sleep, when he would take no comfort from me.

As the wind blows hard, I know that the enemy of our souls pushes against the faith of us all. Please hide my family in Your holiness. Take my hand, Father, keep it in your mighty one, and lay me down in Your green pastures of rest.

Your daughter, Eva Jo

January 1902
Dear Nettie and Eva Jo,

I'm amazed that neither of you knew how unhappy I was before I left. I've been angry for a long time, but I guess you never noticed. I didn't like my life, Eva Jo. Farm life suits you, but I don't like the outdoors and I definitely hate cleaning out barns. You must admit, I did not complain. But when Papa hired Cal and Shepard to help, and we girls were sent to school, I began to see another way to live. I wanted to be done with the hay, the mucking of stalls, carting water to horses, and especially the sticky mess of birthing animals. I've yet to rid my mind of the picture of you, Eva Jo, with your right arm all the way inside a calving cow. Disgusting!

When I had more time to read, inklings of a better life took form. While the two of you became involved with church activities, I began to keep a scrapbook of all the places I would travel. Teacher gave me a book about California, and I used to borrow Meg

Scheurman's fashion magazines. I wanted so much to be like the ladies in those pictures. During your times out hunting with Papa, I was planning a completely different life…the one of my dreams.

So when I met Jake and he told me about his California life, and then said he'd bring me here to marry, what would you have done? I knew my family would never get used to the idea of me leaving Yacolt. But I'm eighteen now and fully able to make decisions for myself. Jake held out a diamond engagement ring to me on Christmas Eve. If I wanted it, I had to leave that night. I just knew I'd never see him again if I hesitated. I made the one and only choice I could.

Dear sisters, go about your lives and do not fret about me. I don't miss Yacolt, but like I said, I do miss you. Getting married is a big step for me without the blessing of my parents, though I just know Papa and Mama would approve of Jake, if only they'd give him a chance. In a year, when we visit, the whole town will approve.

Nettie dear, I know it was especially hard on you to have me leave on Christmas, but I'm sure you understand better now why I had to. You're strong, and you'll be just fine. We'll return next Christmas, so keep my gift until then. I hope you liked the book I got for you. Did you unwrap it?

Papa and Mama are worried about me for nothing. Please tell them I'm in good hands here. Jake even spoils me. Whoever would have thought I would have servants? Just today I was fitted for a splendid green velvet gown and a hat to match. I'm to wear it to the horse races next month. Jake goes to every single one and is looking to buy a thoroughbred himself.

Did you know I took something besides clothing with me? Remember the locket that was Mama's? It has a picture of her in her wedding dress. Well, someday it was to be my inheritance, for reasons between our mother and I alone. I don't know why, but early Christmas Eve day she gave it to me. I was greatly thrilled to have it, of course. She'd even put it on a new lovely chain.

While examining it on the train south, I discovered a small mystery. I had no idea there was an inside compartment. It has a tiny latch that pops open just like the outside one. There are delicate words inside, but I haven't taken take the time to read them yet. Oddly, I'd never noticed the small bird engraved on the back. It's quite the dear piece. The entire insides are lined with gold, so likely it's valuable. I'll have to inquire further when I'm more settled. Don't think for a moment I'd ever sell it or anything; nevertheless, what's mine is mine.

Our wedding plans continue and yesterday was the bridal dress fitting. It's white satin with Battenberg lace on the sleeves and bodice. I will have a long train. Jake won't step foot in a church. Thus we'll have a civil ceremony! He's made that very clear. We'll have professional photographs done, of course, and I'll send one as soon as I can.

I sympathize with your inclimate weather. We've had only a day of rain since I arrived. The Angelenos are happy to see it in this desert climate, for the crops and orange trees that are everywhere. Jake took me for a ride on the Arroyo Seco road. Despite driving the horses at breakneck speed, the countryside views were exquisite There are English walnut trees, acres of grapevines, exotic pomegranates, and field after field of oranges, lemons, and melons ripe for harvesting. A land of Eden.

We stopped at an artist's colony, where I bought Mexican pottery to plant flowers for our generous porches. Street musicians played sad songs on guitars and women dressed in bohemian clothes talked at outside cafes. Though they looked foreign, the English they spoke was every bit as American as my own. Of course, some of them can speak Spanish, too. One woman smoked a cigar!

On the way home, we had our first discussion about what I will do with my time. Jake thinks my hands should never get dirty, but I told him I was from a farm, after all. So he's agreed to allow his wife garden time, as long as I protect my skin from the sun with a large hat. He doesn't want me looking like the native or Mexican women. I think their skin is lovely, but he wouldn't want to hear that. Strange I think, because his own complexion is quite dark and his brown eyes are every bit as mysterious as theirs.

We also discussed having children. I dream of many, but Jake told me in no uncertain terms that he didn't want any for a long time. Our conversation ended abruptly when he whipped the horses, and the buggy shot forward. My hat blew off, rolling over and over on the road behind. It was my favorite, but Jake refused to stop. Surely he'll purchase another.

In celebration of our wedding, Mr. Emory Hudson is sending a box of oranges to you via his railroad. You may pick them up at the

Portland station, since the railway connecting Yacolt is just starting to be built. Enjoy the luscious fruit and think of me. Mr. Hudson is a gracious father-in-law to do this for my family, don't you think? My earlier impression of him was an obvious error. What a relief.

I want to address your concerns about the "Black Rider." How dramatic of Will and Percy. They actually saw Jake perhaps, once or twice. Those two pests discovered our meeting place at the oak tree and spied on us. I must admit to being shocked when Jake brought them up on his horse, their little legs flailing as he galloped away down the road. Though they never returned, you surely cannot believe their tale of being threatened. What Jacob spoke to them is unknown to me, but certainly he would not deliberately frighten two small boys. How absurd! Besides you know they've always been full of too much whimsy. Ignore this tall tale. Black Rider, indeed!

Well, I'm needing to finish and post this letter.

Reveling in happiness,

Grace

P.S. There's so much to do here. We've been to the beach, and Jake even bought me a swimming suit. Yes, mixed bathing! Aunt Etta would not approve, but the ocean water is most refreshing. Jake also likes to go to Vaudeville Theatre. It's great fun, even shocking. I've lost count of the parties we've been to. So many, in fact, the dressmaker will be kept busy until I have enough proper clothing.

Three

PRAYER JOURNAL
NETTIE

Father God,

I haven't been able to sleep all night. Gracie's latest letter just backs up what I found in her journal. I know I shouldn't have read it, but I did. I guess she left it behind on accident, but when I found it, my curiosity took over. I can't believe how unhappy she has been, when I didn't have a clue. I adore her and thought that she knew she could tell me anything.

I'm shocked at the times she's felt left out of our family. She believes Eva Jo is Papa's girl and I am Mama's favorite. And the boys, well...they're the "boys." Does she resent me? Maybe she was just pretending to love all of us.

Oh Lord, how many mornings did we quickly do our chores and rush over to Eva Jo's, just to spend time talking, teasing one another, and dreaming? Even as old as we are, we still enjoyed our silly games while walking through the woods. And our tea parties—wasn't she having any fun?

She's always been an important person to all of us. I've shared everything with her. Eva Jo loves her just the same. But Lord, she doesn't see it that way. She said she sometimes feels invisible. What do

I do…now that I know the secrets of her heart? My heart is heavy with Gracie's sadness, but still angry too. Maybe she really will be happy with Jake. I hope so.

Please bring comfort to my soul. Please let Gracie see the truth. Let her feel our love.

Nettie

February 1902
Dear Eva Jo,

Since you're the married sister, I'm writing you alone this time, because you're better able to understand the longings of this smitten heart. You love Ephraim, therefore you must understand the depth of my love for Jake. He's promised to show me the world! Los Angeles is only the beginning, you see. My dreams are coming true.

Our little sister will be leaving home soon too. After all, she's sixteen. Then perhaps she'll have a bit more compassion for a runaway sister. We came of age while barely being noticed by Papa. He still thinks we're freckled girls playing in the orchard. For sure I was the thorn in his side. I was, you know. I can hear your protests, but I believe a person's mind knows the truth of one's own heart.

I'm hoping my communications are making you understand why I left with no regrets. This road's been traveled in my mind for at least three years. Mama thought I was never content, an unhappy "dreamer" of a girl. Well, this girl now has contentment…in a new place, with new friends. And best of all, a noble husband-to-be.

Last night, my prince charming took me to the Opera House. What a palace. Chandeliers lit the entire place like nothing I've ever seen. The carpets oozed between my feet they were so thick. Wooden floors of our old farmhouse beckon me no more. Such gray drabness, compared to the rainbow colors of this new life.

I've made good friends with a girl named Amanda Hutchinson. We've gone shopping together and had lunch several times a week, since we met. She and William, her beau, have gone with us to the theater a few times. She's known Jake for five years, after he returned from boarding school in Switzerland. It's nice to know that she thinks he's a good man, too.

"You'll never find another man quite like Jake," she told me.

"Well, I think I'm the luckiest girl in the world," I said.

She had a rather odd look on her face, but I took the opportunity to ask her if she knew anything about his mother.

"Oh Grace," she said, "I wouldn't ask him about her...not ever."

"But she's his mother, after all."

"That's exactly the point," she said with a finger to her lips. "A real mother would not have abandoned her only child."

I pretended to be nonchalant over the conversation, yet the entire story of Jake's mother remains unsettling. Well, I'm trying not to concern myself with the weightier issues of life, in order to keep attentions turned on my own delicious priorities. My wedding! You and your wild horses couldn't tear me away now, Eva Jo.

Other things occupy time, of course. As a recent volunteer at the Ladies' Aid Society, responsibilities abound. I can tell I'm often the topic of conversation, all because of my betrothal to Jake, no doubt.

I don't think Papa and Mama would ever be able to leave the farm and come to a place like this...fish out of water, so to speak. They should be glad for me. I've come up in the world. Who knows but we might one day rise to such prominence that I would be able to help our family with the financial burdens of keeping a menial farm business afloat?

You'd love it, Eva Jo, I know it. Your adventuresome spirit was made to explore the beauty all around here. For instance, there is a plant called a Bird-of-Paradise. How exotic! The flower looks like an enormous sharp-billed blue and orange bird. I know a friend who has a hat made to look like it. I want one.

What I love most is the air, free of anything rural. No barnyard smells since our stables are well away from the house. At night the scent of tropical flowers and salty ocean breezes waft through my open bedroom window. Something new is always blossoming, sunsets are glorious...inspiration enough to take up painting. Summer linens and straw hats can be worn at this time of year. Is it any wonder I'm thriving? Perhaps, too, because of the abundance of fresh fruits. I have only to walk outside and pluck a juicy ripe orange from one of a dozen trees. No more wandering about in Mama's dank root cellar for stored apples.

I will confess that my thoughts do stray to wondering about continuing life in Yacolt. Are your little ones growing like weeds? I imagine my brothers will be taller than me in no time. When I come home in December, I'm sure I'll scarce recognize any of them. I do wish I could hold Lulu; her sweetness is remembered fondly.

Eva Jo, I welcome your letters. Continue your writing, but please try to understand...without judgment. This dreamer's wishes are coming true.

Your sister forever, Gracie

P.S. All remains proper between Jake and I; you can be assured about that.

February 1902
Dear Gracie,

I appreciate the letters we've received. Despite the distance between us, every word keeps you close, and images dance in my head surrounding your adventures. I want you to know that you're wished only God's richest blessings, and prayers that Jake Hudson will be the man to make your dreams come true. Hopefully he'll not take after his father. Emory Hudson sounds like a man too full of himself, lacking any Christian morals. Although sending the oranges was a kind gesture from the elder Mr. Hudson, what if your first impressions of him were accurate?

Mama has said nothing about the locket. If she gave it to you, then of course it's yours. I do remember how lovely it was, but only vaguely recall the etching on the back, and I never knew of the other chamber.

If you're thinking my handwriting looks peculiar, you'd be right. I broke my arm. Imagine! I've been riding horses since a little snotnosed kid and never hurt myself too bad. Well, unless you count the time I got bucked off old Blue and hit my head. You're the only one who knew I couldn't remember two plus two for a week. (Thanks for never telling Mama.)

Anyway, I was helping Kizzy Ruth with her birth. Her mother was supposed to be here, but the Columbia flooded, and she sent word from Portland that she'd most likely not make it. Kizzy Ruth has always used Jewel, the Indian's midwife, and asked me, did I want to help? I figured since Kizzie had four already, and I had three, I maybe could be a comfort while I labor-sat. I know what you're probably thinking, Gracie, but how many calves and lambs did you and I help come into this world? Now, of course I know that human babies can't compare with birthing farm animals, but I thought, *Just how different can it all be?* That was then.

Turns out that labor "sitting" didn't involve sitting at all. That Kizzy Ruth walked around the whole muddy boundaries of their farm *twice*, before she said she was "ready." Despite the cold, we worked up quite a sweat after all that walking. Made me ready for sure. (I've got to quit eating so many of my own biscuits.)

Once we got back to the house, Kizzy said she was perking like a pot of good coffee as we helped her up the stairs. She started saying, "Oh my, oh my," just as we got her back to bed. Then quick as the shake of a lamb's tail, that little baby started to make its way into this old world. Things moved mighty fast and with me and Jewel so involved, we didn't hear Samuel, Kizzy Ruth's husband, come up the stairs and into the room. We figured later that he strolled in just about when his baby's head came popping out. I say "figure" because we don't know for sure, only seeing him after we heard him. When he fell flat forward, landing right on his large lumberman's face, we came very close to dropping that baby right then—a huge-sized squalling boy—being so startled and all.

Since Kizzy Ruth and Jewel were way busier than me, I was the one who went to check on Samuel. He was kind of moanin' soft and low by the time I got to his side. That's how I knew he wasn't dead or anything as extreme. He then rolled over, lifting his head still real dazed-like, looking towards the bed. I guess the sight of his wife in the process of giving life to another large baby boy, was too much 'cause he passed out again. This time he didn't make a sound. I was just as surprised to see a second child coming from such a little woman. But since Kizzy Ruth was laughing with joy and Jewel right along with her, I knew it was a good thing.

Torn between helping the dad, or helping the mama, I left Samuel right where he fell. It was a delight wrapping those babies tight and placing them on each side of their proud mama. They were all red-faced and pinched, but of course she thought they were the

46

sweetest things in all God's creation. I've never seen such a look on a woman's face, but then I guess all women since Eve have had a similar one, don't you think?

When Samuel started coming around again, he said he needed a little fresh air before he checked out the new family addition. Kizzy Ruth was all involved in getting the babies to nurse and didn't seem to notice her husband's need for revivement. As I helped him down the stairs towards the front door, he started asking me about the baby, apologizing the whole time for his "weakness."

"Well, Samuel," I said to him, looking right into his large, embarrassed face, "don't you mean...ba—bies?" I spoke that part nice and slow, emphasizing the double blessing. Since I was so close, I saw his eyes begin to roll back into his head right away. But it wasn't soon enough to brace myself for his fall, because all of his manly weight landed on top of me. Pushed me hard to the floor. That's when I heard the snap in my wrist.

As soon as I shoved him off me with the good arm, I managed to make a sling from a flour sack. It really hurt, but the sight of that man crumpled in a heap for the third time caused me such a fit of laughter that I can honestly say I felt little.

That was four days ago. Jewel gave me some white willow to chew on and it works to take the pain away, unless I try to do too much. Doc Barlow braced the break real tight, and says I should be good as new in a month. I told him that if I didn't keep up around here, in a month my little ones would have taken over the entire place, and Ephraim would find him another wife. Actually Mama took the boys, leaving Lulu here with me. The ladies from church brought enough food to keep us, and Ephraim, bless his undomesticated soul, has been a big help.

I'm wishing to see your face, Gracie Rose. Just looking into your eyes since the day you were born brings me peace. I'm not sure why that's been such a pleasure. Maybe because I could see you needed me. I always liked that. I never once remember being jealous of you or the others. You were a gift from God to me just the same as to Mama and Papa. You'll always belong to my heart because that's where I keep you. Place your hand over your own heart, Gracie. Feel it beating? That's how often I think of you...well, it seems that way to me.

I'm saying good-bye. Eva Jo

Hey little sister,

This is Ephraim. I'm taking care of your big sister. Wanted you to know even though she broke her arm, her mouth works just fine. Ha, ha. I think this is only the third or fourth letter I have ever wrote. Hope you are doing fine.

Your brother,
Ephraim

P.S. Your friend Mertie Johansen was one who brought food. Good thing she's pretty, 'cause she sure can't cook. Oh well, the chickens didn't seem to notice. Love again, Sister.

PRAYER JOURNAL
EVA JO

February 1, 1902
Lord,

It's late and the lamplight is weak, but I'm needing to share my heart thoughts with You. Even though my arm throbs, I did not want to forget a single thing of what I witnessed. My praise reaches to the Heavens for the double blessings Kizzy Ruth and Samuel hold in their arms. New life! Two babies! I'm laughing out loud in recognition of the goodness of Your hand. Thank You for allowing me the privilege of being part of it all. What joy my heart contains! Childbirth is difficult, but the birthing miracle is almost beyond description. I've never been more surprised than when that second boy was born. Kizzy Ruth is probably still smiling. Sure hope Samuel has recovered, 'cause when I left, he was pale as skimmed milk.

Life is hard, bringing us to our knees, yet right in the middle of it all we see Your almighty, perfect plan. You are a good God, yet I must confess my doubts and continuing fears for my sister. Forgive me that I doubt Your provision for her. If Your eye is on the smallest of birds, then I should trust You know all about Grace, even as I write. Help me to remember that she is the apple of Your eye. Right now I'm a stranger in her life, so surprised am I by her actions. Can one human ever really know another? Of course You, my Lord know everything…each time we sit or stand. My now, that's a lot of knowing.

My pain is worsening. Please help me keep my home and family together until this arm is healed. Help me to be the woman You've called me to be—the wife, mother, daughter, and sister You desire.

I want to serve You with a heart filled with gratitude, not fear…a submitted heart full of trust and obedience. May Gracie's heart be submitted to Your perfect will.

Your daughter, Eva Jo

February 14, 1902
Gracie Dearest,

My first postcard! Yes it's true I've finally seen the Ocean! We took a lovely ride on the Clamshell Railroad, down the Long Beach peninsula, close to where Lewis and Clark trekked. I struggle with words to describe how it made me feel. Who would have thought that winter at the ocean could be so lovely.

Love, Eva Jo

P.S. Oh, and happy Valentine's Day, and of course Happy Wedding day—how romantic. All my love goes to you for your new role as wife and forever companion.

PRAYER JOURNAL
EVA JO

At the Beach
Oh Lord,

I am overwhelmed with the sights and sounds all around. Never have I seen You so big, or observed myself to be so small. Such beauty is a constant reminder of Your magnificent presence in my life. Who am I that You should bestow such blessings? It makes me purely humbled. Why am I surprised? You have blessed me without measure my whole life. I admit I've not always seen what You've put on my plate as just that, yet in the reflection of this place I tell you, I believe it is so. May I bless others with the same measure. May I pour out grace as it has been poured into my life.

On the horizon I see a fishing vessel. I wonder, are those aboard aware of who fills their nets? Do their lips give You praise for what You provide? Forgive me for the times I've not been grateful, or taken things for granted...taken You for granted. Sometimes I wonder why You ever chose me in the first place. I'm laughing inside with the joy of it. Joy to the world...joy to me.

May Gracie be reminded of You as well. Please don't let her shut us out though she has a new life and a new love.

Your grateful daughter,

Eva Jo

February 14, 1902
Dear Gracie,

Today you're getting married...you were my first thought this morning. Although I'm sad because we're not together, I do love you and pray for your marriage. I want you to be happy...we all do. Eva Jo and I long to hear all the details. Mama and Papa don't know I'm writing, but despite their pain, and underneath the anger, deep love for you is still there. I just know it.

I have some pretty exciting news! Miss Knatz, our schoolteacher, is engaged. She's getting married this summer to a family friend from Portland. When he came to visit last week, Mama and I happened to bump into them while in town. Miss Knatz looked so happy; whenever she looked at him it was with obvious adoration...she fairly swooned. We ended up going to Uncle Herman's restaurant to have coffee and biscuits. It was a very interesting time, listening to their plans for travel and work. I've no doubt that, together, they'll do just fine. How romantic it all seems.

Here's the excitement part. The most interesting thing they discussed was...ME! That probably sounds horrible. I don't mean to brag. It's just the most incredible news I've ever had. Miss Knatz has recommended me to be the new teacher in the fall. I am simply beside myself. Mama actually gasped and clapped her hands. She acted so proud. I could be head mistress of Good Hope School. ME!

Can you believe this, Gracie? The schoolboard meets Friday, the twenty-first. I'm to present myself to them, along with an essay on why I should be hired. I'm very nervous. At least I'll look good because Mama is going to whip up a dress out of some material she's been saving for a special occasion. It's really more your color than mine but, still, I'm grateful. What would I do without Mama? She's going to help me practice my presentation.

I couldn't wait to tell someone else, so I ran right away and shared the news with Cal. He seemed excited for me and liked the idea that I would be teaching his daughters. I'm sure you remember him; he's Papa's farmhand—the widower with the twins.

"You're the perfect woman for teaching, Nettie." He extended his hand with the congratulations.

My face went hot, but I managed an awkward thank you, anyway, before pulling my sweaty palm back.

"What will your pay be?"

"What?"

"How much will your salary be?" He leaned closer, like I was hard of hearing or something.

Suddenly, I felt foolish. Grace, I never even asked.

"Well now," I said, "I don't know, Cal."

He threw his head back and laughed.

My face grew hotter. "What's so funny?"

"Well, Missy, here you are, all grown up and ready to step into your first job, and you don't even know the money you'll be making. Maybe they want you to work for nothing."

Then he was rude enough to laugh again. Only when he saw I was getting riled did he stop. Real quick like, he took off his hat and apologized. But he was still smirking. Then he just stood there, looking at me. Goodness, his eyes exactly match the Lewis River's deepest pools. Did you ever notice that? Maybe it was the way he looked at me that made them so full of interest. Or maybe it was because he called me a "woman." I've only ever been the boss's girl who played with his children, even though I've had a crush on him from afar. He's had patience as a good listening ear all along, even though Papa always keeps him busy. But today was different. Sometimes I think I might be too dramatic.

Oh well, I won't bore you any further with news from Washington, since your experiences in California are far grander.

I'm wishing you were here this very minute, though, because writing doesn't take the place of talking...you know how I love to talk. Guess that will help me in my teaching. Oh, I hope I get the job, whatever the pay.

I have to go now—I'm watching Eva Jo's oldest while she and Ephraim are having a holiday. When her boys are together with Will and Percy, they are more than a handful. I can't imagine having them all in one classroom with others as well. Oh, I think I'm getting a headache.

Write soon,
Nettie

PRAYER JOURNAL
NETTIE

February 1902
My Father in Heaven.

I need desperately to climb upon Your lap and feel You hold me close. I'm being considered for a very grown-up job, but I'm feeling small and unsettled inside. What is wrong with me? Is it Cal?

Only You know how smitten I've been with him, since the moment I ran smack into him in the barn, and we both ended up slipping into a mucky puddle, way last fall. His kindness and laugh when he helped me stand made my heart jump. Today I felt something from *him*.

I've tried to avoid thinking about the two of us, but I'm older now and may have a working position. Plus, he called me a "woman." Does he see me different than when he first came to work here? I think the answer lies in that look he gave me. Long and silent. My unspoken dream (even to myself) has been that someday he would fall in love with me.

Hmmm…Lord, have I ever taken the time to ask You if that is Your will? I mean, would it be okay if Cal were my husband?

I am feeling intimidated at this moment. He is, after all, "Papa" to Cassie and Sissie. If we were to marry, I would be a "Mama."

Lord, I can scarcely bear that thought right now. I'm not feeling well; my heart is aching, and my stomach's tight. I just don't know, Lord. My feelings are strong toward him, but I am just a kid. I haven't had to be responsible for anyone; my parents take care of me.

It hurts to realize I may possibly have to let this dream die. If it's just a silly child's dream, I'll need Your help to let go. For sure, I want to make a better decision than Gracie did.

I also need to know if it's Your will for me to be a schoolteacher. I was so excited about the offer, but it pales in comparison to maybe having a life with Cal and his girls. Could I do both?

Perhaps I am borrowing needless worry. It's not like Cal has even asked to court me, or anything close to that. It was just a "look"…and my dream. Still…

Lord, You are faithful. Help me leave the dreams of my heart in Your hand. It's late, and I truly need to practice my schoolboard presentation.

In Jesus' name, amen.

Nettie

February 1902
Dear Gracie,

I'm still not believing that I, Eva Jo, have been to the ocean. My sweet Ephraim arranged the entire trip for my birthday. Nettie was kind enough to come in to town to watch the boys. Lulu stayed with us because I'm still nursing. I was nervous some, since I'd never left them before, but our little sister did a wonderful job. She's certainly grown up now. I'm very excited about her maybe being Good Hope's next teacher. What a girl!

Well, back to the ocean. Of course I know you practically live on the water, yet for me it's been life-changing. In some places it was very busy with the fishing boats coming and going. But when we got away from the hustle, the beauty was inspiring. An old fisherman told me some "special" people can actually tell when the tide changes between "coming in" and "going out." Imagine the very instant! Ephraim laughed his head off when I told him that one. But I don't know???

The bigness of the Pacific gave me thought right away to the Lord. And oh the noise! It was more than the winds sweeping through our little valley off Mt. Saint Helen's...steady, sure, and powerful.

I actually skipped along beside the water, playing tag with the waves, finding incredible shells...little houses for sea critters. God is so creative...what pleasures He gives. There's one snow-white shell, round and almost flat, with a star like design on top. Do you know it? A sand dollar. When I showed Ephraim, he called it a "dollar of the sand." Felt like a piece of the ocean in my hand. Still does.

Lulu seemed mesmerized when we took her to the water's edge. She's amazing!

I couldn't wait to show my treasure to Lucas and D.J. They had more questions than I have energy to answer. When I told them you lived near the very same water, they were most jealous of the fact.

While wading in the grand water, I was thinking that maybe some of those very same waves had touched shore where you live. I know I have quite an imagination, but still that intimate reminder of you satisfies. The Bible says that God's thoughts of us are too many to count. Well, Gracie, I've lost count of the many love thoughts I have of you.

Nettie and I cannot wait to hear the details of your entire wedding day; we want to know about it all. A photograph would be wonderful. I hope it won't take long. My curious nature makes me restless, and the slowness of the mail is beyond frustration...it's maddening.

I've felt a prompting deep within the last few days to keep you in prayer. I'm sure it's because of all the new responsibility you're bearing as Mrs. Jake Hudson.

As always, Eva Jo

P.S. I've saved every letter you've written, tucked in the little trunk you gave me at Lulu's birth.

February 16, 1902
Dear Eva Jo and Nettie,

Congratulations, Nettie. No doubt you'll make a delightful teacher...Mama always thought so. I can understand her pride. Be sure and tell Miss Knatz I send hearty best wishes. Seems you have better news than I.

There's been a postponement. I'm not yet married. One of Jake's friends in San Francisco needed him. He sent word a few days before the wedding, so Jake left for a week or so. I begged him to tell his friend "our" day was set, but he pulled away from me, and the train took him northward. I sought comfort from my friend Amanda.

She knows Jake's family and said there was business that only Jake could attend to. I've cried buckets of tears, not understanding what could have been more important than our wedding. The ceremony was to have been in Amanda's mother's garden. I was embarrassed, because I know a lot of preparation had gone on, and they must be upset.

When Jake returned yesterday, he was in a foul mood if ever I saw one. I haven't approached him about setting a new wedding date. He stayed in last night, smoking cigars down in the study, pacing the floor until very late, and sleeping on the leather couch. I saw this through the keyhole. This morning, he was gone, and hasn't returned. I'm a little afraid, Sister; he's so changed. Something must have happened in San Francisco to make him this way. I've questioned Amanda, but she thinks his mood will pass.

I've paced a distance in my bedroom as well. Mrs. White, our cook, always has a smile for me, making her a welcome sight when I ate my lonely breakfast this morning. She maintains a peace and calm that permeates the kitchen. It's my favorite place in this whole friendless house.

Dinner tonight was another meal alone, my thoughts constantly on Jake and his whereabouts.

"Will you be all right, Miss Grace? I could stay a while, fix a cup of tea, if ya'd like."

"No thank you, Flossie. I'm sure Mr. Hudson will be along shortly."

"I've not said anything, Miss Grace, but I'm real sorry about your wedding plans. Postponed and all, I mean."

"Thank you for your kindness. It's most welcomed."

I was embarrassed by my unstoppable tears, but she seemed not to notice.

Mrs White has often described her pleasant cottage near the harbor area. So apparent is her contentment, I'm wondering if she has a secret. As soon as she finished dishes and was gone, I wished her back.

Must close….there's loud pounding and shouting at the front door. Jake must have forgotten his keys.

Grace

Prayer Journal
Eva Jo

Midnight. Something's wrong with Gracie! Lord, You woke me to pray. Protect my sister's life. Oh God, have mercy on Your wayward sheep. Give my sister courage to stand against what evil comes against her.

E.J.

Grace's Diary

February 17, 1902
Dear Diary,

I've made a terrible mistake. I thought Jake loved me. I thought he wanted to marry me. I am so, so foolish. Oh, how I wish I'd stayed in Washington…on the farm. At least I was loved there. I want to go home, but I know I cannot.

Last night was a horror! I scarce can bring myself to face this…Jake forced himself on me. He was drunk, stinking of whiskey, and caught me by the hand the instant the front door flew open.

"What do you think you're doing?" he shouted, "locking me out of my own house?" He was a madman.

He grabbed one shoulder, twisted my arm behind my back, and shoved me into the study. He pushed so hard, I lost my footing and landed in a heap on the floor, the breath knocked out of me. With my long skirts, I couldn't get up, and in a flash of pain, he was on top of me, tearing at my clothes. The smell of him made me gag, I screamed and tried to reason with him, but he said I owed him.

"Who do you think you are anyway, Miss High-and-Mighty? I paid for all your new little trinkets, now you owe me."

"Please," I begged, "Jake, I love you. I left my family for you."

I'll never forget his laugh. It was the devil himself cackling over me. He became a possessed animal.

I continued fighting, but there was no one to hear my screams.

"We'll get married when I say so, but tonight will be the honeymoon."

I begged and pleaded some more, choking on my own sobs. One hand on my throat, he struck me full in the face. I must have blacked out.

When I woke, I was confused as to my whereabouts. I tried to move, but every inch of my body ached. I groaned and made an effort to sit up. I was still lying on the floor, parts of me shamefully exposed. The last of the lamplight sputtered, and I supposed it must be close to dawn. How I longed for the terrible blackness of the night to be ended.

Then I heard it. Breathing!

I turned my head slowly. I was looking right into Jake's face. My flesh recoiled at the sight. Because his hand yet rested on my chest, I dared not move, for fear he would awake, only to violate me again.

Summoning every ounce of strength left, I gingerly picked up his arm by a sleeve and inched away, the carpet chafing my back. Trying to stand, my legs refused to hold any weight, and I crumpled back to the floor. He stirred. Nightmarish scenes flashed in my mind, and I wanted to shriek, remembering all he'd done. I clamped one hand over my mouth for fear of crying out. Pain shot through my body.

Oh no, oh no. Please no. How dare he? How dare he take from me what I was so willing to give after we married? My stomach churned with memory as foul bile rose, burning my throat.

Terrified he might wake, I forced myself upright. The room swirled about, like a bizarre carousel. Grabbing furniture, the walls, whatever was available, I limped to the hallway. Quivering with fear, I dragged the sordid remnant of who I used to be up the stairs, listening for the beast. Only ragged snoring came from below.

Every step brought safety closer, propelling me onward. I avoided the reflection passing in the mirrors along the stairway. What would a woman of scorn look like? I wasn't ready to find out. It was all my fault. For an instant, I wanted to hurl myself to the bottom, ending it all. But imagining Mrs. White's horror when she came to work was too much, and I abandoned the thought.

I want my mother, my sisters…my family. I should be there now, wrapped in my quilt, reading and laughing with Nettie. I should be brushing down horses and mucking out stalls in the misty rain of home.

Instead I'm in this room, a prisoner of my own choices. After getting my repugnant clothes off, I buried them in the back of my chifferobe. I'll burn them later. There was little water left in the washbowl, but I managed to remove some of Jake's violation, before dumping talc on myself from head to toe. I rubbed it in so hard that my skin burns with the effort. But how do I cleanse my heart? Worse yet, how do I cleanse my soul? I'm ruined from the inside out. No one will want a used, willful girl.

I don't know what to do. The shame of what's happened weighs on me like lead.

Mrs. White brought me breakfast in bed because I'm pretending to be sick today. When she asked me about the bruise on my cheek, I said a book had fallen from a library shelf and struck me. She's suspicious, but some things must never be shared. This hurt is consuming. How will life go on? Jake terrifies me, but I heard him leave the house at least. Obviously he has no remorse for his violation…my violation.

G

Four

Dear McLeod Family,

Ya do not know me. I'm Mrs. Floss White. I'm sending this letter, so's ya might find some comfort beyond your sister's misfortunes. I begged her to write her family, but I've no way to know if she did. Sad though it is, my conscience begs me tell you a few things, just in case.

Part of my great fondness for Miss Grace comes from her being so young and all...a child really. I've watched how the mister's treated his betrothed and well, now I feel guilty. Looking back, I should have done more because I suspect his cruelty has taken a toll, greater than she's willing to tell.

He was drinking and gambling for days on end, coming home only to rant and rave, then pass out in drunken stupors. For those reasons or not, his father fired him, told him to get out of town even.

The younger Mr. Hudson left Miss Grace standing in the street with a pitiful pile of belongings and small suitcase, after his father's hired men put a chain and padlock on the front door of their house. Just got in the buggy, whipped his horse, and left. Good riddance, I say, and I believe your sister feels the same, though her heart be now broken over her fallen fortunes.

"Don't you be crying over spilt milk, Miss Grace," I said. "There are other fish in the sea."

"You mean sharks," she said.

But there was no mirth in that remark. She crumpled to the ground at my feet, watching Mr. Hudson, till he was gone from sight.

"Miss Grace," I said, "come home with me. My place is small, but I've got a cot you can land on."

I helped her stand and walked her to my place. She's sleeping like a baby, now, so I must close, in order to post this. Any letters you want to send, mail them here, and I'll see she gets every one. I sense something in her little spirit. I'm guessing she won't stay put here long. Despite the many hurts, she's determined to make her choices right. Them's her words.

Said to me: "Mrs. White, somehow I have to make my choices right. Otherwise, my leaving home would prove to be a waste entirely. I cannot let that happen. Please understand."

I told her I did understand, but I'm telling you, I don't. Watching her sleep makes her look even more like a little wisp of wind. She'll not survive in this town without some help. Despite her leaving all of you behind, she speaks of you every single day.

Enough of my babble. I'm a Christian woman, and live the best I can, standing on the word of God. I'll do right by your girl. I promise.

Miss Grace's friend and yours,
Mrs. Florence White
25 Harbor Lane
Los Angeles, California

March 15, 1902
Dear Gracie,

How are you? We are worried sick after receiving a letter from a Mrs. White. Have you left her shelter? If you have, maybe you're on your way home. My heart's burdened to the depths over thoughts of your being out on the streets somewhere.

Mrs. White gave us permission to send our letters to her. I must continue writing since it is the only way I have of reaching out...of reaching you. Putting words on paper somehow frees my mind of too many bad thoughts surrounding your well-being.

Today I took old Blue out riding, hoping to take a break from fretting. Oh, of course you don't know; Papa finally gave in to my love-nagging. Blue is mine.

I put Lulu in the willow papoose carrier Papa made for her when she was born. She loves it...snug as a bug in a rug. I promise you, that old horse noticed I looked peculiar, with a sleeping angel on my back. I was determined just the same. The boys stayed behind while Ephraim worked, so they didn't notice I'd left. Managing all three would have been impossible from the back of a horse.

I had indeed been going stir-crazy with all the winter rain, toddler's colds, and the demands of our little princess. (That's what all the menfolk call my Louisa Grace.) Anyway, I figured Blue needed to get out the same. I was right. He lifted his head and tail, like a young colt, instead of the old man of twenty his teeth say he is.

The roads were sorely wet, forcing me to take it nice and slow. I didn't want to miss anything on my first journey into spring, because I always feel closer to the Almighty when outside. I even saw an early trillium...thrilling! It was absolutely perfect, set aside by the dark woods behind. I was carefree during the entire ride, not wanting to finish. The warmth of the sun on my back was altogether comforting. With soft breezes lifting my hair, I clean forgot about the chores I'd left undone. Ephraim said to take my time, we could have a breakfast dinner and he'd not even notice.

I felt God giving me a gift. Well, me and Lulu that is, although she slept through the gifting. Someday I'll take her for her first walk in the woods, just like I took you, Gracie. Of course I'm not sure what kind of guide I was, me being five and you only two. But you wanted to go where I went, so I gave in. Everything we saw made you laugh. You were the happiest child, making my life special. Your giggles were catching. Sometimes you'd laugh so hard, you'd fall on your behind. Then of course, the rest of us laughed even harder. Papa said he and Mama must have named you Grace by divine guidance, because having you was a showering of God's grace contained in one little human bundle.

Though riding put me behind a day, I've been getting one of the Indian girls living outside town to help me now and then. She's become right special to me. Tiny for her age, she's smart as a whip, with eyes like shiny rocks washed in Fargher Lake. She's patiently kind with the boys and Lulu adores her. The best part is she's got a hungry curiosity about our Lord and wants to know more each time she comes. If we can make room, I'm thinking of asking her parents to let her stay with us on a regular basis so I can school her some. Little Dove's her name...it fits her.

Mama said she believes you'll be home soon. All of us hope for that. You'll be shocked at how big Percy and Willie are getting. Papa is teaching them to hunt with dogs. Those two have a way with animals. Papa says that's good and that's bad, because if you make a pet of a hunting dog, he's no good for the chase. Just last week Mama caught Birdie, their new coon pup, snuggled down as comfy as could be, right in the middle of both of them. Bet she never did tell the "Mister." (Did we ever figure out why she calls him that? She probably wouldn't tell me if I asked.)

Goodness, I can barely see to write. I'm tired and the lamp is sputtering. Night, sweet sister.

P.S. Because you and I used to ride double on Blue, lots of my time was taken up with thoughts of you. I wonder if you miss the simple things that once made you happy??? I do enjoy your letters, yet I'm thinking there's much left unsaid. Even thought I saw holes in the paper. Ha. Ha. Hope you're not feeling too sad with the way things worked out for you and Jake. He was not worthy of you. God has a better plan, and someday, if you trust Him, it will all be revealed.

Eva Jo

March 17, 1902

I'm back. We've still not heard a word from you, which causes tears of frustration and frankly, makes me crabby. I'm trying to be the strong "big" sister for Nettie and the boys, but there are days when I can hardly manage for the wondering.

Two days seems like a short time, but circumstances can come barreling through and upset things in three shakes of a lamb's tail.

The night I wrote you last was nice enough to leave the window open a crack in our bedroom. I must have heard "it" first, because I woke up real startled like and had my feet on the floor before I knew it. I was thinking to myself, perhaps I'd heard Lulu, but when I checked, she was sleeping peaceful, as were the boys.

I didn't see a reason to wake Ephraim, since he was slumbering hard and heavy. Anyway, when I got downstairs, I first went to the back door to check the porch. All I saw was the washtub turned over and figured that must have been what woke me. Sometimes a whole family of pesky raccoons makes a night-time visit. The moon was almost full and the sky clear, but I saw nothing around the barn or anything in between. Finally I went to the front door and opened it full wide. I thought I must have been dreaming, because what I saw was nightmare-sized. There standing—I say STANDING—in front of my face was the biggest black bear I ever saw!

I don't know who was most startled—me or her. She looked at me, and I looked back, then opened my mouth and yelled as loud as I could. (Mama always said I could wake the dead with one scream.) Well, maybe the dead, but not my husband...or his children. It was just me and the bear, Grace, just me and the big bear. After screaming, I slammed the door right in its face as hard as I could. I heard only some loud grunts and my own panting as I leaned my ear to the wood. She must have been listening too because she stayed put for a long time, breathing loud and steady. I was afraid to get Ephraim, thinking the bear might break in and wreck the whole house.

When it finally got quiet, I backed away to look out the window. I could see her meandering ever so slow-like, right towards the smokehouse. When she got there, she began rocking with all her weight on the door. Since I'd seen a bear knock down a huge evergreen, I knew what damage could be done to a little old building.

That's when I made my decision. I went for the gun.

Looking back, I guess I should have taken the time to fetch Ephraim. Instead I grabbed the old shotgun we inherited from his Grandpa, jammed a shell into it, and headed out the back door to sneak up on that thieving beast. I would have had her too. Only too late did I realize she wasn't alone.

I heard them before I saw them, but she spotted her cubs coming from behind me. That old sow bear had three, and when they heard her slamming on the storehouse they came running like the devil was chasing them. The whole thing exploded so fast, I'm still piecing it all together. Right when her attention was toward the cubs is when she saw me, immediately losing interest in the food. She started at me about the same time I saw the cubs and for a second I was torn over shooting her because of them. Yet I didn't want my babies left without a mother or one that was torn up and useless.

Now all this thinking was going on while I lifted the gun to my shoulder, took aim, and fired. What happened next is a blur, and my ears are still ringing. I guess it had been a long time since Grandpa's old relic had been fired, because when I pulled the trigger there was a slight pause before a huge flash of light went off right beside my head. I hit the ground harder than a steer at slaughter, being totally stunned for what seemed like an eternity. I heard nothing and could only make out hazy shapes. I sat up, shook my head, and looked around for my intended target. Mama and her cubs must have hightailed it to the woods because I couldn't see hide nor hair of them in the moonlight.

Catching sight of some kind of movement, I turned my head in the direction of the house. Thinking the bears had circled around I prayed, asking the Lord to make it quick, knowing by now that the she bear would be enough riled up, I'd be easy pickings. Thankfully it was Ephraim carrying a squalling Lulu wrapped in a blanket. I guessed she was crying, because Gracie, I could hear nothing, except the loud ringing like Easter morning still going on in my head. Ephraim said something, I mean, I saw his mouth moving and all. He got real close to my face when he noticed I couldn't hear a thing.

"Eva Jo," he says, screaming in one ear, "why are you outside in your nightdress...sitting on the ground?"

Really Gracie, what did he think I was doing? Picking spring daisies? Right then's when he spotted the gun laying beside me, split open like an overripe melon. He handed the baby to me and ran over to where I was pointing and saw the smokehouse door hanging off the hinges. He rushed back, scratching his head.

"Only thing that could do that would be a bear. Ha, my wife the bear hunter!" He looked proud and worried at the same time.

"Are you all right?" By then, my hearing was returning and I reckoned I was. Only I started laughing so hard I could hardly stand, even with Ephraim's help. See Gracie, he'd been in such a hurry to run outside, he forgot to pull on any trousers. I'll never forget the sight of my husband running around in the moonlight in his unmentionables. At first I guess Ephraim figured the explosion rattled me more that he thought, 'cause he had a most puzzled look on his very serious face. That being the case, I laughed even harder. I was trying to hold on to a squirming baby with one hand and point with the other.

"Oh my sweet jackrabbits," says my modest husband when he

realized he was missing something. By that time both boys were on the porch, wondering if their parents were moonstruck. They came running out, and all of them helped me back into the house.

With everyone wide awake at one in the morning, I got out some leftover cornbread and Basket Flats honey the bears would've loved. By the time I finished telling them what happened, Lulu had fallen back to sleep and her brothers were yawning. I was feeling mighty sore all over, ready for bed again myself.

After all the children were tucked in snug, Ephraim and I had ourselves another spell of laughing before finally saying good night.

I hope my family talk is not boring you. I'm only wanting to stay connected. If I share my daily life, then I feel you're nearby, instead of miles beyond me. Every day with the sunrise, I beg God to watch over you, directing you in His ways. God's heart is huge, compared to mine, and when I think of how much love is contained there for each of us, I weep. I've shed many a salty tear for you, little sister.

Love,
Eva Jo

GRACE'S DIARY

California

Dear Diary,

I have stayed with Mrs. White now for three days. I fear Jake might come looking for me, but hopefully he does not know where I've gone. Mrs. White is not wanting to interfere, but she can't help giving me some of her sage advice.

"Dearie, use your sense," she said. "You're young. You should go back home...start over with those who love you. Not that you are not welcome here, mind you."

I listened, but she knows nothing of what Jake has done. And if she did, I'm sure she'd not want the likes of me under her roof. I began to cry and couldn't stop. I might stay a while longer here. It's cozy clean, every corner scrubbed. I'm just not sure what to do. But I know I'll never be able to go back home. My papa was right to declare me dead because I might as well be. When I walk out of this house, all will see what I've become. Should I have Mrs. White create a huge letter *A* and wear it about my neck as I well deserve?

Whatever happens next will be my fate.

Gracie

March 1902
My dearest Gracie,

I'm sending this letter to your friend's house. Even though the way Jake left you was cruel, I am not surprised. Now you can see exactly the kind of man he is, and you are free to come home. I'm hoping you'll do so. Even though you might arrive soon, I can't wait to share some exciting news. Wonderful things have been happening lately.

First of all, you may congratulate me officially. I will be the one replacing Miss Knatz as teacher after she leaves and fall class begins. I certainly never realized how much training there is, but with Mama's help, I'll be ready. You won't believe all the silly rules they have for me. Eva Jo and I have laughed hours over the entire list.

Now there's even more news. I have been spending a lot of time with Cal. What do you think of that? Well, it's only because I've had more contact with his daughters. Still, a girl can dream.

After Papa bought the Sniders' farm, he and Cal have had more work than ever. They leave before sunrise. Since I need to be with the girls when they wake up, we've had some sweet early morning conversations. I love helping them dress in their frills...so different than Will and Percy.

I'm not sure how it happened, but one day I found myself there a little earlier, and ended up making Cal his breakfast. I sat down with him while he ate. It was nice, and he really seemed to like my griddle cakes. Ever since, we have breakfast together several mornings a week. He's not like Papa in the mornings—Cal talks more. (But not as much as me, of course.)

A lot of times he and the girls have supper with us at the big house, but once, when Cassie was feeling poorly, I fixed supper at the bunkhouse.

"Eat with us," the girls begged.

I sat directly across from Cal. After he prayed, I looked up to find him staring at me with those river-colored eyes.

"Penny for your thoughts," I said. Wasn't that a dumb thing to spout?

He cleared his throat. "Uh, I...," he stammered.

I was astonished. Cal stammering? It was usually me being the awkward one.

"I don't mean to make you uncomfortable, but I was just noticing that, well, uh..." He stopped and smiled. "You have turned into a very pretty lady. One with a job and everything."

I'm sure my face went red. I know I felt hot all over. I was a little uncomfortable but more than pleased for the noticing. "Cal, I don't know what to say."

"Say thank you to Daddy," Sissy said.

"Thank you, Daddy."

Both girls burst into laughter...so did Cal and I. Something wonderful happened in that moment.

Oh Gracie, when I am with him, there's not a care in the world. I love working around his place and caring for the girls. My heart beats faster whenever I know he's due home. When we say "good-bye," I'm already looking forward to our next "hello."

Life couldn't be better for me, and I'm sure it will be better for you...especially without Jake Hudson. You probably don't want any advice from your younger sister, but I believe it's true just the same.

Love to you,

Annette Louise (Nettie)

P.S. Since I have employment and all, I think I'll start going by "Annette." What do you think?

Dear Sisters,

Just a postcard to let you know I am fine. I've moved to a nice room over a business, doing laundry and ironing until I find real employment. I'm not coming home, but please continue your letters sent to Flossie's address. I'm on another adventure. I will survive. More to you later.

Gracie

GRACE'S DIARY

Dear Diary,

I've sold what belongings I had, getting next to nothing for it all. I'm holding on to Mama's locket…a small link to home.

I feel the walls in this wretched place closing in like a coffin. I'm lonely, but somehow I have to prove I can make it after the disaster of Jake's violation and abandonment. I saw several of his friends on the street yesterday. They pretended not to notice me, but when I passed, I could hear their bawdy laughter and insults. I've got to shut out this hurt, keep it at bay, or it will win, and I'll lose. I can't let that happen. I won't.

Voices constantly invade this room from the tavern below. Last night I heard drunken sailors on the stairs. I ran to the door with a kitchen knife, my heart pounding out of my chest. I must have gotten up too quickly, because I felt faint with the effort. I sat in a chair for hours, listening. I did fall asleep later, with my weapon underneath the pillow. Morning came too soon, the rising light dull and ordinary. Only a short while ago, I couldn't get enough of the California sun, now the brightness mocks my mood, refusing to penetrate this darkness.

I long for something to read, but this dismal space holds not one book. Of course most days I can only fall into bed, exhausted with the labor of my work.

Whatever shall become of me, whatever indeed?

G

March 1902
Dear Gracie,

I've had many sleepless nights lately. Mostly over you. In my spirit, I feel something is dreadfully wrong. Helpless to actually know, my prayers are continually for your safety. There's an overwhelming sense that you're in harm's way. I've even had a mind to come down and look for you, but home responsibilities demand otherwise.

At least you've found a job, but will it get you by? You certainly can come home, Sister. Ephraim and I have money ...you just have to send word, and we'll get it to you.

Grace, don't let stubbornness get in the way of good thinking. We love you...all of us. Even Aunt Etta agrees we're not the same without you.

Sorry this is so short. All of us have colds and I've so much to do.

Love to you, Eva Jo

Five

Dear Gracie,

I've been asking God to keep you in the shelter of His wings. Are you somewhere safe? Do you still have friendship with Amanda? Hopefully you have all the books you need to keep you company at day's end. A book to you was like the out of doors to me, a magnet.

Just this morning when thanking the Lord for all the blessings He's given, guess what was close to the top of the list? Reading! I never thought that being able to read was a gift— guess I've taken it for granted all this time. Truth is, I can't remember when I couldn't read. Some of my earliest memories are of Mama reading to us with the last light of day, beside a smoky lamp. Now I realize what a sacrifice she made in sharing the privilege. Some days I'm so tired I fall asleep with my clothes on, yet our mother never seemed to tire of seeing her children catch on to the special magic treasured away in the weathered reading primer. You, of course, became a bookworm. Ha!

I've been reminded of the blessing a lot lately, trying to teach Little Dove. Her English has improved bushels, and I've been as proud of her as I could be. Still, where to start loomed at me big. Mama's been helpful in giving pointers and finally after weeks of struggle, we've made a breakthrough.

Little Dove has courage that inspires me. No matter how hard the struggles, her strong inner spirit shines through. Though young, she's considered a woman in the tribe, so soon she'll be expected to marry, though maybe because of her smallness, they'll hold off a year or two. She's got great patience for learning.

You'd like her, I know. Maybe the reason I'm fond of her is because we met right after you left. I see that as a gift from the Lord...to fill an empty spot in my heart, I mean. Oh, don't get me wrong, your place can never be filled. Yet the loneliness of departure left a hole the size of Fargher Lake, and I believe God's hand brought Little Dove to this little home. With all the work, there's never much time for sitting. But when my three darlings hit nap-time together, I manage a few minutes for instruction with her.

Ephraim calls her "Dovie," an endearment that makes her head drop and eyelids flutter. Her parents work hard and though they love their daughter, there's not much time for pleasantries. If my life is hard (not a complaint), then hers is ten times more difficult. One day when we went into town, I was showing her our family burial plot and she broke down sobbing. So many of her people have died, there's no way to count them all. No wonder her mother's face seems a mask of sorrow, with having to bury child after child. I think Little Dove makes her proud, but she struggles with the expression of it.

Lulu said her first word yesterday. Well, maybe. I've been a little worried because she seems to take no interest in talking. I mentioned it to Ephraim, but he says she's got so many people chattering around her all the time, she doesn't stand a chance. I think I'll ask Mama what she thinks, just the same.

I swear the boys seem bigger in the morning than when I put them to bed at night. David John has decided he wants to be called "DJ." Just woke up one morning and made the announcement at the breakfast table. His father reminded him that he would answer to whatever his parents called him. Ephraim winked at me, and has called him "DJ" every since. Those two have a special kind of connection. Makes me think that Ephraim gave birth instead of me. Ha, Ha! He's more strong-willed than Will and Percy put together. I believe the Lord will call him for something special. I know for sure he's got a unique connection with animals...and not just the ones around the house, 'cause he's always bringing home wild things. The other day I found a baby coon in the bottom of his bed. Scared me right into the next room. Then the nasty thing hissed at me like I was in HIS way.

Lucas is a fresh wind. He's Lulu's little protector, with a Heaven-sent bond. He hauls her around the yard in our old wobbly wagon.

Quite a responsibility for a boy not yet four. You can hear her giggles and his laughter from everywhere. Sure reminds me of our growing-up years.

I'm hearing some loud thumping in the direction of the stairs, have to close for now. Sometimes when I hear light steps on the front porch, I think it might be you…coming back to me…coming home.

Your big sister, E.J.

April 1902
Dearest Gracie,

There's not a day goes by that I do not wonder what you are doing. But of course I'm more concerned with *how* you're doing. Laundry and ironing make for hard work…are you sure you're strong enough for it? Whenever Eva Jo or I come to town, our first stop is always the post-office. I worry our letters are not getting to you. We don't really know Mrs. White, though she sounded responsible and caring enough. Please, please, let us hear from you. It's my final prayer every night.

After all that's happened to you, I've been thinking a lot about marriage. Do you remember when we were younger and would play make-believe in the woods? My favorite was pretending to be lost. Every time, we'd be rescued by two of the world's most handsome men. We never had names for them until Shepherd and Cal came to work for Papa. What fun that was, so innocent.

Now I realize I've never taken time to think about all that is involved in a long, grown-up relationship. I find myself wondering how I could possibly ever marry. I'm very selfish, not a good quality for marriage. There's more.

Whenever I'm with Eva Jo, I see complete devotion to her family. Not only is she up before dawn, making breakfast for Ephraim and the children, but she opens her home to others. She doesn't seem to notice that extra mouth to feed. She mends clothes, wipes tears, laughs at jokes, and milks the cow.

When Ephraim is inside, she's able to continue doing all these things and still pay attention to his conversation. What an encourager, especially to me. No matter how busy she is, we are able to have sister fun. One day she coaxed me into helping churn butter. Yuck! But even that boring job wasn't so bad with Eva Jo.

Funny how I've always seen her as being more like our papa, but now I realize she's learned all she knows about home and family from Mama.

I'm just afraid that I've not learned enough. Enough for Cal and the girls, I mean. I've daydreamed of marrying Cal since near the day we met. Now my dreams appear to be coming a reality. I've some concerns because Cal is older than me. And there are children to consider. Can I be the mother they need, while being the wife Cal expects?

I've got to trust God more...only He has the bigger picture. I see that with all Eva Jo has to do each day, her life revolves around what God wants...same with Mama. More and more I believe that if there's a "secret" to life, they have it. "Life is hard, but God is good." How many times have I heard Mama say that?

Oh, I don't mean to babble, Grace. I'm just concerned about where my life seems to be going. Even though, you're not here, at least when I share things in a letter, I feel almost like you are.

Well, I must go before I get myself all stirred up, and not be able to sleep. Hoping you walk in God's blessings, I am forever your Nettie. I love you.

P.S. Enjoy the lavender sachet I'm sending. Eva Jo and I made them when we were together last.

P.S.S. More than once Shepherd McFarlane has inquired about you. Eva Jo and I are considering sharing your letters with him, if you don't mind.

April 15, 1902
My Dear Sisters,
By now you're aware of my severe misfortunes. It is with a heavy heart that I continue corresponding, but I feel drawn to give in to the pleadings of your letters.

Of course, you know Jake has left me. Until just a few days ago his complete disappearance remained a mystery. Not that I cared, but now I'm resting easier knowing he's gone for good.

My work and lodging are in an area Jake frequented, so many people know him. Yesterday one of them stopped me on the street.

"Ho there!" he said, "you're Jake Hudson's woman."

I tried walking around him, but he grabbed a sleeve.

"Let me pass."

"Well, ain't ya the high-and-mighty. Just thought I'd give ya a friendly bit a'news."

"Sir, what is your news to me?" He was drunk, but I listened.

"Thought you'd like to know that cuss of your'n ain't in L.A. n'more. He's gone ta sea on the *Asian Pearl*, bound fer foreign soil. Ain't gonna see him fer a long spell. M'be never."

I cannot tell you what relief I felt, knowing I don't have to deal with him—ever. Every remnant of him gone. I'm free to build a new life. You know I've a strong constitution, so not to worry.

Stop looking for me on your front porch, Eva Jo. I'll not be stepping foot there anytime soon.

Nettie, I find it strange you should mention Shepherd McFarlane, because he's barely given me notice since the day Papa hired him. If there's one thing I've learned from all of this mess concerning Jake, it's this: Men cannot be trusted. I find it odd though, how we seem to need what they have, regardless. Under no circumstances are you to share one word of my letters with him...or anyone else.

From time to time, I do find myself homesick...for you, sisters.

Love, Gracie

GRACE'S DIARY

Dear Diary,

I've just posted my first letter home since Jake's departure, but I could not burden my sisters with the true state of my life, nor the shame. Never could I have imagined living over a tavern. Laundry hangs everywhere in this cramped space, and as it heats up, humidity sometimes chokes the breath out of me. Stepping outside helps little; the stench of dead fish and crab steals away any comfort from the ocean breezes.

I couldn't share about Harvey either, after my declaration that "men cannot be trusted." I still believe it, but I'm much more wary now. Harvey's father owns the establishment below, and I met the son during the rental transaction. Now I have his laundry business. Gentle, with a soft-spoken manner, I find him a different man altogether. I wanted to repay his kindness to me in a small way, so I made him an apple pie in the tavern's kitchen yesterday. His mother watched me the entire time, wearing a scowl matching the tartness of the apples.

I have no more tears to cry, yet sadness is my constant companion. The letters from home are bittersweet. They bring little comfort, but the thought of not having them causes panic within. There's no doubt I'll never go back, so why do I need them?

I took Mrs. White's invitation to church to heart, and attended last Sunday. It's not far from here, so I walked, rather than spend money for the cable car. I sat in the back, looking for Flossie's straw hat in the crowd, when a bold nausea overtook me. There was not enough air in the church, I believe. I had no choice. I left. Several people stared at me like they knew I really didn't belong anyway. I don't know if I'll go back.

G

April 1902
Gracie Dearest,

May this letter find you well and not working too hard. Maybe by now you'll have found a better job. With all your knowledge and love of books, I can easily picture you as a librarian. Ephraim and I are convinced of it. Have you any contacts there? Perhaps one of the friends you made earlier could point you in that direction.

Life is hard...hard and sad. (Of course I'm not telling you anything.) The misfortunes of life are never sparse, it seems.

I don't remember if I told you that Little Dove's parents found work recently in a logging camp near Chalatchie Prairie. Their family has prospered from this, since not many Indians are given such responsibilities. Little Dove's mother, Winnowett, and her mother's sister, Mawnee, were hired as cooks, while Wolf Heart, her father, worked a pair of mules. His job was to haul logs from where they were cut. We were blessed to keep Little Dove.

Wolf Heart's reputation was held high for working long and tirelessly, with talent for the mules, and sure hands to direct them, even in the rain. All logging of course is dangerous, as many loggers' widows can tell you, but Wolf Heart's skill seemed destined to assure him safety in the woods. Not so.

Albert Wilkes, the cutter on the tree Wolf Heart was pulling, testified the log was half up a hill when the mules began dancing around nervously. With some hearty coaxing, Wolf Heart had gotten them calmed down and back to hauling when a huge bull elk crashed into the clearing. Both jacks sidestepped, dragging their handler like a toy. Though he planted his feet into the ground, talking and whistling to calm them, nothing worked. When the elk pawed the ground, threatening to charge, the team bolted. Exactly how Wolf Heart ended up underneath is a mystery, but when the mules stopped, Mr. Wilkes found his broken body. Only God knows the number of our days, Albert said. Wolf Heart's added up to less than thirty years.

This has greatly affected Little Dove and her family, as you can imagine. Although the camp owners agreed to let Winnowett and Mawnee stay on, they don't make enough money to keep a home and with no family support, they'll be living at the camp. We are happy to keep our precious girl, but watching her sadness weighs heavy upon us. She seems to take comfort from our prayer time, although sorrowful tears drench her pillow nightly. When Lulu knows Little Dove is upset, she'll get her attention, begging sweetly to be picked up. I know Dovie finds consolation in this because her face reflects it like the July sun. Still a youngster, she sometimes lets herself go giddy with the children. It's then I hear her laughter above the others. She's like my little sister and my child. I wish you could look into her doe eyes and see the soul I see. It's an old one.

Ephraim and I pray for the right time to ask Little Dove to make a commitment to Christ. Even though she's open to the gospel, she's worried about disappointing her mother because of their culture. The tugging is fierce.

Recently I heard the boys asking her questions about her father. D.J. wanted to know if Wolf Heart was dark brown all the way through.

"Through what?" Little Dove asked.

"You know...through his insides."

Little Dove thought before answering. "Though my father's skin was dark...like mine, inside he was same as your father."

"Oh!"

That's all my questioning offspring said. Her answer satisfied and he let it go. Sometimes I wonder what's going on in that blond head. Maybe it's best I don't know.

We're all so different, aren't we? Even in families the contrasts are wide, yet our love creates a sameness that can't be denied, especially our love for the Lord. Maybe that's exactly how God intended it. That way we'd stay connected regardless. Am I making sense? See, if you were here, I'd wait to have this conversation over some good strong coffee or tea, and watch your face for signs of agreement...or not.

I'm needing to go.

Later.

In the midst of the sadness over losing Little Dove's father we've had some good news. We had no way of knowing where Wolf Heart was regarding the Lord since he'd not been open to listening to any part of the gospel from Ephraim or I. The whereabouts of his eternal soul weighed heavy on our hearts...until the burial.

Wolf Heart was from the Chinook tribe, which meant that when he died he was to be laid to rest in his canoe, then placed on a high platform or in a tree. When we arrived, we saw nothing of his canoe, only a plain casket with something laying on top. We must have had a puzzled look on our faces, because Mr. Wilkes hurried to greet us.

"Have you heard?"

"Heard what?" we asked.

He proceeded to tell us that while working together, Wolf Heart had many questions about the white man's God. For months, Mr. Wilkes had the privilege to answer every one, all the while praying for wisdom to make himself and the gospel clear. Just a few days before his death, Wolf Heart finally understood, and Mr. Wilkes, with the forest as quiet witness, prayed with him to accept Jesus as his Savior.

Oh Gracie, we were so relieved. When we stepped closer, we could see what was laying on the coffin...a beautiful carved cross from Mr. Wilkes' own hand. God is faithful! Wolf Heart's service was full of hope, although Little Dove looked uncomfortable...stiff and out of place, as did her mother and aunt.

We gained some understanding into the spiritual practices of the Chinook after talking to Mr. Wilkes—Wolf Heart had shared a great deal during their talks after work. Especially interesting is the "spirit" walk children are supposed to make by age ten. They are expected to go out, looking for their "guardian spirit." They make these trips alone—boys and girls. Regardless of terrain or weather, they're to search until they find what they believe is their own personal "spirit." This might be an animal or even an inanimate object like a rock, the wind, or perhaps water. Every child in the village is expected to do this, regardless of class or status.

No wonder Little Dove has struggled with Christianity! She's been torn between her culture and our faith in Jesus. She's probably had pressure from her family to make her spiritual journey because she's close to a year past ten already.

The gospel is so simple, yet the enemy of our souls can complicate things greatly when truth and years of cultural superstition come face to face. Hopefully, knowing her father died a Christian will be great comfort to Little Dove one day. We shall be praying for Winnowett and Mawnee as well.

I've not felt such a burden for this many souls, making me believe I've too often taken my faith for granted. It's a comfort to rest in God's faithfulness, knowing He will guide every word that's shared.

So many chores left undone today. I'm happy I'm not being judged on what I accomplish in a single day, because some seem fruitless. I must learn to keep an eternal perspective.

Lovingly, Eva Jo

Six

Dear Gracie,

Thank you, thank you, thank you, for your letter. I am so excited. I've read it over and over again. Oh, but Gracie, it just isn't enough. I'm disappointed that so little took so long to get here. I promise I won't share anything with Shepard, if you're sure that's what you want. You know you can trust me, and Eva Jo as well, but I have to tell you, he's been very insistent.

I'm sad that my entire image of you in the BIG city was destroyed. It sounds as if you have to work just as hard in the city as a person does on a farm. I imagined you living a life of luxury with the man of your dreams—like a fine lady. Oh, that reminds me. Aunt Etta came by the other day for tea and the latest "news." (That would be "news" of you, of course.) Mama, in her very kind way, let her know that if she came to get fuel for gossip about her daughter, that tea would be over quickly.

I was standing outside the door.

"Well, I never," huffed Aunt Etta. "I never indeed! I expect an apology."

"You'll be waiting until the cows come home, Aunt Etta."

"How insulting, Louise." This time she nearly choked on a huge huff.

"I'll tell you what's insulting, Etta. It's insulting that you would want to turn my deep sadness into fodder for town busybodies."

With that, Mama took Aunt Etta's arm, pulled her from the chair, and escorted her to our front door. I peeked out the window while she stood on the porch, sputtering. She then turned on her heels and stomped to her buggy. By then she was so flustered she could barely haul her chubby self inside. Now here's the best part. She headed down the road...in the WRONG direction.

Mama came back in, closed my gaping mouth, and the two of us laughed so long that when we looked again, she was out of sight. Of course, in a little while, Mama was feeling guilty enough to go look for her. I say good riddance. I'm just not as nice as Mama.

Later, she said she shouldn't have handled the situation the way she did. We prayed together for wisdom to know how to handle the likes of Aunt Etta.

Love to you, Nettie

PRAYER JOURNAL
NETTIE

Oh Lord! Today is the day Cal plans to ask my papa for permission to court me! I am so excited. My dreams are coming true.

I believe with all my heart that this is Your will for my life. I confess to fears about my ability to be a good wife and mother, but Your Word clearly says, "I can do all things through Christ which strengtheneth me." I'm going to trust in that strength and lean on the Holy Spirit each day, no matter what.

Oh Father, I see Cal walking across the yard. It's time! Jesus, go before him, I pray.

Afternoon

My eyes are burning, my insides feel raw. I can hardly think. How could Papa be so cruel? I don't understand him. Where is the encouraging man I've admired all my life?

"Absolutely not!" Papa's voice rang through the house this morning. "She's too young to marry and too young to be a mother."

I raced out my room and down the stairs to see what the commotion was about. Surely, he couldn't be saying this to Cal. But he was.

"I expect you to stay far away from Nettie, until whatever fantasies you have put into my child's mind are gone. I shouldn't have allowed her to watch your children so much." He turned to Mama. "Louise, she is not to go over to Cal's from now on."

"No, Papa, no," I begged as I entered the room.

He turned toward me with a stern look, his face red as a beet. Cal lowered his head.

"Nettie," Mama said, coming to embrace me.

"Enough of this foolishness. I won't hear another word." Papa spat out those words right before leaving Mama, Cal, and I standing in awkwardness.

Cal spoke first. "Guess I'd best get back to work. Thank you for your time, Mrs. McLeod." He began to leave without saying a word to me! I was sinking into the dark hole forming beneath my feet. He turned at the door and looked at me with tenderness. Oh, how my heart yearned for this man I was now banned from seeing.

"Trust God, Nettie. Trust God." He tipped his hat towards me before stepping outside, letting the screen door bang behind him. When I started to run after him, Mama held me firmly in place.

"Nettie, listen to him. He's a wise man," she whispered.

When I looked into her face, I knew she honestly believed that. So much was said with those few words. Needing to be alone, I kissed her on the cheek and came back to my room.

Lord, what is wrong with my father? Please touch his heart and give him understanding. Take away any fear he has for me because of Gracie. I truly believe Your will for Cal and I is to be married. Open Papa's eyes to the truth. Oh, how I pray he would see the truth.

Evening

I tried to study my teachers' journal earlier this afternoon but instead found myself staring out the window, waiting and hoping for a glimpse of Cal and the girls. My heart leapt for joy when I saw them, then filled with pain, knowing they would no longer be in my life.

Father, is that why Gracie ran away with Jake? Did she know Papa better than I do?

After dinner Mama called for me to go for a walk with her.

"Nettie." She held me close as we meandered to the creek. "I know you are hurting, but please listen to Cal and trust God."

I couldn't hold back the tears. "Mama, what do you think Cal meant when he said what he did to me?"

"Well, I think he truly believes you are the one for him, and he's willing to wait for God to work it out. It's plain as the nose on your face, Nettie."

Joy filled my entire being when Mama said those words. Cal was willing to wait for me!

"Mama, how much patience do you think Cal has in him? Papa's more than stubborn. It seems hopeless to me."

Mama stopped in her tracks. Turning, she had a firm, yet endearing look on her face. "Nettie, what's important is what you believe about Cal. Through this test, you'll be able to see the faith God has put into him. Ask yourself if he makes decisions based on what God wants or what he wants?"

"Cal prays about everything."

"Do you believe this marriage is God's will?"

I could only nod.

"Then ask for strength and faith. Life isn't easy, and this is only the beginning for you and Cal. Mark my words, there will be harder times. You can lean on your emotions, or trust in God's power. You choose, my Annette." She kissed my cheek.

"Mama, of course I choose to lean on God. But it doesn't make sense why Papa would be so hard on Cal. I love him, and those girls are like…like my own." I felt anger rise and spoke through gritted teeth. "I've done a good job taking care of them these few months. Papa can't know me at all, or else he'd see I'm not a child."

Mama smiled and drew me close, gently rubbing my back while I sobbed on her shoulder. "Then it's time to give your papa a chance to see his little girl has grown up." She lifted my chin, wiping away tears with her apron. "It's hard for fathers to let go of their children, especially daughters. But they do…eventually. Now, let's go talk to your papa."

Walking back, I was scared to death. I hadn't had this kind of confrontation with Papa before. Mama asked if I would agree to watch the girls in our house and have Cal take his meals there. Of course I said yes. I would do anything, if it meant we could be together.

Papa was in his favorite chair, watching Will and Percy play dominoes. Mama went over and quietly asked him to meet us in the kitchen. With only a few words and her constant smile, she convinced Papa to agree to her plan.

She finished. "She's not our baby girl, anymore, Jim. Look at her. Remember me at that age when you came to call?"

I felt uncomfortable when he glanced over at me. For a moment he looked startled.

"Papa…" I hesitated, twisting a hankie round and round.

He nodded for me to continue.

"I don't understand your answer to Cal. Is it because you don't realize I'm capable of being a wife and mother? I love them. I truly believe God's will is for us to be a family. Please Papa, take some time to pray about this. Get to know Cal and I together. I want to marry with your blessing." Taking a deep breath, I was afraid of what he would say.

He stared at the floor for an eternity, slowly lifting his gaze to Mama. She smiled and walked to his side, wrapping her hands around his arm.

"I'm sorry, Nettie. A decision this important should be made with prayer. I spoke too soon."

"Oh Papa!" I started toward him.

"Wait!" He put up one finger. "I didn't say yes. I said I would pray, and I will. Cal and the girls can come to the house, but only with supervision."

I threw my arms around him. I know what answer he's going to get from You, God. What peace to be in the center of Your will. Thank You for Mama. She certainly knows what's best for her family. I want to be just like her.

And, thank You too, for Papa. He's a man going hard after You.

Your daughter,

Annette

May 1902
Dear Gracie,

We've had so much rain, I could almost set sail for California—if I had a boat, of course. My thoughts are forever floating off to where you are anyway, so it would be nice if my body caught up. You can tell how much we still miss you, right? Though busy, all of us think of you daily.

Mama and Papa celebrated their anniversary this week. Eva Jo and I surprised them with a huge cake after church. Mama's face blushed like a new bride, and Papa was grinning from ear to ear. You know he's not much for public affection, but he actually kissed our mother in front of everyone. Then he cleared his throat, and the room got very quiet.

"I'd like to say something," he said. Mama never took her eyes from his. "My wife has put up with the likes of me every day for the last twenty-five years. And...and...well I'd just like to tell her thanks."

There wasn't a dry eye in that entire place, I can tell you for sure. Big Jim McLeod was crying himself. You should have seen the looks on Will and Percy's faces.

Cal was standing right beside me, holding my hand. I couldn't help but blush when we exchanged looks. I want what Mama and Papa have in their marriage. I must say, I don't believe Cal is as stubborn as Papa, by a long shot. Well, I hope not.

Even though there is much fieldwork to do, I manage to find time to study my Teacher's Preparation Guide. I'm sending you these silly rules I have to memorize.

The Standard Guide for Employed Teachers

1. Teachers each day will fill lamps, clean chimneys, and anything else that needs Godly attention.
2. Each teacher will bring a bucket of water and an armful of wood for the day's session.
3. Make your pens carefully. You may whittle nibs to the individual taste of the pupils.
4. Make sure your own horse, or that of any student(s), is properly corralled with adequate water.
5. Men teachers may take one evening each week for courting purposes or two evenings a week if they go to church regularly.

6. After ten hours at school, teachers may spend the remaining time reading the Bible or other good books.

7. Women teachers who marry without written permission of the elected school board will immediately be dismissed.

9. No teacher, male or female, may chew tobacco.

10. Any teacher who smokes, uses liquor in any form, frequents pool or public halls, or gets shaved in a barber shop will give good reason to suspect his worth, intention, integrity, and honesty.

11. Every teacher should lay aside from each day's pay a goodly sum of his earnings for his benefit during his declining years so that he will not become a burden on society.

12. The teacher who performs his labor faithfully and without fault for five years will be given an increase of fifty cents per weeks in his pay, providing the Board of Education approves.

Of course, I will have all summer, but I find it hard to concentrate on books when I'm more interested in things of the heart—MY heart, of course.

Oh Gracie, I'm a complete ninny when it comes to Cal. How can he love such a scatterbrained girl? I swear I was not this way before I knew his feelings towards me. Yesterday morning I burned an entire pan of scrambled eggs while daydreaming at the stove. He laughed, but I felt guilty feeding he and the girls cold biscuits and milk for breakfast. At least Mama's Basket Flats honey added some pleasure. I'm trying to imagine Cal and I twenty-five years from now. Oh goodness! I just can't see it.

Well, the lamplight is weak, and I'm very tired. I'm praying you find all the rest you need for yourself, dear sister. Most of all, rest for your soul.

Your little sister,
Nettie

May 1902
Dear Gracie,

Praying this letter finds you. I'm sure you're not feeling well has more to do with your emotional state than anything else. Such upsets would make anyone sick. Maybe a good old-fashioned tonic would help. Mama's combination of molasses and cod liver oil ought to do the trick. Dandelion tea, made strong, helps rid me of leftover winter doldrums. Since they grow everywhere, you should find some.

We're moving forward here, with most days flying by, though with all the spring work, they're never quite long enough.

Today I struggle with the hardness—no, wickedness—contained in some people's hearts. You'll recollect how I've sung the praises of Little Dove, and the progress she's made in her reading. She's excelled so quickly, in fact, that I'm no longer able to do her right by my teaching abilities. So I looked into putting her on the school roster at town school.

Miss Knatz was gracious to say the least, upon listening to my request, and made arrangements to meet Little Dove.

Dovie was nervous, and I was afraid her shyness might get in the way of the revealing of her intelligence. She came decked out in a beautiful buckskin dress with delicate beadwork around the sleeves, neck and bottom. Her braids, the color of raven's wings, were woven with ribbon I'd given her, but it was the smile on her face that stood out the most. How I love that face.

The sun came out just as we reached the school, a symbol that things were looking up for my star pupil. I squeezed her hand tight as we climbed the stairs.

Miss Knatz met us at the door. The look on her face puzzled me and caused Little Dove to step back. She was not alone. Behind her, in the shadows, stood Mirval Abbot, the schoolboard president.

"Mr. Abbot," I said, "what a surprise."

"Please, call me Mirval." His voice was cold. "Eva Jo, I'm needing to speak with you."

I waited, watching how nervous Miss Knatz was, her hands now shaking like a leaf.

Mr. Abbot stepped outside to the porch. "It has come to my attention that you are wanting to enroll an Indian child in school." His lip curled ever so slightly.

"Yes, Mirval, that's exactly what I'm doing...today."

"Eva Jo, your intent is indeed admirable, but highly unacceptable...dear."

Now my hands shook, and a spot near my left eye began to twitch.

"Explain unacceptable," I replied in the strongest voice I could muster. I straightened to my full height, glad I'd worn my boots, since they make me a plumb six feet.

"What exactly about the word *unacceptable* do you not understand?"

"Mr. Abbot," Miss Knatz weakly tried to intercede.

"Miss Knatz, contain yourself. Your place is inside the classroom."

"Mr. Abbot, I've come to enroll Little Dove so she can have the proper education she deserves. She's bright and can already read...beyond the basic primer."

He stepped closer. "Where's her mother, I might ask?"

"Little Dove's mother doesn't speak English that well. But I assure you, I have her permission to enroll her daughter."

"Eva Jo, I'm beginning to think you do not understand English all that well either...dear," he nearly snarled.

"Mr. Abbot," I said in a slightly louder tone than intended, "this little girl will be educated in this school if I have to sit beside her every single day. And, by the way, I'd like to remind you that you sit ...in the front pew...every Sunday at my church." My forefinger now punched the air, directly in front of Mr. Abbott's face.

Then he starts to sputter and stammer, like he forgot how to talk. "Nn...nn...now, Eva Jo, I don't see what that has to do with this...this...situation."

I took a step backwards, hoping he knew I was NOT intimidated by such rudeness, but rather I needed to escape flying spittle.

"First of all, Mirval Abbot, this is NOT a situation," I said. "This is a child who needs an education. A flesh-and-blood person. One that Jesus died for. Tell me, Mirval, did Jesus hang on that cross for all people, or only the white ones?"

By this time tears spilt onto my cheeks, hot as late August. Dovie was well entrenched within the folds of my skirts, while Miss Knatz fanned herself with one hand.

"Well I..." Saliva sputtered again from Mr. Abbott's enraged, gaping mouth. Just for an instant he reminded me of a huge catfish we once pulled from Fargher Lake.

He removed his hat, ran his fingers around the brim, then

cleared his throat. Said absolutely nothing for what seemed like forever. Then his eyes began to bulge.

"Eva Jo." His voice was ice, and if looks could make a person disappear, his would have sent me all the way to Portland. "Eva Jo, you're totally out of line in this matter."

"Really!" I said. My knees began to knock.

Mirval dropped his hat.

Little Dove walked from behind my back, inching towards him. Bending over, one hand still clutching my dress cloth, she picked up the hat, looking up at him with utter innocence.

"Here's your hat, mister."

He roughly snatched it, causing his hand to brush against hers. A shadow passed over Dovie's face, right before she returned to the refuge in my skirts.

Mr. Abbot's eyes flashed with anger and something vile. He stuffed his hat back on his head and shook a fist right in my face. "Eva Jo, you and I are not finished with this."

Before he turned and walked away, he spat on the ground near me, then removed a big, red handkerchief from his coat pocket. With exaggerated motion, Mr. Abbot, upright citizen, wiped the hand that had touched Little Dove.

I was angry enough at that moment to wish myself a man. I would have knocked him clean into the middle of next week.

Miss Knatz broke her silence with a loud sigh. "Eva Jo, you're my hero. I can't stand up to that man."

From folds of fabric, Dovie hugged me around the waist, shivering, but not from cold. "Want to go home," she whispered to my back.

Bringing her round front, I said, "Oh, my sweet girl, you're going to blossom in this very place, just like a big old apple tree. Don't be afraid, Little Dove. I'm not the only one who'll be sitting beside you in school. The Lord will be with the both of us."

I have to confess that my words were braver than my insides.

Miss Knatz sent her off to explore the classroom before speaking to me again. "Eva Jo, there will be other Indian children who'll want to enroll now, and I don't mind. But are you prepared for more ignorance from this town? Today's incident might be mild, compared to what could happen."

"Miss Knatz," I said, "I believe the Lord prepared the way for

Little Dove to come to this place, at this time. Have no doubts. He will complete the same preparations for the others."

When I went looking for Little Dove, I found her sitting in a desk matching her size. She was wearing a grin, though her eyes were closed.

"Dovie?" Calling her name made her jump. "What are you thinking?"

"Not thinking. Dreaming."

"About what?" I asked.

"Books." With that, she got up, ran her delicate hands over the buckskin skirt. Eyes brimming, she stood before me. I knelt down to look full in her face.

"Thank you, Eva Jo."

"For what?"

She placed both her hands on each of my wet cheeks. "For being like Little Dove wants to be."

"Oh, you're so very welcome, my little bird. So welcome indeed," I said.

She ran outside, but I needed time to compose myself. I'm willing to do anything to make her life easier. I cannot let her suffer from the ignorance of others...I will not. I know Ephraim feels the same, but I've yet to share with him my plan. And trust me. I do have one.

Your forever sister, Eva Jo

May 1902

Dearest Gracie,

How I wish you were here to share in this wonderful thing unfolding in my life with Cal. I miss you more than ever before. Sometimes I actually pretend to sit and talk with you over the day's events.

With you still gone, poor Eva Jo gets her ear chewed off whenever we're together. She is missing you as much as I am, although she said she's glad to be here for me. I'm learning more about our sister every day, especially after hearing what happened between her and Ephraim before he started courting. Maybe you have heard this before, but it was news to me. Eva Jo always has some hysterical, funny thing happen to her in any given situation, so I was not surprised with this escapade.

When she first saw Ephraim, he took her breath away. How romantic is that? NEVER had any Yacolt boy affected her this way. A boy was just a boy, unless he wanted to take her on in some kind of competition, of course. Then he became a challenge. Most the time she'd come out on top, so there was always the next "one." But the first meeting of Ephraim was totally different.

She'd gone with Papa to buy a new horse from a new family in the valley. After all, who better than Eva Jo to pick out the perfect one, her being such a horse lover and all?

Anyway, they pulled up to the barn and Eva Jo hopped down from the wagon just as Ephraim walked towards them. He stopped her in her tracks. She couldn't move. Papa was calling her to come along, but she was frozen in place. Finally, she took a breath, though she was still feeling fluttery like, and took a hearty step forward. That's when she heard a ripping sound. (You know how much Eva Jo hates cumbersome skirts.) Well, half the thing was hung up on the buckboard. You can imagine how Eva Jo felt, discovering her backside was now totally exposed. She grabbed the material, trying to figure out a way to recover some modesty. She somehow managed to keep it all together by pulling torn fabric around to the front, holding it in place with a death grip at her waist. Of course this now greatly limited her movements for horse stock examination.

Papa kept giving her the opportunity to get involved with the purchase but gave up when her growing awkwardness made no sense. When she refused to even touch one, he told her she might just as well have stayed home. Her faced blushed bright red with Papa's scolding, especially when she noticed Ephraim stealing looks as they moved from horse to horse. Once he smiled, catching her off-guard completely. She only blushed more.

Papa never mentioned how odd she looked walking backwards from the barn to the wagon, but Ephraim did when he came by the next day. He thought she was just shy or something. Well, that set Eva Jo laughing her head off.

"Ephraim, that would not be a description of me," she said.

"Really?"

"No sir, not me."

When she told him the entire story of the ripped dress, he threw his head back and laughed...until he cried. She said that was the moment her smitten heart went deeper with feeling.

When he asked to come back, Eva Jo didn't hide her pleasure. She said yes immediately. And, the rest is history.

I'm happy we have the big brother Ephraim's been. He's still able to laugh at all of Eva Jo's misadventures.

I had the same strong heart feelings from the moment I laid eyes on Cal. You remember how I fantasized about marrying him.

When he first asked Papa's permission to court, Papa threw a tizzy. It was a real test of my faith, for sure. Right now Cal and the girls are taking all their meals at the big house with the rest of the family. Cal has way more patience than I do, but I think he's earning Papa's trust at a different level entirely.

I can hardly believe it. Life cannot get better than this.

I hope and pray you are well, Gracie dearest. Someday God will give you all the desires of your heart. I just know it.

Love,
Annette

Late May 1902
Dear Gracie,

Some days are diamonds, some days are stones, Papa always says. I now have enough big fat rocks to equal the size of Mt. St. Helens! I'm sorry to dump all my frustration on you, but writing is the next best thing to talking with you. Sometimes I imagine you're sitting at the table as I pull the nib across paper.

We'd worked weeks getting the garden started, plowing the dirt until there was no daylight left. Even our boys helped while Lulu spent hours strapped to my back even though she's too big for the pack. After all that labor, we looked forward to the planting, but when we went to get our stored seed, varmints had beat us to it. The gunnysacks were scattered as leaves in the wind, each bearing holes like a pincushion, only mouse, rat and squirrel sized. I sat down hard on the barn floor...crying. So much work went into gathering and storing. You know exactly what I mean. Remember all the long hours we spent saving corn kernels and shucking beans and peas for Mama? I especially hated the beans...made my hands frog-green for days.

Ephraim was faithful to rescue me from my own attitudes, but even he was discouraged. Well, when Mama heard of our problem she packed up the wagon along with Percy and Willie and came sharing her bounty. Her seeds survived because she stored them all in glass containers, which made me feel even worse since I'd skipped that part.

It started to rain on a Friday, never stopped on Saturday, and Sunday we stayed home from church because of the relentless downpour. We knew the garden would flood over, so in the soaking wet, we dug escape paths. By late Sunday afternoon we could see that our plan was failing...little seedlings floated in the lake that had once been our confident food source.

I was devastated. Ephraim said nothing. He left for the barn and when I went to find him he was kneeling, head in hands. I thought he was weeping, but then I heard him pray. I got down beside him, and together we poured out our hearts to the Lord, our pleas matching the intensity of the weather. Coming out of the barn, the rain stopped. That's when we saw a stream of sunlight pushing its way out of a dark cloud, striking the ground all around. Ephraim and I looked at one another in disbelief. Then we wept.

It took days for the land to dry out, but we found at least half of the garden was still growing. Our resourceful mother called on all the neighbors after the storm. Even though most of them had suffered losses as well, each gave us a little seed, and when it was all said and done we were able to replant most everything.

My little mountain of stones is worth more than diamonds because it's a stout reminder of God's faithfulness.

I don't know why I worry so much. I'm trying to break myself of the habit.

Funny thing now is, we're having such a dry spell we've got to irrigate everything. Life is hard, but God is good.

Shepard McFarlane is ever inquiring of you, but true to my word, I've shared nothing with him like you asked. But Gracie, if you could see his face when he's here, I believe you'd change your mind. I've never seen anyone so sincerely interested in another's welfare. Though quiet, he's solid in the Lord and works hard as two men,

Papa says. After buying the Snider farm, Papa's put Shep in charge of all the supply buying, stock management, and even keeping the books.

I hear my name being called...need to close.

Love to you,

Eva Jo

Seven

JUNE 1902

Dear Sisters,

I confess I did not remember Mama and Papa's wedding anniversary. I guess it just proves further that you two deserve to bear the title "daughter" in our parent's eyes. You say you want me to come back, but you don't understand how I feel. I can't come home. Not with the way things are between Papa and I. I feel badly, but fact is fact, and I've got to live my life as I see fit.

Life continues here—work and more work, with money a continual thought. I'm desperately needing new shoes since my last pair has already worn through. Laundry work demands standing on my feet the entire day, so the boots Jake bought me do not support my feet well enough to suffice.

I've met a nice man named Harvey Stubb. Harvey is coming to take me out tonight. He's intelligent, witty and clever. He really wants to go to college, but can't because he has to mind the tavern whenever his parents ask. What social injustice! He deserves a better life, and the ability to do what he wants. Through no fault of our own, we are at the bottom rung of city society, he and I.

Harvey has lived here since childhood, playing amongst the patrons, while beer and wine flowed freely. His three brothers have escaped to work the railroads, leaving Harvey behind. His parents are kind enough, but don't show it openly. Mr. Stubb is a burly man, with a large protruding middle. He wears a white apron like a butcher, and speaks gruffly to everyone, but I see a good heart. His wife, Jane, is the manager of the business. The men do what she says, and when, believe you me. She intimidates me, but I manage to stay out of her way, except when she brings her laundry. I'm grateful for the work, so I avoid any conflict. Most times she sends Harvey.

Harvey seems lost between the two of them. He's like a little puppy. I don't think they know how unhappy he is.

Today he gave me a chocolate bar. How I savored every bite! After the falseness of the gifts Jake gave me, Harvey's offerings are purely from his heart, small though they are. Harvey is the complete opposite in disposition from Jake, his gentle ways a sharp contrast. He's just as fastidious about his dress, for sure, but will talk with me for hours, like a true friend. As good a friend as Amanda ever was. He's never even tried to hold my hand. What a gentleman!

I miss talking with you, sisters. Maybe that long-awaited telephone will make its way to the valley. Good thing I'm not holding my breath. Love, Gracie.

P.S. Thank you for keeping my confidences to yourselves.

May 1902
Dearest Gracie,

I pray this letter will find you doing well. Every day I seek the Father for your circumstances. As hard as it is for you, my heart's longing is that you will find your way back to us soon. I'm sure Papa will forgive you when he sees your beautiful face once again. He's really only angry because he misses you. Eva Jo and I think he believes he's failed you somehow. I was angry for a while, but now I just want to hold my sister again.

Life is very busy now. I start the day watching Cal's daughters. Then, when Miss Knatz is finished with school, she comes here to familiarize me with the curriculum for next year. That has been somewhat of a challenge since Eva Jo has found local Indian children of all ages that are unschooled. Most speak little English.

It won't be easy to meet all the needs of all the children. I certainly don't want the Chinook children to face teasing because they've not been educated like the others. It's going to be hard enough for them to attend. Some of the white parents are quite upset that an Indian child may be sitting next to their son or daughter.

Miss Knatz said it is already an issue during class. One boy dared to walk up to her desk and sneer. "Indian lover. You're not going to get me to sit by any of 'em."

"Indeed! I do love Indians, and so does our Lord. You will sit where I tell you or you can sit outside," she stated calmly.

"I won't!"

"Good, that settles it. You will sit where I tell you." When she got up and turned her back to write on the chalkboard, she heard his footsteps walking away. He was muttering under his breath.

Fortunately, Will, Percy, DJ, and Cal's girls will already know some of Indian children. For sure, our bunch will make them feel welcome. Little Dove has been upset ever since her run-in with Mirval Abbot. I hope it doesn't scare her mother from allowing her to attend class. Eva Jo has become well known all over the valley for her stand on equal education for all children. But passion is rising, and Ephraim has made her carry a pistol whenever she goes into the hills.

On a different subject, my favorite as of late...Cal. Since the majority of his courting takes place on the front porch, we've had long hours for talking. He once lived in the city like you...Portland, Oregon. He ran the family store before his wife passed. After, he needed to get away from her family, who actually blamed him for her dying. He left the girls with his sister and headed to Seattle for work. He ran across Papa in Vancouver, and after a lengthy conversation, Papa hired him on the spot. He really hadn't planned on staying as long as he did, but he was close enough to visit his children often. And then after their first visit, Mama thought it'd work out for them to live at our place. Remember how surprised we were when he brought the little lovelies? Like two peas in a pod they were. None of us had ever seen twins before!

I really never thought to ask anyone where he'd come from. Of course it didn't matter, since I had such a crush on him. But listening to his story brings doubts. Oh, not about his love for me...I can see it in his eyes. I struggle with how I compare to Delilah. She was beautiful, Gracie. I've seen a picture of their wedding day. Her dress was perfect and they made a dashing couple.

One afternoon I took the girls for a picnic lunch. We spread out a blanket and filled our plates. The girls were arguing over who got to sit the closest to me. I wrapped an arm around each of them.

"Can't get any closer than this, girls. Only problem is, now we won't be able to eat all this wonderful food I brought. Cassie, you scoot over a smidgen and Sissy, you do the same."

With a few moans and groans, they finally settled down and allowed me to dish up their plates. They were silent while they shoveled food in their mouths. And when I say "shovel," I mean it.

"Hey girls, slow down, there's enough for both of you. Besides, you're going to choke."

Giggles were their reply. I leaned against the tree and started on my own plate. Goodness, it was delicious...if you don't mind my bragging on myself. I've always loved to bake, but a family cannot live on baked goods alone, so I've been practicing on my general cooking.

"Are you going to be our new mama?" Cassie asked, looking at me from under thick, pale lashes.

I coughed. It was so unexpected. "What makes you ask that question?" Both girls hid their faces behind delicate hands.

"Daddy said he loves you. He loves you like a mama."

I could feel the heat in my face. It was pretty awkward. Cal and I hadn't discussed what to say to the girls.

Sissy had cleaned her plate and was now chewing on a piece of sweet grass. "Daddy loves our mama lots...even though she's in Heaven."

"I'm sure your daddy will always love your mama. After all, she gave him the two of you and you're the most special girls in the world."

"Daddy told us he fell in love with Mama when he was as old as we are right now. Did he tell you that, Nettie?"

My food suddenly lost its flavor. I wasn't ready to have this sort of conversation, especially since I was already struggling with comparisons. The girls had more to say. They went on to share their Mama and Daddy's love story. It's their favorite bedtime ritual.

"Mama lived on the farm next to Daddy's Grandma," Cassie began. "It was love at first sight." Cassie rolled over onto her back dramatically, hugging her arms to her chest.

They went on about how whenever he visited his grandparents, he'd make his way through the woods that separated the farms and knock on the door.

"Then one time..."Cassie looked over at Sissy with a smile. Sissy stood up, put her hand on a hip, then flung back her hair, looking at us over a shoulder. "An angel from Heaven answered. Her hair was let down, lit from behind. It was beauuutiful, wavy blond, floating all the way down her back." She strung out the word *all* with a dramatic gesture, tilting her head back to make her own golden locks even longer.

"All day he tried to make her laugh. That wasn't easy, 'cause our mama was the serious type. When she finally cracked a giggle, the sound set his heart to beating faster." Now Cassie was on her knees pounding her chest. She reached over and broke off another long blade of grass, using it as a wand. She was her own director of story time.

"Delilah, I have loved you since the day I first saw you with your hair a'floatin' in the sunlight. Do you, by chance, have like feelings for me?" She reached over and tickled her sister. Sissy laughed and ran behind a tree.

"Oh Delilah," she said in the most masculine voice she could muster, "don't leave! I didn't mean to scare you!" she cried out.

"Why Calvin," Sissy's eyelashes fluttered up and down, "I have to go, or I might just let you kiss me." Sissy sprinted off with Cassie right behind.

They began to spin in widening circles, their arms imitating flight. "When he kissed her, butterflies flew all around the two of them...hundreds and thousands of them." They danced and twirled until they fell to the ground, dizzy with the telling of their parents' love.

"Is that the most beautiful story you've ever heard, Nettie?" They both were looking at me with expectation.

Suddenly lunch felt like lead in my stomach. I managed to get the picnic mess cleaned up and the girls back to the house. I was drained. I couldn't shake the impact of Cal and Delilah's story. She'd been his first love. I felt like second choice would never measure up. Was I destined to always be the spoils?

I helped Mama with dinner and left, muttering excuses about needing "fresh air."

I needed to talk with Eva Jo, so I rode over, my mind in a muddle. She met me with arms open wide before I hit the porch. Even from her kitchen window she could see I needed her shoulder to cry on. She understood my pain, she said, because she could not imagine Ephraim ever having loved another. But, she reminded me, I knew that from the beginning.

"Cal is a good man, Nettie. Delilah will always have a special place in his heart, but she's gone. That's not his fault. He had to learn to say good-bye to what he believed would be his for life. I could never see God asking me to just forget Ephraim."

"Eva Jo, how will I fit, then? There isn't anybody in my heart but him."

"Honey, I guess it's hard to understand without walking in Cal's boots. Remember when you were little and you had that loveable dog, Curly? He went everywhere with you."

"How could I ever forget? When he died, I didn't know what I'd do. But then you brought me one of your squirming puppies, right?

"Did you stop loving Curly?

"No. I still do. I even still miss him. Okay, Eva Jo, I get it. I'm being silly."

"Well, you've always been silly, Nettie."

She pulled me close, rubbing my arm. "Don't be so hard on yourself, my girl. You're just in love. You may feel these doubts again, so I think you need to decide. Is he worth it? Would you rather live with him or without?"

How obvious. I can't think of my life without him in it. I kissed Eva Jo on the cheek and gave her a hug.

Suddenly I missed Cal. Eva Jo gave me a leg up on Chester's wide back, then slapped him hard. I took off at a lope but pulled to a stop as a rider came bearing down hard towards me. Cal!

He jumped off and ran to me, stopping short. Eva Jo gave a shout from the porch, before going back inside.

"Nettie, I just heard what the girls told you today." He reached up and helped me to the ground. "I...I need to explain. I only want the girls to know how special their mama was. They have no other memories."

I understood, but I waited for him to finish.

"They never knew her. I tell stories and make them sound as wonderful as I can. But...Nettie, that part of my life is over." He had my hands in his. "You're my life now. I want you, Nettie. I want you for my wife."

My eyes filled. "What about the girls?"

"They love you. Don't you know it?"

"Yes, but..."

"There are no 'buts,' Nettie. You're the one for me, and for them. I think you're the only one with doubts."

"No, Cal, I don't have any doubts. Not now." His face was so close to mine, I could feel his every breath.

We heard a huge round of applause coming from Eva Jo's front porch. The whole family waved sheepishly. They all came running at once.

"Aunt Nettie, you got to tell him yes." D.J was jumping up and down. "Say yes! Say yes!"

"Yes!"

"Oh boy, now you just have to ask Papa." Eva Jo laughed.

Cal's face burned bright, but I knew he wouldn't hesitate.

He pulled me even closer, looked deep into my eyes, and whispered my name. When he brushed his lips against mine, time refused to move. There may have been butterflies for Delilah, but my sister and her clan were cheering at the top of their lungs as the sun danced its way down the sky to end the most perfect day. I   can hardly wait for Cal to talk with Papa and Mama, so we can plan our wedding.

I love you, Gracie, and hope you're able to see God's love for you.

Annette

Prayer Journal
Nettie

Three days later!

Dear Lord,

PAPA SAID YES! I'm going to be Mrs. Cal Stewart. Mrs. Cal Stewart...Mrs. Calvin R. Stewart!

I don't know exactly what Cal said to Papa, but when I came downstairs after their "talk", they were shaking hands and Mama was wiping her eyes.

God, You are so good. Thank You for how You've brought Cal and I together. May I be the wife and mother you want me to be.

I'll never be able to sleep tonight.
Your loving daughter,
Annette

GRACE'S DIARY

Dear Diary,

I'm not able to comprehend the mirror's revelation. The person I remember scant resembles the face looking back at me now. It's gaunt, with eyes that haunt me, even when I look away. They belong to someone I've never dreamt of being. This can't be Grace Rose McLeod, happy girl, joyous bride-to-be! And this, the most dreadful part, the reflection has a voice that taunts.

"You are lost to your past, frozen in despair by forces beyond you."

I'm afraid of what I see, and too ashamed to share my thoughts, save in this journal. But sometimes a glimmer of hope rises above the condemnation, and I hear something different.

"Come home."

The second voice is firm but kind. I'm so confused and completely weary of the battle going on in my mind. Am I slipping into insanity, doomed to a life of madness because of the sordid things I've allowed to befall me? I've no hope. Well, except that one, still, small voice that begs me follow to a place lost to me.

If it were not for Harvey, I fear I could not go on. He's a dear friend and my life begins only when he takes me down from this work chamber into the lively streets.

He says I'm dressing rather like the gypsy I am now. He's right. I love the brightly colored skirts, worn with a peasant-type blouse. I do so admire these Spanish Californian women in the artist colony. They are free-spirited! Being around them makes me feel the same, allowing my mind to forget the face and voice in the mirror. When I'm with them, I'm no longer a laundress. I've learned to smoke like them, and the wine they offer brings with it a gift. Forgetfulness! At least before I have to return to my room. Until then, I trade in the old, remaking myself into whatever the moment provides.

I'm going to become an artist, as soon as I save enough to purchase supplies. Harvey thinks I have talent. He's grand entertainment and makes me laugh with happy little trinkets. Once I saw him pocket one without paying for it. He's daring like that, but only for me.

He worries about me too, continually sneaking food from the Tavern. I'm needing to refuse his generosity because I'm adding to my girth, though my legs and arms remain spindly. I wouldn't hurt his feelings about the food he brings, but often it just comes right back up.

I'm meeting Flossie tomorrow. Hope to have letters from Eva Jo and Nettie. How I long to see them, touch their dear faces, and hug on their necks.

G-

June 1902
Gracie Darling,

We wait with anticipation for more details of life on your own. I'm sorry you have fallen on such hard times. If only you don't despair...please be brave. Won't you consider, really consider, returning to us? There's no life left untouched by sadness, Grace, and so it is with Ephraim and I.

I'm writing with tears held back only by my strong will. Since Lulu was born, there's been something different about her. I realize now I've not wanted to see the truth right under my nose. Neither has Ephraim. She makes no response to our voices, and now we know for sure that Lulu cannot hear. Oh Gracie, my heart is broken for our precious little girl. She'll never hear her name, or the words of love we share daily. What will happen to her? My thinking is so clouded by sorrow I must stop. I'm going to my knees before the One who made her...I have no other place to go...

Your Eva Jo

Eva Jo's Diary

Lord,

My hand shakes, yet I must pour out my longings to you, or perish with the effort of holding back. My baby, Lord. My baby girl is never going to hear. What does it all mean? What good can come from this? Ephraim and I have never even met a person without hearing. Lord, why did You choose us to be her parents?

Please heal my baby, Lord…give me her deafness…willingly I'll exchange my hearing for her silence. I'm trying to be brave, but I'm falling into despair. Rescue me from my own pity. I'm thinking nobody knows my weaknesses more than you, yet you've given me this special little girl, just like you gave me her brothers.

Even as I ask the questions, I feel Your assurance bringing comfort. All the whys don't seem so important when I choose to trust. I trust You, God. It's me I don't trust. I'm ashamed of my own doubts.

I have such fierce feelings towards this tiny girl, Lord. Is that how You feel about Your children…about me? I know every thought You have of me is good, and there are so many they cannot be counted. I want to believe I'm strong enough to be Lulu's mother. I want to believe she'll be all right. Oh Lord, help my unbelief. Every time I feel doubt creep in, I'm going to sing your Word to my own ears. If I don't know a melody to go with the words, I'll just make it up.

Take away my sorrow
Take away the fear
Take away the doubts I have
And take away the tears…Please…

Father, thank You for the presence of Your Spirit. Thank You that Ephraim and I are not left alone to parent our children. I'm thinking You've never intended it any other way.

Your loving daughter, Eva Jo

Two days later
Dear Sister,

Once again I'm crying, only now with different tears. Gracie, I believe God is so good! What I once thought was about the most sorrowful thing to happen to a child has turned into something else indeed. My little girl was not created as an object of pity, but made in the image and likeness of her Creator. She was made to love Him and serve Him and I believe with all my heart that she will.

After ending my last writing, I threw myself on the Lord's mercies, begging and pleading for Him to heal my baby. I even asked that He take my hearing and give it to her. I was laying flat on my face beside the bed, having exhausted myself with weeping.

I got up just as the sun was setting, on fire with evening light...the kind that takes your breath away. As I walked to the window, shafting light struck me full in the face. I was awed by the brilliance and in an instant realized the bigness of God in a whole new way. "Oh Lord," I whispered. "Not my will...but Yours be done."

Gracie, in that very second, the most incredible peace I've ever known filled me from the center of my being. And there, with the last light of day warming my body I felt...joy. For sure, a small seed, but can you believe it? Joy!

I ran to find Ephraim, who was rocking Lulu with her head resting on his chest. It's always been her favorite position, and now we know why. When we talk or sing, she can feel it in our chest. He was holding the Bible and handed it to me. "Read Psalm 139, Eva Jo. Read it out loud beginning at verse 13." I could see where his tears had fallen.

There, Gracie, on those thin, worn pages I saw the truth for the existence of us all.

For thou hast possessed my reins; thou hast covered me in my mother's womb.
I will praise thee; for I am fearfully and wonderfully made. Marvellous are thy works, and that my soul knoweth right well.
My substance was not hid from thee, when I was made in secret, and curiously wrought in the lowest parts of the earth.

Thine eyes did see my substance, yet being unperfect; and in thy book all my members were written, which in continuance were fashioned, when as yet there was none of them.

Oh Gracie, do you see like we do? Louisa Ann was formed...just as she is, by the Lord God of the Universe, who knew her before any of us. He knew she wouldn't be able to hear, He knew we'd love her, and most of all we believe He knew we'd come to this place of trust.

We prayed over our little girl right then and there, putting her to bed with new tenderness, thanking God for His gift of our precious child.

The whole thing was quite a shock for the boys and they've been sneaking up behind her for days, yelling at the top of their lungs to see if she maybe could hear something. Doc Barlow says he thinks she might hear some deep, low sounds, but for sure she doesn't respond to voices.

I think God's gifted her in other ways, Sister. She watches my face when I hold her. I mean she looks deep into my eyes. There's a wisdom there I've never seen in a child yet so small.

We shared the whole thing with Little Dove, of course, and she took the news real serious. Hardly said a word about it. Then when she and the boys had Lulu in the wagon out collecting eggs—Lulu loves the chickens—I saw Dovie grab up a hen and take it over to the wagon. When the baby reached out to touch it, her face lit up like Christmas. Little Dove let the bird go, making a peculiar hand motion. She kept doing it over and over, the chicken not much willing, while Lulu watched every move. Curiosity made me find out what was happening.

I knew the Indians had some kind of hand language, but I never realized that the children knew it. That's what Little Dove was doing in the chicken yard. She was teaching my stone-deaf little girl how to talk...with Indian signs. She told me she'd learned dozens of them before she could even talk. Seems families have their own special ones that only they use. It's their special language.

She and I have been practicing every day. Imagine, my student has now become my teacher! She and Lulu have a special bond that's hard to describe...it's a connection that is God-given for sure. It's no surprise that when Lulu had an awakening, it was with Little Dove.

Lulu was sitting in her high chair while Dovie fed her. Lulu kept pointing to her cup of milk and grunting, but Little Dove would not budge to hand it over until her student made the proper sign for drink. Lulu's cries grew louder and shriller, her face contorted with frustration. I was about to make Little Dove give in since Lulu looked so pitiful and all, but I waited.

After a few minutes, my ten-month-old-daughter asked for her own cup. Those chubby little hands formed the sign for drink. You'd have thought she was given pure honey by the look on her face. She grinned from ear to ear. Little Dove and I whooped and hollered (me being the loudest of course). You should have seen the look on Lulu's face. She knew she'd done something special because she kept signing that word over and over. The boys and Ephraim are so excited that now they want to learn Dovie's signs. Isn't God good?

I pray that the Lord is blessing you, honey girl. Whatever you're doing, whatever you're thinking, I hope you have the same sweet thoughts of me as I have of you. I have your picture on my bureau, but you know I have you in my heart as well.

Lovingly,

Eva Jo

June 1902

Dear Gracie,

We had such a grand time on the church picnic this year that I wanted to share it with you. First off everyone was asking about you. Since Mama gets upset when anyone mentions your name, and Papa won't speak of you, people kept approaching me. Guess maybe because I'm the oldest.

Anyway, of course Aunt Etta came idling by to "chat," she says, all nice and cozy. Butter would not have melted in that woman's mouth. I know the Lord wants us to be charitable to all, but Gracie, just watching her walk toward me made me want to head for the hills. The first thing she just had to mention was Lulu's riding in the papoose pack. Never mind my daughter loves it there. Aunt Etta claimed she heard it could make a baby's legs grow crooked. Some old wives' tale! Then she looks me up and down, with her eyes finally resting on my middle, and asks in a butter-wouldn't-melt voice, "Oh Eva Jo, expectin' so soon?"

I just wanted to throw her in the lake, but thought better of it, being how it was the Lord's day and all. The nerve. Like I don't know I've gained a few pounds.

You know what I'm saying, Grace. Bet you can even picture her in that crazy hat she loves so much. Remember how we marveled at how it stayed on her head, what with all that petrified stuff stuck on it? Must weigh as much as a full sack of corn.

This year, I hope you're ready for this...she added a bird!!!! Not just a small sparrow, either; this one looked ready for the Sunday table, it was that big. Mama said she sent for it from mail order, but I say she found it under somebody's wagon wheel and dried it by the fire. It had beady little eyes that fascinated Lulu, but frankly gave me the creepies. I kept checking to see if they blinked, which made it difficult to follow all of what she was saying. She still talks faster than a crow can caw!

Anyway she finally dragged the talk around to you. Said a friend of hers thought she saw you one day on the streets in Los Angeles. This friend had met you when she lived here in '86. She was certain it was you, because she never saw another human being with the auburn hair you have. When she crossed the street to hail you down, you'd turned a corner and disappeared into a doorway. Aunt Etta kept pressing for more information about what you were doing— well, more like *how* you're doing. I assured her you were doing right fine.

But those words were for her only, little sister, because I fear for you something awful. I pray every night the Lord would protect you and hide you in His very holiness. I ask Him to send big angels to wrap you in wings of protection, so that not one of your feet should stumble.

The other night I dreamt you were adrift in the Pacific Ocean, crying for help. I jumped in for the rescue, but every time I got close, you drifted away. When I woke, I had the most empty feeling. Grief overwhelmed me until I couldn't breathe...or sleep neither. Ephraim prayed, and I finally drifted off, fitfully.

Love,
Eva Jo

P.S. Don't know if Nettie has written, but Papa said yes. She and Cal will be getting married in October. We're not sure of the exact date yet, but there's plenty of time for you to come and help with all the planning. We need you! I need you!

June 1902
Dear Sisters,

Congratulations, Nettie. You'll make a beautiful bride. You worry too much; you have all the family there to support you. Cal will do right by you, I'm sure.

Eva Jo, you are so brave. I'm tearful over Lulu's plight...poor, poor baby girl. I hear no pity in your letters, so I'll have none. But, still it is sad. I'm very sorry, but I do believe Lulu's intelligence mixed with her cleverness will see her through this hard life.

Hard life indeed. I am beside myself with worry. Harvey is missing! Four days now! Worse yet, his parents are blaming me for his disappearance. I don't think he ran away like Jake. Harvey is a steady sort of fellow, very courteous in spite of growing up on these mean streets. I'm needing to write down exactly what happened. Perhaps, when I see it on paper, I can make sense of where he's gone. I was certainly with him the last day he was seen.

It was Sunday, my half day at work, so we went to Echo Park Lake in the afternoon. All week I looked forward to this picnic, which Harvey made himself...ham and cheese with sarsaparilla beer. After renting a boat, we rowed around the lake, though Harvey's not a particularly strong man. We glided slowly through the water, resting every now and then to take in the peaceful quiet and watch the swaying palm trees overhead. I took my turn at rowing. (Since I've been scrubbing clothes for a living, my arms are muscular indeed!)

The entire rest of the day was spoiled by some boys on the bank, throwing rocks at us. I thought they were just street ruffians, but they called out, "Harvey." When he heard his name, he rowed in the other direction. The young men walked to the marina area where we had to return the rented boat. We'd had the dinghy past our allotted time, but Harvey was afraid and kept rowing and drifting, sweat now pouring from under his white cap.

"Harvey," I said, "we've got to return. It will cost more money to keep the boat out any longer."

"I know, but..."

"Who are those boys?" I asked. All innocence, I assure you.

Harvey cowered lower and lower into the bottom of the small rowboat. His shoulders heaved and he sobbed into his hands. Finally, he looked up with red eyes, nose running, and said, "You've got to believe me, Grace. I didn't do anything wrong. They know something...a...a secret. I can't tell you. Not now."

"Harvey, why are you so afraid?" My heart was pounding.

"They're out to get me, Grace. They're out to get me."

It'd been a whole extra hour by the time we got to the spot where we'd launched. From the shadows under the bridge, I watched as the boys talked to some rough-looking old sailors standing around the docks. They pointed their fingers in our direction. Harvey watched until the younger boys left. We took the chance to tie up and get out, our legs rather shaky after sitting so long.

I pulled out my pocketbook, finding enough money to pay the man for that extra time. He wasn't too happy, because we were supposed to pay upfront, of course.

"Whatsa matter?" He nodded towards Harvey. "He sick or something? Some sailor he'll make." He laughed, revealing a mouth void of teeth.

He turned his attention to me. "Where'd he pick you up? You don't know the likes of his sins, a young thing like you." He winked at me, grinning his toothless smile.

"Leave her be," Harvey said, his protest weak.

"Hey, Master Sulky, you'll get your comeuppance soon. You'll see!" He laughed again, saluted, and disappeared into the stinking boat shack.

We left in haste. It was almost seven, and we had promised to meet Harvey's friend Rudy at a tavern. On the way there, Harvey was so anxious, I thought he was going to fall to pieces. Shaken by the incident, he looked over his shoulder and into every shadow the entire way before coming to the Mermaid's Roost—or something like that...there's a carved mermaid on the shingle. Harvey lay his head on the table and asked for a stiff whiskey. I thought my friend a bit dramatic and strange. Rudy didn't come, at least while I was there.

I didn't know how to console Harvey. Too much sun had made me a bit dizzy, and I told him I needed to return to my room. He urged me to go, apologizing for not being the best of company. He said he'd wait for Rudy by himself.

That's the last I saw of him.

Every day his parents berate me. They insist I know more than I'm telling. I really don't know what Harvey meant when he said the men were out to get him. I've told them just what I've told you. I think the boys really hated him and meant to hit him with those rocks. Maybe they found him at the tavern and killed him. I know he's either dead or...beaten somewhere. I'm going to look for Rudy. He must know something.

I send you my best greetings. I miss you all.

Your sister, Grace

Dear Ones,

It's been a few days since I wrote, and I've shattering news of Harvey. The police have found evidence that he's been shanghaied. They found Rudy in the hospital and he told them what happened.

About an hour after I left the tavern, Rudy entered Mermaid's Roost. It would've been ten o'clock, getting dark. Harvey was quite drunk by this time, barely able to talk. Rudy decided to take him home.

They crossed the street closest to the harbor, taking a shortcut down a narrow alleyway. I'd taken that way myself, only hours earlier, in full daylight of course. Someone was following them. Rudy said they just looked like a gang of boys, so he thought it was nothing. Harvey was terrified and tried to run.

Like a pack of wolves descends on their prey, the young men came at them from all directions. Harvey had no chance of escaping. They put a blanket over his head and carried him off, leaving Rudy for dead.

"He's going to make a fine sailor." They laughed and joked. "A perfect cabin boy for the ship!"

"Maybe they'll put him in the galley for a scullery maid," they mocked. "He'll be paid for all his trouble before he hits Shanghai."

Rudy heard all this before he blacked out. Now it's the talk of the harbor. Kidnapping and forcing men to work on ships going to China is not uncommon. Maybe that's what happened to Jake. Maybe...he didn't really want to leave L.A. for good.

Now that this has happened, Harvey's parents have put me out on the street. They told me I've been a bad influence on their son and ruined his morals. His mother took my best aprons in payment for "stayin' on here without so much as payin' a dime," as she put it. And I thought they were kind when I first came.

I look forward to every letter waiting at Flossie's house. Continue to write me there. With Harvey gone, I've have nobody here but Mrs. White. She's always good company, but I don't have time to visit, and since her husband is back from sea, there's no room for me.

I'm staying with all the unmarried laundresses in a dormitory near a huge washhouse. It's a sad place, noisy with comings and goings all hours. There's no privacy and not so much as a shelf to put my things...little that I have. I dare not leave any belonging on my bed, or it fast disappears. I'm learning quickly not to trust a soul. I wear Mama's locket day and night, fearing it might be stolen. One girl gave birth a few beds down from mine, but the child didn't even make it through the night. The mother cried for hours, but now she's silent...like her dead baby. I suppose she needs comforting, but I've nothing to give. What a pitiful human I am.

I miss Harvey, but not nearly as much as I thought. I think I know the unbearable secret he couldn't tell me. The hatred on the boys' faces spoke volumes.

I'm in a bad way here. But I guess I can be grateful I wasn't shanghaied. Sometimes I dream of home in Washington, yet when I awake I know I'm living out my fate. And well I know how much I deserve this.

Please pray for Harvey.
Love always,
Your sister, Gracie

June 1902
Dear Diary,

I'm filled with fear. All encompassing, compared only to how I felt after Jake's attack. I wanted to be done with him, finished forever. But now I know that will never be.

G-

Eight

❧❧

NETTIE'S DIARY

Dear Lord,
I've gone from "Little Nettie" to Miss McLeod. Teacher. You know how I've struggled with wanting my family to treat me as grown up. Suddenly I'm seeing the other side of the coin. Growing up is hard, and I wonder if I'm ready for the adult world, especially now that my name on the school house door says I'm already in it.

Miss Knatz never did officially put Little Dove's name on the roster for the fall, but that's the first thing I did after accepting the job. No one on the school board said anything to me about who to register (or not), and since Mr. Abbot was out of town, her name was added.

Eva Jo traveled all over the valley and into the hills, searching for school-aged children, especially those who've had no book learning at all. Remarkably, she discovered eight, half of them Indian.

I was not prepared for the complications that arose. It feels as bad as skunk cabbage smells...awful and lingering. I guess that's a good comparison for ignorance. It stinks. How can people be cruel enough to give one child less than another?

Little Dove and the others will have an education, or my sister's name is not Eva Jo. Her name is on the registration list for Good Hope. Hers and Ephraim's. Now how's that for a kettle of fish? I guess Mama will have to watch Lulu, because there is absolutely no more room in that little building for another child.

Mama has a good ear for listening, and she stands by my adult decisions, but still I'm feeling awfully young and inexperienced right now. Then, of course, there's Cal. I suppose if I'm grown up enough to teach school, I'm grown up enough to know my own heart. For sure this girl's heart belongs to him. But marriage is BIG!

Oh, now my head is spinning. I'm sorry to be such a whiner, Father. Make me to be strong in heart AND soul.

Your daughter,
Annette

July 1902
Gracie Darling,

I'm in Eden! Well, it feels like paradise, waiting for sunrise to hit the valley floor...wondering what the Psalmist was viewing when he wrote Psalm 139. When I read of the "wings of the morning," I imagine he was waiting, same as me, for the sun to re-stake its claim on the sky. Then when those first rays take flight towards heaven...that's the wings he's talking about.

God is everywhere this morning; my senses are more alive somehow. I can see the mountain, smell the sweetness of our garden, taste the morning mist, and hear the birds' sweet melodies. I'm at peace, grateful the Lord allows me breath in His creation. I love the way summer births its mornings...innocent...pure...like children. They are rich with promise and so is my day. Oh, for a greater mind to capture with grander words the whispers of my heart.

I hope you don't mind my use of pencil for this script. It's too tricky to manage pen and ink on a porch swing. Ephraim excused me from morning chores, even though there's more work during this season. I hear him singing to the ladies down in the barn...a rousing rendition of "Bringing in the Sheaves."

We're on alert these days since spotting a big mountain lion by the creek. He's brazen as sin and just as big. Ephraim had taken Willie and Percy with him hunting, when he shot a fine buck. It didn't drop right away, so the boys took off when it did, afraid he'd be lost in the brush. They followed him straight to the creek, but when Ephraim caught up they stood still as statues, pointing.

What a sight they described. A huge cat was dragging their kill through creek water like a toy. Even when Ephraim shot in the air, it didn't let go. He decided against chasing him anymore, especially with the boys there. They settled for several already bagged rabbits.

The boys were chattering like squirrels when they got back. Every time the story's told, the cat gets bigger...of course. They're calling him Old Nick because he's got a chunk of flesh missing from one ear. My, aren't they clever! D.J. made his dad promise to take him hunting next time. I'm thinking he's still too small. No matter the size, males have it born in them for danger, I reckon.

Papa says that in all the years living in this valley he's never heard of a cougar being so bold. He and Ephraim figured maybe it's old, injured, or the logging on Roan Mountain drove him down. I heard one yowling once, out at the Vanderdyk's place. Made my skin crawl.

We had Percy's birthday celebration on Sunday with a picnic after church; had lots of folks. All the children were playing a game when I spotted the birthday boy off to the side.

"Percy, this is your day. Go play."

"I don't wanna." It's all he'd say. But I saw a tear slip down a freckled cheek before his head bent down.

"What's wrong, mister man?"

"I want Gracie! She's never missed my birthday, Eva Jo. Never. She's not ever comin' back."

With that, he grabbed me in a hug, sobbing on my shoulder.

You've been gone more than six months now, Gracie. Somehow, someway, I know God is going to bring you home, despite Percy's doubts. Don't be angry. I know you're a grown woman and can make your own decisions. It's just that I've begged God for so long, I believe He'll answer just to shut me up.

Good-bye for now.

Later

I love the longer days, gives me more daylight for finishing tasks and letter writing. I'm still journaling to the Lord as well. Are you?

Since my incident with the old shotgun, Ephraim's been working to teach me the ways of a shiny, newer rifle he bought from Doc

Barlow. I'm suspecting Doc wanted me to have it, otherwise afraid I might bring him more business.

I've been shooting at crows mostly, but the other morning I spotted a big whitetail buck, eying my garden. Usually the dogs keep them away, but they were gone with Ephraim and the boys. There he was... Mister I'm-free-to-eat-all-I-see. Little Dove was playing with Lulu on the porch, so I snuck around to the barn side of the garden. I think he heard the click of the hammer because right before I fired, his head came up quick. He fell with one shot, kicked a little dust, then lay still. I still had the gun on my shoulder while walking closer, grinning from ear to ear with the pride.

That's when I heard one small snap of brush. The hair on the back of my neck stood up and I froze. Spotting a slight movement out of the corner of an eye, I turned my head only slightly. Old Nick!

He was stalking this body the way a barn cat stalks a shrew, slow and sure.

Lord, help me, I prayed. Then as deliberately as possible, I pivoted, pulling the hammer back while raising the gun into place. My whole body quivered as I breathed deep, swallowed hard. He took his leap and I felt as if the devil himself was pouncing. My shot caught his belly midair, felling him like a duck. I walked over to where he lay. I found him equally intimidating up close on the ground...his tongue hanging out one side of a huge mouth. I've never even seen a mountain lion, let alone touched one...or smelled one.

Fright drove me to my knees right next to the scarred body. That's where I was when Ephraim found me. He was sweating. From exertion or concern I couldn't tell.

"Eva Jo, every time you pick up a gun, something awful happens."

"I'm sure," I said, wondering if he thought that a character flaw.

After helping me to my feet, we inspected the prey. Ephraim was so rightly impressed with the dead cat, at first he never noticed the deer. After walking the distance, he let out a low whistle, proudly wrapping both arms around me. I was basking in the pleasure when we heard something low, ominous, unfamiliar. A growl? A moan? Both!

The lion still lived! By the time we understood this, he was on all fours, shaking his head while continuing those frightening sounds. Exactly when we noticed the cat's revival, David John came running around the barn. He was not twenty feet away when Ephraim shouted for him to stop. Without hesitation he did...not a muscle moved once he saw what was happening. In a lightning flash, Ephraim had the gun to his shoulder. Firing on the run, his shot met the target dead on. What could have been a disaster ended. The only sound remaining was that of our breathing....then I heard D.J. shouting with complaint as to the grip his father had on him.

Needless to say, the talk around our dinner table was long with excitement. Me? I've had all the excitement I'll ever want. For once in my life I was actually speechless. It's true. I'm in complete amazement when I think of all that happened and how differently things might have turned out. Praise God for His divine intervention.

At least we have wonderful venison to cure and an adventure tale to pass along. Ephraim gave the cat's hide to Adam McIsaac from church. I never want to see it again.

I'm confiding this much, Grace. I'll never look at a cat of any description in the same way again. When I see one of the barn cats running for cover, chills trail down my spine like winter wind. Perhaps with time, it will pass.

Even though we've always felt safe, living close to town and all, we have to be vigilant...I've learned a powerful lesson. Who knows how long that animal had been watching us? The Scripture that describes Satan as a roaring lion, looking for someone to devour, has deeper meaning now. We need to be ever aware of the damage Satan wants to inflict. The older I get, the more I see the wisdom of Scripture and the practicality of it all.

Oh my, never a dull day around this valley.

From my heart to yours, Eva Jo

PRAYER JOURNAL
EVA JO

Dear Lord,

What a fright we've had. Thank you for your divine protection. Though Life is hard, You are ever with us. I know I get too comfortable sometimes, please forgive me for taking you for granted.

That cat was bigger than my worst nightmare. Well, not as big as the big old sow bear, but huge just the same, and for sure, as mean and dangerous.

I can't shake the feeling of horror at the thought of such a creature watching us, maybe even stalking us. How long had he been doing this? What a picture in my head of Your love and protection. Give me eyes to see through the wiles of the devil. And while I'm asking, could you please give Grace that kind of vision to see the mess she's really in? Satan appears to be having a field day in her life. My sister's heart can't understand this kind of running away. I weep at what Mama and Papa must be going through. Mama says so little. Out of respect for Papa's wishes, I'm sure. How would I react if one of my children left home like Grace? Oh Father, I hope I never have to know.

How your heart must break over the disobedience of Your children who go astray. I beg You, Lord, to keep this stubborn woman on the right path. Make me the woman You want me to be.

I do love You,

Your Eva Jo

GRACE'S DIARY

California

Dear Diary,

Work is making me hardhearted. So great is my aloneness and fear that I have shut down to my surroundings in order to survive them. It takes little effort now to ignore what doesn't concern me. To be involved at any other level might consume too much of me, and thus I might disappear. I think often of disappearing. I'm torn, because now I know there is another within me that would be gone as well. Surely this new, small, and helpless creature would be better off. What kind of mother could I be?

G-

Middle of July
Dear Gracie,

I'm choosing to walk by faith and not by fear, since not hearing from you for so long. You'd not believe the many times God has led me to pray for you. My mind reels with the possibilities of why you've not written. Perhaps our letters are not getting to you. It's a worrisome thing for both of us.

Yesterday it was 90 degrees...in the shade, according to the old thermometer on the barn wall. If there are marks on this paper, it will be from my sweat. Despite the heat, we scheduled woodcutting with the neighbors.

Ephraim suggested the "ladies" stay home, but when Henry Bottemiller's new wife insisted on going, what could I do? I admit to a sorely bad attitude...you know me and hot weather.

We loaded all the brood but Lulu into two wagons, heading for the little creek on our back twenty. Parking the wagons in the shade gave me relief from the rising sun, while the children found theirs playing in the water.

I was pleasantly surprised at the downright friendliness of Mrs. Bottemiller...Agnes Ann, and we hit it off. Turns out she's the late Mrs. Bottemiller's cousin. She stepped into quite the responsibilities, with having three small toddlers and a husband to care for. They're real sweet little guys, and played well with mine, even Lulu.

I felt my mood lift, enjoying the conversation with the labor, when a bloodcurdling scream tore through the air. Despite the heat, I had a terrible chill. It was the oldest Bottemiller boy. He came running from the creek, arms flailing. At first we didn't see what he was running from, but as he got closer, we heard what followed him. Bees, thousands of them!

For a few seconds neither Agnes Ann nor I moved. Then she took off like a bullet and grabbed that boy off the ground, heading back towards the water. I screamed as loud as I could for David, and he and Mr. Bottemiller came quick as deer. Ephraim yelled for the children to get back in the water. My boys had sense to grab their little sister before I got there. Even with my skirts hiked up, wading in was slow going, but dunking did the business for the bees and they

119

flew off in a swarm.

Everyone had stings, but none got as many as Nathaniel Bottemiller. His body looked like an unearthly patchwork quilt...bright red and puffy. You couldn't lay a finger on any place on his body where there weren't ugly welts. Right off his dad slapped creek mud all over him.

When all the commotion had settled down, I heard heavy breathing and Lulu's quiet sobbing. We all walked out of the creek, Agnes Ann and Mr. Bottemiller carrying Nathaniel, who appeared unable to stand by himself. They laid him on the ground, and right before our eyes his face and upper body began to swell like nothing I'd ever seen. His breathing became labored, getting slower and slower.

"He's having a bad reaction to all those stings," Agnes Ann shouted.

As soon as she said that, Nathaniel went still as snow and just as white.

"Is he dead?" a brother whispered.

Now I was shaking like a cottonwood.

Mr. Bottemiller threw himself on top of his dear boy's body. Agnes Ann, kneeling right beside, suddenly started praying as loud as anyone I've ever heard. She begged God to give back their special boy, who meant so much to everyone. She took her hands and placed them over his heart and began kissing his face, all the while pleading with the Lord.

We were all in tears, sobbing out loud, when Ephraim joined her in supplication. Mr. Bottemiller's lips were moving, but no sound came out. I held Lulu tight, while both D.J and Lucas clung to my wet skirts, bravely ignoring their own red splotches.

We must have been praying for a full minute (though it felt like time eternal), when a faint moan came from the ground. At first I thought it was Agnes Ann, but then Nathaniel's eyelids fluttered, and opened. He looked all around and to everyone's amazement, he smiled. A huge big grin spread from ear to ear. As soon as the boy was full awake, he asked for food.

Although still covered with stings, all the swelling was gone and he had color. He sat up, moving his hands and arms, then stood, hopping from one leg to another. He kind of circled around the spot where he had once laid motionless, looking bewildered but alive. His two brothers jumped up and down hugging each other and their father. Agnes Ann had a most satisfied, relieved look, tears remaining on her red, marked face. She kept repeating over and over her praises to the Lord. Mr. Bottemiller didn't know who to hug first...his son or his wife.

The four adults were totally awestruck as to what happened, making us speechless. Now you know that doesn't happen with me often. Had Nathaniel really died? Did God truly bring him back? When we were finally able to talk, our mouths were filled with praise, for all agreed that, yes, we'd seen a real miracle. Right in our midst, the Lord God of Heaven reached down and answered a cry from His helpless children.

Ephraim and Mr. Bottemiller took water-soaked branches mixed with dry, forming smoky torches to burn out the bees they'd disturbed.

The rest of the children had lots of nasty red spots, but none seemed any the worse for wear. They'll remember this incident for a long time. I'll venture to say that Nathaniel will never forget. He stayed right by Agnes Ann the whole rest of the day. They've a new bond that's sweetly apparent.

Ephraim and I slept outside that night...under the stars. It seems we're closer to God when out of the house. We're connected deeper because of what was witnessed on the banks of that creek. A miracle...a miracle! Since that stream never did have a name, we're calling it "Miracle Creek."

I've been thinking a lot about miracles, Gracie. There are some right under my nose, for sure. Like me and you, for instance...we're miracle siblings. Maybe you never thought of this before, but the fact we're related is a divine occurrence. A Heavenly happening, you might say. God made it so! He's the one that put our family together...His choice...His plan. Do you see it? I admit, until you left, I often took you for granted. Mama and Papa too...all of us. My eyes have been opened to many things since the Miracle Creek incident. I will never be the same. It's right up there with becoming a born-again Christian. I'm born-again to the almighty power of God. More miraculous than our earthly bonds is the fact that you and I are part of the family of God. Because we're sisters in the Lord, we'll be Heavenly sisters as well. I'm overwhelmed with the revelation of it all.

The same mighty God that saved Nathaniel Bottemiller watches over you, my miracle sister. May He bless you and keep you, and may His face shine upon you.

Love, Eva Jo

EVA JO'S DIARY

Dear Diary,

I am beyond exhaustion, but I cannot end this day without coming to you. How do I process what my eyes saw yesterday today? The privilege of observing something so holy goes beyond words. It's humbling even to close my eyes and watch it happen all again. I want to store it in my memory, keeping it fresh and alive. Of course, from now on, whenever I see Nathaniel Bottemiller, or even hear of him, I will relive the day of his deliverance from a death too soon. Did you bring him back for some great deed? Was this miracle as much for those who watched as for this boy? Perhaps You wanted to build our faith. I feel exactly as small right now as I did standing on the shores of the Pacific Ocean. "What is man, that thou art mindful of him, O Lord." What, indeed!

Lovingly,
Eva Jo

GRACE'S DIARY

July 4, 1902
Dear Diary,

I watched the 4th of July parade from my window in the dormitory. There were decent people all below. I didn't belong. It seems long ago when I was one of them: a normal, innocent girl. I wish

I were still.

I saw Flossie White yesterday on the street. I think she checks on me sometimes. She says I ought to come and live with her. She guessed my condition.

"I see you're in a family way," she whispered. "Oh, Gracie, stay at my house. My husband's out to sea again, and I could use company." She reached for me and I collapsed into her arms like a lost child.

"I can't, Flossie," I sobbed.

"Dear Heart, have you told your sisters yet?"

"About the baby? No! I can't. If my papa finds out, he'll hate me."

"Grace, he's gonna find out anyway. You need ta write your family."

I completely broke down at that point. She walked me back to my sleeping quarters. Sitting on the bed, she said, "Oh, honey, look at this place. How can you live here? This is no place to have a baby."

I was struck with fear remembering the baby that had died, just feet away. "Flossie, I know I need to go home, but I just can't. You don't know where I'm from. It's a small town, and now my family's name is in the dirt. All because of me."

She looked deeply into my eyes and lifted my chin. "God is with you. Who, pray tell, can be against ya?" She got up and kissed my cheek. "You know where I live, dear. Come see me soon, won't you?"

Oh, diary, I wanted to get up and go with her right then and there. But something kept me in this infernal room, despite the smell of sweat, dirty bedding, and...degradation.

My swollen belly reminds me I have to write Eva Jo and Nettie. They will understand. But I won't tell them that Jake...raped me. They can never know that.

G-

July 1902
Dear Eva Jo and Nettie,

I cannot keep my secret any longer, though I've tried to deny this with all my being. I'm going to have a baby. There, I've said it. I know now there is no hope of Papa ever wanting to see me again. Most of the people in Yacolt will shun me as well. You've encountered their deep prejudice already. Imagine how they'd treat a pregnant woman with no husband. Aunt Etta will cast me away like one of her old hats. Mama will be further heartbroken, even though I grieve over causing her more hurt.

I'm unable to tell you exactly how it happened; regardless, I'm "used goods" now. My life has taken a new direction with the revelation of a child in the future. I beg you both, sisters, try to understand. I must bear this alone.

Of course it is Jake's child. I cry as I write these words, because there are more secrets. At this moment I don't have the strength to share them. I will tell you this: I never knew that a man could be so cruel. I'm intending to go to his father's office to claim money for this, his own son's child. The Hudsons should bear some responsibility. My living as a laundress is hard, making me think about the future more clearly now.

My friends drift away from me as they learn about my condition, although Mrs. White remains faithful. She's offered to help me with some different clothing...for this...state. Thankfully, aprons cover most of my girth, because I have to unbutton the tops of my skirts now. A loose peasant blouse still looks well, but I've just one.

If only Jake had truly been the man I saw in the beginning. If only we could have been husband and wife and raised our child together. I think about it all the time. What a fool I've been!

As I wash the clothes every day, my hands red and raw from the strong lye soap, I still feel dirty...as though I've been rolling in a filthy pig-sty. But then I think about bringing a new life into the world, and a little measure of hope wells up in my heart. How sweet the memory of Eva Jo's children lingers. I wish this little one could grow up with cousins, and aunts and uncles. Yet this child will always be different. Things are so wrong...all wrong...upside down.

Know, sisters, that I am determined to pull through this by myself. I don't need any one else. It's hard for me here, but I cannot come home like you want. Don't you see now? The shame and prejudice of having a baby out of wedlock is too great for me in your little valley. Here in California unwedded mothers are more plentiful, especially in the society I keep.

I dream that a rich gentleman might sweep me off my feet one day. Men used to admire me when I was on Jake's arm. But I've fallen so hard and so deeply that they look right past me now. They see my belly and have no desire to court a pregnant washer woman. I know no man willing to raise another's child. It's a disgrace. Maybe that's what I should have as a name now: just call me DIS-GRACE. I am not Grace Rose McLeod anymore. And the new me cannot ever come home.

Your sister of disgrace

Prayer Journal
Eva Jo

August 1902
O, Lord,

I need to be on my face before You for Gracie's sake. I should have known she was pregnant, been able to read between the lines all this time. Father, what will become of her now? I'm frightened. She's so vulnerable...no husband, no family. What kind of monster could leave her like this, and what about the secrets?

I'm helpless, living this far away. Please rescue my sister, make a way where there appears to be none. Keep her safe from the enemy who seeks to destroy her very life. I anguish over how to tell Mama and Papa. Ephraim thinks I should, but Papa's not receptive to anything having to do with talk of Grace. I've no idea what he'll do. Ephraim and I will pray tonight.

August 1902
My sweet Gracie,

I've thought long and hard about this letter, praying over and over about what to say. I love you, Grace. I love you regardless of what you've done, or what's been done to you. More important than my love and that of your family, is God's love for you. You are precious above your circumstances. Please sweetheart, please come home. Don't believe you have no worth...that's a lie. The enemy of your soul would have you think we're through with you. That's not possible. The same is true of God. He says that even if a nursing mother could forget her young, He would not forget you. All these many months you have survived. The McLeod women are tough. How many times did we hear that growing up?

You have the same toughness in regards to your spirit as well, little sister. Even though your dreams have been shattered, God has a plan, regardless. I still remember how determined you were when anything new came along in the way of our schooling. If I thought it too hard...I'd quit. But not you, not ever. Determined to conquer the new arithmetic Mama had laid out, you once fell asleep at the table. Papa carried you to bed...with the pencil still clutched in your little fist.

Maybe you'll have a little girl. She'll have red hair and be smart and beautiful. And full of Grace. If you have a boy, he'll be bright, love to read, and have a curiosity for life that will match your own. Grace, God will redeem whatever you've done. More than that, He'll restore all that's been lost.

I know it will be hard returning home to face the entire town. But love can conquer all, my sweet. Believe me, sister. Believe Him.

Love to you,
Eva Jo

PRAYER JOURNAL
NETTIE

August
My Father, who is in Heaven...Whose eyes are on all men. You alone know what is in the depths of one's heart. You are the Creator of all

things and have designed a time and place for everything to begin.

I must rest in Your truths as I sit and wonder at the words I've just heard. Gracie is pregnant. She's all alone. What disgrace this man brought upon my sister, Lord. Does she walk in shame or is she clinging to You?

Oh, dear Jesus, give her the strength and courage needed for what is ahead. I wish I could be with her. I want her home. I'm yearning for days like those before she left. Life was simple and we were protected from awful things.

Despite the pain these past months, You, Lord, have been faithful to bring about many blessings. Thank You. And even now in the midst of Gracie's troubles, You have blessed her with this special little someone. It will be hard, but I pray for Your presence to be made known to her. You are her Maker. Please let her see You will be her husband.

All my love,
Annette

Dear Gracie,

I love you, dear sister. I always will. You know that I pray for you every day, and now, I will add your baby to my prayer list. May the Lord cup your precious child in His hands forever.

While walking today, I spent time thinking of bygone days, and the journey our family's been on. I lay down under our old oak tree where the ground was cool and the grass tickled my legs. Looking upward, the sunlight created an amazing complicated patchwork as it bounced off the tree. But no matter how thick the branches were, the light still managed to make a grand impression. Exactly like God's Word. It says that trials bring good things to our character: perseverance, patience, hope. I want to believe that, even when bitterness and hurt close in on me.

A sparkling turquoise sky shown through the canopy, with birds flying by every few minutes or so. How free they were...free to just get up and go wherever, and whenever they choose. I felt just like that when I was younger...carefree and singing, able to enjoy being God's child. We all did.

Oh, my lovely Grace, if only you could fly home to our nest...to be protected and cared for. How much more heartache can you take? Your baby needs family. We can make lasting memories of simple things...like pictures in a book...to look back on when times get hard. Our life used to be so good. I refuse to believe it won't be that way again.

I know you have your reasons for not wanting to be here, but do those reasons stand firm in light of present circumstances? Is it better where you are now than where you have been?

Gracie, please come home. You need us, but most of all, you need Mama. She can help you. I'm begging God to bring you back to us.

I'm your forever sister,
Annette

August 1902
Dear Grace,

I hope you've gotten my last letter. When I wrote, I desperately needed you to know how loved you are because I believe that "I love you" are the most important words in the world. I know you think that nothing good can come from what's befallen you, but that's not true. Your life IS hard right now, but I want to share this, Grace, because you know that life will always be hard for Lulu as well.

My little daughter told me she loves me this very day. My Lulu understands! I was frightened that she might not ever realize how loved she is, and now I see she does. She was just finishing breakfast this morning when I looked right into her beautiful blue eyes and signed *I love you*, like Little Dove taught me. Lulu's eyes studied my face for fleet seconds, looking deep into my heart, I believe. I was about to turn away when she signed back to me...*I...love...you*.

Sometimes she'll mimic a sign even before she knows what it means. But Gracie, she knows...it was all over her face. She loves me, understands that I love her, and now she can tell me so. I'm writing this down before any of the others know, because I wanted to share it with you first. I'm going to put me and Lulu on Old Blue and ride out to Mama's and tell her.

There have been several times lately when it's surely evident that Lulu is trying to talk. One of the ladies at church was telling me something she read about placing the deaf person's one hand on their own throat and the other on the speaker's mouth. I tried that with the word pear. It took some time, but I believe she's catching on. The look on her on her face said it all.

What a little clown she's getting to be. Makes a lot of noise...real loud sometimes. We think she feels the sound. She's caused a few anxious moments in church lately because of it.

When we took her to Jenny Case's wedding, the whole place was in an uproar.

Right when pastor says: "Speak now or forever hold your peace," out of the silence, Lulu lets out one of her war whoops. Oh my, was this face red. But then everyone started laughing...even the bride and groom. Only Grandma Case shot us a look.

Lulu seems to be a special girl to lots of people, always knowing who needs extra attention. Widow Vida Brooks took a fall and was missing from services for weeks, but the minute Lulu saw her, she nearly jumped from my lap before I could set her down. She wrapped those baby arms around the woman's legs so tight, I thought she'd cause her to fall again. The Widow Brooks must be in her 80s, but she bent over and picked Lulu off the floor like she was a spring daisy. Lulu laughed out loud and wouldn't let go of the poor woman's neck, kept planting kisses on her cheek with wet slobbery enthusiasm. There wasn't a dry eye in the church, including the Widow Brooks.

Grandma McLeod used to say that God is altogether good and only does good things. I for sure didn't believe that when we found out about Lulu's lack of hearing, but now I can see His plan becoming clearer each day. He's blessed her with the ability to connect deep to others. I want you to know her, Gracie. In some ways she appears fragile, because she is after all still a baby. But she possesses a spirit that's tough. Tough enough to not only endure what life gives her, but to prosper in spite of it.

I'm feeling restless today. We've had fierce winds...makes it hot, dry, and dusty. There must have been some lightning strikes in the woods because for days there's been an acrid tinge to the air. Even the stock act strange, especially Blue and the other horses. They keep running up and down the fence line, noses nose high in the air, shaking their heads something fierce. Well, soon the fall rains will come and we'll have relief. Next thing you know, I'll be complaining about how wet everything is. And you know how long that lasts.

Gracie, we've always talked about raising our children together. That can still happen. I refuse to think anything else.

All my love to you, Gracie Darling,

Eva Jo

PRAYER JOURNAL
EVA JO

Dear Lord,

I so dreaded facing Mama and Papa over Gracie's revelation, but after Ephraim and I prayed, we both felt the need to tell them. I never expected the reaction that followed.

I waited until after church was through, hoping for more courage. Your perfect peace washed over me, as Ephraim and I asked Mama and Papa to walk us to our wagon.

"What's wrong, Eva Jo?" Mama asked, looking right into my face.

"Well…"

"Eva Jo, has something happened to Gracie?" Papa's voice was filled with worry.

"Yes."

"I knew it," Mama cried. "Is she hurt? Oh, God, please." Her hands were clasped together, looking as distraught as the day Gracie left.

"She's not injured. She's…Grace is having a baby." My words were a whisper.

Mama walked over to Papa, collapsing against him. He enfolded her into his embrace and looked at me over her back. Silent tears spilled onto Mama's shoulder.

"It's my fault." He spoke, never taking his eyes from mine. "I was wrong to be so hardhearted." He stepped away from Mama, took his

Sunday handkerchief, and blew his nose loudly. "Louise, get the children."

Papa is a man of few words, but he'll come up with a plan. I expected him to be beside himself with anger, but his tears said something entirely different.

Oh, Lord, please pour out Your comfort and mercy on this family. Give Papa wisdom and discernment where Grace is concerned. Please continue to make a way where there appears to be none. Protect my little sister…hide her in Your holiness. Bless the child she carries, and most of all bring her home. Bring *them* home.

I'm so dreading Aunt Etta's reaction when she hears about this. Help my attitude with her.

Your loving daughter,

Eva Jo

Grace's Diary

California

Dear Diary,

What an odd experience I've had. Yesterday's dawn was unusually cool so I left the stifling hot dormitory to take a quick walk in a fine neighborhood close by. I had stopped to tie an undone shoelace, when out of the corner of my eye, something of color flashed. Fleeting though it was, curiosity begged me find it. I stood in front of a stately home, the grounds well-groomed. Had I only seen a brilliant blossom tossed about by wind? Perhaps, yet I needed to search further.

Hesitating at the grand gate until I made sure no one watched, I entered. Enraptured by the splendor of beauty and the morning, I never noticed the gardener until I nearly tripped over him where he worked.

"You're trespassing." He was old, his voice hoarse. His ancient straw hat jiggled when he spoke.

"Oh, excuse me," I said. "I'm not meaning to be rude. It's just that I've witnessed an incredible blaze of color I've never seen before.

Perhaps a bird?" I felt foolish, talking to a complete stranger about a fleeting vision of sorts.

"Oh."

I waited, arms folded, while he continued digging the loamy soil with a silver-colored claw.

"It's a bird. Scarlet Tanager."

"How perfect," I said. "I don't believe we have those in Washington State, where I'm from."

"Don't have them here neither." He paused only long enough to spit something brown and foul towards my feet.

"But you just said..."

"I know what I said. I said it's a bird ya saw, and it's called a Scarlet Tanager. Don't live here normally, but once in a blue moon, a couple of 'em fly up from South America. Now if ya don't mind, I need to finish."

"Oh, I don't mind at all. Would it be all right...I mean, do you think I could take a few minutes to look for it?"

He spat again, barely missing my right shoe. "Suit yourself."

I had little time left before work, but something compelled me to search out the elusive gem that had created such a disturbance in my otherwise mundane life. I walked about in the fading dew of the lawn, looking skyward for those dazzling feathers.

Suddenly I heard a melody calling from the bougainvillea that smothered a side portico. Distracted by abundant blossoms, I looked in vain. Then I spied him.

A flame with wings. I dare not move, lest he take flight, and my eyes be denied his beauty. Why was I so enthralled? California was filled with opulent flora and fauna, yet this small wonder caused a stirring within that would not be denied.

He was free! Far from home, he had freedom, I did not. He was flourishing in his surroundings...his song proof enough. I was a bird who'd left the nest too soon, pounced upon by a predator and abandoned to fate. Though his surroundings were strange and unfamiliar, he still had a song. Where was mine? Where once music had held daily joy, there was only silence, memory dead to its filling power.

When I raised a hand to shade my eyes from interfering sunshine, the tanager flew from its rest, making escape upon the wings of the morning. With melancholy, I turned to leave. It was only then I realized he'd left something behind. His song.

G

Nine

Dearest Sisters,

Yesterday, I summoned enough courage to see Mr. Emory Hudson at the railway office. My desperate circumstances finally overwhelmed my pride. I need help.

I wanted to look as presentable as possible, so I wore a hat, and the one piece of clothing that covers me decently. A steward led me into the inner waiting room after taking my name, but not before looking me up and down.

I found Mr. Hudson's workplace no less ornate than his home. Red velvet curtains and gilded carved ceilings fairly shouted to the wealth of its owner. I was so enthralled with my surroundings that I didn't hear the steward return.

He cleared his throat politely, startling me. "Mr. Hudson is not available at this time, Miss McLeod." He tipped his head in dismissal.

"But he has to see me," I wailed, unable to control pent-up emotions.

"Mr. Hudson was quite specific, Miss."

"You don't understand. I must see him." I removed the cape, revealing my obvious condition. "I'm having his grandchild."

I only wanted for Mr. Hudson to have mercy on his own flesh-and-blood, if not on me, dear sisters.

The steward's face blushed crimson, as did mine. He turned on his heels, headed back to Emory Hudson's inner sanctum.

How I longed for a sip of cool water, something to refresh my wilting spirits. In spite of this agitation, my eye caught a peculiar modern painting hanging on the wall opposite my repose. It was a mother and child, painted in broad strokes of lightly colored paint. "Breakfast in Bed." A woman artist! Her name was in the lower left corner, "Mary Cassatt." The mother looks like you, Eva Jo, reclining on fluffy white pillows. Sitting near her, on the edge of the bed, is a toddler, clutching some food in a chubby hand. Curls wreath her head, and she's dressed simply in white. Her eyes gaze outwards, away from the mother, who looks quizzically at her offspring, as if to say, "Who is this child of mine, and what is she thinking?"

I saw myself in the painting, not as the mother, but as the child. I, too, always looked out from the comforts of home and family. Distracted by the wide world, I yearned for a different life. I confess I dreamed of riches, even fame. But I wanted to scream at the child before me, "Look out! Your mother loves you. She wants you. Don't look anywhere else for what you need. Don't leave her!"

My thoughts were interrupted by the steward's greeting.

"Mr. Hudson will see you." He spoke without a hint of what was waiting down the hall.

I managed to pull myself together in some semblance of decorum. Mr. Hudson was standing when I entered the room. "Miss McLeod," he said abruptly, pulling out a chair, "sit down."

"Thank you."

I looked at his face, and truly, sisters, his eyes were cold and hard, as I had remembered, though his lips formed a smile.

"So, Miss McLeod, what is it you want? You do want something from me, am I right?" He paused, running his hand over a neatly trimmed goatee. "Everyone does."

"I've fallen on some hard times, because your son...your son..."

"Come now, Miss McLeod, I'm not blind. You're pregnant." His right hand fingered the elaborate diamond ring on his left hand. His eyes glared into mine. I was his prey. "You're having a child, and you want me to believe it belongs to Jacob."

"It is Jake's baby, I assure you."

"Grace—" his voice lowered, and I thought he was about to speak something of comfort—"I have only your word as to the paternity of the child you carry." He spat out the words like they were bile.

"But there's no one else. No one." I was on my feet now.

He came around his gigantic desk to stand over me. "Like I said, I've only your word." He cleared his throat before continuing. "I miss very little in this quaint town, and I've many friends about. Friends who've kept me abreast of your bohemian ways, Miss McLeod. Your loose, careless ways."

"What are you implying?"

"I'll make it as clear as possible." He paused, then ran his ringed hand over his beard another time. "I don't know if you're having Jake's bastard child or not."

The absolute truth of that word slapped me back into the chair. I was faint with horror.

He closed in, placed both his giant hands on the arms of my chair. I was now looking directly into his face. "My dear girl, go back to the simple farm you came from. Forget this ever happened." He waved his hand at me as if I were an insect, then walked towards the window.

I spoke to his back. "I am not a liar, Mr. Hudson—something your son could never say. He was not man enough to speak the truth."

He had more to say. "Jacob is gone. We are all better off for his leaving. I have no son." He cleared his throat. "Your child deserves better, as do you, but you'll receive no help from me...none." He turned from the window with deliberation and walked through the double doors without a glance in my direction.

I was alone. Alone as I've ever been.

I expected the steward to come and escort me to the door, but when he didn't return, I left. I couldn't help but pause and look at the painting in the foyer, one more time. I whispered to that dear, innocent child in it, "Don't leave your mother! It's too soon. If you jump off into the world, go back. Go back to where you belong. And may God help you if you don't."

Emory Hudson knows the truth about my baby, but still he's refused my pleas. At least I have Mrs. White. I'm considering accepting her offer for shelter because the dormitory is more than a nightmare. Just today, a fire started below, and if not for the quickness of several people, the whole place would have been an inferno.

Perhaps it's my nervous state that makes me edgy, but I had the strangest feeling I was being followed today, when I left the railroad office. More than once, I stopped to look around, but the street was crowded and no one in particular stood out. Although an older woman looked somewhat familiar when she caught my eye. She turned her face immediately, so it was only a fleeting glance...still...

Thanks for your most recent update on Lulu. You're right about the importance of love, Eva Jo. How sweet and timely for your daughter. Yet I can't help wondering: if the God you always talk about is all loving, why did He make Lulu deaf in the first place? If He loves children so much, why did He give my baby to a mother who's a complete failure?

Surely you know I don't believe in the Bible anymore. Please don't write me if you're going to tell me about "what the Bible says." I know it all, and I'm weary of it. The Bible can give me nothing right now. God, if there is a God, is not who I thought He was. Just because I don't believe in God the way you two do, doesn't mean I don't believe in you. I do love you both and would give the stars to have not caused you so much pain.

Love from me always,
Gracie

P.S. If I do move in with Flossie, she'll be an old mother hen. She doesn't approve of my drinking because of the baby. I assured her I really don't drink more than a sip or two of wine. It's the wonderful atmosphere of the Old Town taverns where women are equal to men that I like. Fortune tellers abound, and card dealers play their games. There's gambling behind dark curtains marked "Forbidden." Well, it's not forbidden to me...I'm free of those rules. With a snap of my fingers, they're gone in a poof. I don't need any scraps from Emory Hudson's table. There are other ways to make money.

My mind aches with the effort of thought. I'm not able to write another word.

G-

GRACE'S DIARY

Dear Diary,

I've just realized why the woman I saw yesterday on the street looked familiar. The day Jacob left me, and my belongings in front of our house, a stranger walked by and offered assistance. Since Mrs.

White was there, I declined, but I'm almost positive they're the same person. Surely, it was just a coincidence, because what could she want with me? Yet...it's almost like we've met before. It's the eyes I can't forget. I've seen them before.

I have no energy for mystery.

G

My Gracie,

I received your letter telling of your meeting with Mr. Hudson. I'm confused and sick because of the great burden you're bearing right now in order to live. But it's the last of that letter that grieves me the most. You're my sister, Grace. The distance between us hasn't changed that. I've never meant my letters to be sermons, only heart notes.

If God is not who you thought, can you wait? Can you wait for Him to meet you right where you live? Look for Him, because I believe that somehow, someway, He will show up.

I'm wondering about a lot of things, especially the part of your life that seeks so much of the world. I don't understand why you've rejected coming home for tavern life. I don't pretend to have the citified insights that you now have, but with all you've shared, it makes no sense. You don't have to settle for crumbs from some stranger's table, when all you'll ever need is right in our little valley.

Many of my waking moments, and even my sleeping ones are still filled with thoughts of you. Sometimes I think I remember the day you were born, but then I'm not sure. I've shared with you over and over how the memory of you is woven into me like fine, silk thread. I can't—no, I won't—give in to the way you're living. If that makes you even more angry at me...so be it.

You're not a child, Grace, you're about to be a mother. You can stomp your feet and throw a tantrum over life, but you're wasting your selfish energy, little sister. We've begged and pleaded with you to come back, but no more. You've made your bed, and now you can just...well, I'm sure you know the rest.

Eva Jo

PRAYER JOURNAL
EVA JO

Dated same day as last letter
O, Lord,

Perhaps I shouldn't have mailed that last letter to Grace. I was full of anger and frustration over every word she wrote. Maybe it's the heat, but I've run out of patience. What's happening is totally out of my control and I'm at the end of my rope with trying to figure it out. And Lord, You know it's not just my pain and frustration, but Mama and Papa's suffering goes deep. I see it plain as day whenever I look into their weathered faces.

I love my sister, but I've no tolerance left for her willfulness. Yet, even as I write, Lord, I'm convicted. Haven't we all like sheep strayed from Your hand of protection by our own disobedience?

I remember well the time Papa forbid me to take Old Blue out in the beginning of a snowstorm, warning me strongly when he saw it coming. So intent was I to spend time with Ida, I snuck to the barn, saddled up, and never looked back. If I'd once glanced over my shoulder, I would have seen the menacing sky bearing down like Satan himself. When I found myself blinded by the torrent, I remember how utter despair set in.

"I can't see, I can't see," I cried. I was frantic with only my pride and Blue to keep me warm. I know it was Your hand that guided Papa to where I huddled under a fir tree. He blanketed me with comforting hugs when I deserved a good tongue-lashing.

That's a picture of You, my Father. How patient You are. Please pour out Your mercies on my sister. Hide her once more in Your holiness and protection. Save her from herself, and may she realize it's never too late to come home... It isn't, is it, Lord?

Love,

Your daughter, Eva Jo

September 11, 1902
Dear Lord,

There was no dawn today. The sky filled with dark, belligerent smoke. Ephraim tied a wet kerchief around his nose and mouth in order to breathe, while tending stock. We were torn whether or not to stay home or go on to the schoolhouse. I guess we'll be going. With all the turmoil over school enrollment we need to be there. We've had fires before, but this one seems more ominous than others. All the animals are restless. Wild things of every kind are coming down from the hills. This is not good.

Protect us, Lord. Keep this valley safe. Help me not lose my temper with others, and protect each child at school today.

Love to you, Eva Jo

TELEGRAM
SEPTEMBER 12 1902
DEAR GRACIE STOP HUGE FIRE HERE STOP TRAGIC NEWS STOP MAMA LIVES WITH JESUS STOP LETTER TO FOLLOW STOP LOVE PAPA

Prayer Journal
Eva Jo

September
Jesus, sweet Jesus,

My heart breaks from sorrow and tears. Help me before I'm swept away in a river of grief. There's no escape. Save me, Lord, before I drown.

My mama's gone. Oh God, the dearest one of those who loved You has left us. I want to run and hide, but where? My mind cannot comprehend the depth of this loss. What will Papa do without her gentleness? Who will take care of Willie and Percy? Lord, who will I go to when I need help?

Death has roared in, robbing our peace, shaking the foundations of our faith. How unfair it's been. I want to yell and scream, yet I fear if I begin, I might never stop. The emptiness of destruction penetrates every fiber of my being while trying to survive this vale of death. I come to you, void of one more tear, so poured out am I from sorrow. Please Lord, restore me.

We're all exhausted to the point of collapse. Please give us rest. In Jesus name, I pray. Eva Jo

GRACE'S DIARY

Dear Diary,

I see the telegram before me on the table, yet my mind can barely comprehend its contents. I will never see my mama again. My mother, my mother, my mother.

PRAYER JOURNAL
NETTIE

After the fire
My Father, my Heavenly Father,

I want to crawl into Your arms to feel Your strength and comfort. I've never been in such pain. I can't breathe. Can't think. The trees left standing are ink black, the air smoky, and every inch of the sky is charcoal gray. I don't want to be here.

Everything is gone…Mama's house, Papa's barn, the garden. There are a few things down in the root cellar that made it through the flames. That, I don't understand. Why did things survive, but not my mama. Lord, why? How can we begin to write Gracie the details of Mama's death? It's too awful. What will happen to us now? What will happen to Gracie all alone down there?

Willie and Percy have finally cried themselves to sleep. They've both awakened several times tonight, asking for Mama. I heard Papa's deep voice comforting them.

At least we have shelter with Eva Jo and Ephraim. But I cannot go to sleep. Because if I do, I'll have to wake up to the truth. My mama's dead. Keep me strong, Lord, for all the others. Help us write Gracie. Oh, how I dread that.

Nettie

My Dearest Gracie,

By now you have the awful news. I'm so sorry, Gracie. Sorry you had to hear the way you did...impersonal and all. There was no other way, sweet sister, no other way.

I'm writing you since Eva Jo's hands are full, her place bursting with family and strangers. It's all a horror, like the devil himself planned it. We've lost everything. The only thing left was Mama's trunk, half buried in the cellar. The updraft from the blaze picked up Papa's new barn roof, carrying it close to three hundred feet, then it burned completely, right where it landed. There are different stories everywhere about how the fire started and just what was burned. Papa and Cal say we might not know the extent of it for a long time.

I've been replaying over and over the entire day. Despite the smoke, we'd made the decision to hold class. Before nine the sky darkened into night (even the chickens went to roost) and all of us at Good Hope were having trouble breathing. I can still hear the church bells ringing, the wind howling, and the cries of the children. Little Hayley Noelle had a coughing fit so hard she nearly fainted. The entire room was in chaos until Eva Jo and Ephraim took over, gathered us into a circle, and prayed. As they finished, we immediately felt better. Even through the darkness and falling ash, we could see the fire on top of Roan Mt., licking the sky like some wild animal devouring everything in its path.

When we opened the front door, forest creatures were running onto the porch in utter panic. I knew exactly how they felt.

Frantic parents came to get their children. In the turmoil it was hard to keep track of all of them. Fortunately Will and Percy clung to my skirt. I was so relieved to feel Mama's arms grab me from behind in a desperate hug. She urged me to come along with her and the boys, but I needed to check and make sure everyone was gone.

Good thing I did. Little Jonah Waysbee was crouched behind my desk, hidden from sight, hands over his head, shaking. I walked him outside, trying to be as reassuring as possible, praying he wouldn't sense my terror! When he saw Mama, he ran over, grabbed her hand, and refused to let go. He's in her Sunday school class.

She insisted Jonah come with her to look for his parents. I told her he was really my responsibility, but she said he wouldn't be comforted until he was with family. We put Jonah behind Mama on her horse, and Will and Percy jumped in the buckboard with Little Dove, Eva Jo, Ephraim, D.J and me. We headed to Eva Jo's to get the little ones, hoping beyond hope that God in His mercy would spare us. We thought Mama was right behind, since Jonah's family lived close by.

We could hardly see in front of us, but Old Blue knew exactly how to find home. Shortly after pulling into the yard, the oddest thing happened. The ferocious winds shifted, and in a heartbeat, the raging fire beast went racing in another direction. Grace, this could only have been a miracle. We cheered and hugged. In our celebration, we realized we didn't know about ALL of us. My heart stopped. Where were Cal and the girls?

Frantic, I searched the road. Nothing. Then out of the haze, I saw them... Cal, the girls, and Papa, in our hay wagon. A couple of our best milk cows were tied to the back, with a bawling calf tagging along as well. Shepard, directly behind, was leading a string of horses, prancing around in complete panic.

Our relief was not to last. Where was Mama? At first we weren't too concerned because the fire had spared the valley, so she must be safe. Papa sprang into action, ordering us to spread out in different areas to search.

He and I went back to the school, hoping maybe she'd changed directions. It was hard to see anything in the smoke, and even harder to breathe. I was feet away from the building, near that little creek that runs in back. I walked over to wet my kerchief.

Then Mama's horse bolted past me, riderless. Where was she?

Straining to see through the ash, I spotted her. She was lying on the other side of the water beside a tree. Her horse must have spooked and thrown her off. Maybe she was only knocked out. I ran, screaming.

"Mama!" She never moved, but I heard muffled whimpering. I lifted my skirts to cross, willing my eyes to be wrong. She looked asleep, but the odd angle of her neck said different.

The sound I'd heard was coming from Jonah, hiding in the bushes in utter terror. His entire body trembled from head to foot; his face was covered with ash and sweat. I barely recognized him.

"Papa, Papa!" I was hysterical. Oh Gracie, I wanted her to wake up and tell me it was just a bad dream. I touched her face, cradled her head in my lap, while trying to comfort Jonah. He ran back to the school and his desperate parents, who had finally found him. At least there was one happy reunion.

When Papa came, it was awful to watch him. He fell to his knees beside her, moaning more than crying. He placed an ear to her chest. I had to turn away. Papa stayed there for a long time before carrying her back across the creek. I must have been in shock, but I brought the wagon around back to the creek, my hands so covered with grime and sweat I could barely manage the reins. My entire body shook, even though the air was hotter than I ever remembered.

Papa laid our mama in the back with gentle care, just as Cal came around the corner of the school porch with Will and Percy. They right away jumped in beside her.

"Mama, wake up!" Percy was sobbing his little heart out. Will said nothing, just stroked her face and hair, but sorrowful streams marked his filthy face. It was at that exact moment I felt my heart shatter inside my chest.

When we got to Eva Jo's, Cal went to the door. Seconds later, she came charging out of the house, shouting Mama's name. She clung to her, speaking words of love into Mama's hair, trying to brush ash away from her face. I buried my head on Cal's chest, grateful for his embrace.

Oh Grace, I'd give anything to hear Mama say one more time how much she loves me, one more chance to look into her eyes. Such beauty can only be contained in memory now. Hang on to her locket, sweet sister, at least you'll have something.

Mama always said we should never live with "what ifs" and "if onlys." But I wish I'd been the one that went with Jonah. If only I'd taken him. Cal has been a rock for me; his assurance that I did what I could helps so much.

I loved her with all my being, and I can't imagine what we'll do without her. God help us all, God help you, sister. I'm worn out, but Eva Jo and I are getting ready to prepare Mama's body for burial. It's unreal, completely unreal.

I love you, Annette

Prayer Journal
Eva Jo

September...early morning.

Oh Father,

The endless smoke is dense, its lingering a mean reminder of death. As we labor for breath, we struggle to live without the ones who've died. Waiting for them to be counted seems cruel.

Thank You for my husband and children. Thank You for sparing our lives...our little space on earth, our home. It's miraculous. We knew it was your divine providence keeping the fire at bay while praying at the school. We had no time to escape, yet when those devil winds shifted, all fifty-plus buildings in town were spared. No one has been able to explain it, but those of us who name Your name recognize Your hand. Thank You for the seeds of hope You're planting, even in the rubble of destruction.

My Song of Need

Deep calls unto deep, O Lord, at the noise of Your waterfalls.
O Lord, hear my plea.
Deep calls unto deep, O Lord, at the noise of Your waterfalls.
O Lord, hear my plea. Answer me.

For You are my deliverer...the rock on which I stand.
And I know that nothing can remove me from Your hand.
　　—Eva Jo Ehlers

Lord, I'm before You in utter surrender. I want to say I trust You. I want to have continued faith to believe that what You do cannot be wrong, but my faith seems too small for something this big. Lord, help my unbelief. Not my will, but Yours be done.

Your little Eva Jo

P.S. Kiss my mama for me...how I long for one more caress.

September 1902
My Dearest Gracie,

In the tiredness of all that has happened this week, I must take the time to write you. Some might consider this letter morbid, but I'm compelled to send it. Today Nettie and I prepared Mama for burial. We'd had many offers of help, but it was a task we wished to do ourselves. We both knew you would have wanted to as well, thus this letter.

We made up the bed with the very best linens we had, topped with the quilt she'd made before my wedding. Cal, Ephraim, and Shepard lifted her body from our wagon, carrying her quietly up the stairs and into the bedroom. My hands shook like an aspen tree in the wind, while Nettie cried like a newborn.

We weren't able to continue until we fell to our knees in prayer beside my bed. We cried out for grace and mercy because without those things neither of us would have gotten through the laying out. Great peace presided when we finished, turning "duty" into blessing as we worked.

First we washed her hair with the lavender shampoo she'd given me right after Lulu was born. The sweetness of its fragrance filled our senses, pushing the smell of ash and death away while we worked up a rich lather. We bathed her entire body with it. Of course if was difficult, especially since Nettie and I had never seen our mother without clothing in our entire lives.

Somehow remembering the tenderness her body had shown us over the years made it all right. Both her hands were scratched up and death had stolen their warmth, yet they still felt like her when I stroked them gently. Her wedding band slipped off easily, and we set it aside for Papa. I believe it was the most intimate moment Nettie and I have shared as sisters.

I'm not sure who began, but we started humming Mama's favorite hymn while we dressed her.

"Amazing Grace, how sweet the sound
that saved a wretch like me.
I once was lost, but now I'm found.
Was blind but now I see."

How many times did we hear her sing that? It's one of my earliest memories. Funny thing, Nettie said the same thing, because whenever Mama put her babies down for a nap, that's what she sang. Can you remember? If we heard her singing that melody when coming in the house from play, we knew to be still, because Mama was rocking somebody. I wonder if she knew how often I'd sit quiet as a mouse so I could listen. I'm convinced I received the same comfort as the one being rocked.

We plaited her hair and put on her wedding dress, like Papa asked. Unlikely as it sounds, Mama looked young like in her wedding photo. There was not a trace of ordeal or fear, only peace and victory. Make no mistake, death still resembled death, but her beauty took our breath away—an unexpected gift. That is how I'll always remember my mama's face.

Since lacking fresh flowers to surround her body, we substituted many of her favorite things found in the leather trunk that survived the flames: Grandma's wedding quilt, some old photos she loved, her prayer journal, the locks of her children's hair, tucked in white envelopes with scalloped edges, even tiny dark fragments from little baby James. (We didn't have to guess which was yours, Gracie, for your copper hair hasn't faded a bit.) Mama had dried lavender pressed in the Bible from her wedding day. We carefully tucked them into her braid resting on the pillow, forming a delicate crown. Not like the one she has in Heaven, mind you, yet appropriate nonetheless.

Strange how I'm full up grateful for the memory, finding every touch a tender good-bye. All my unspoken words to our mother were contained in those final gestures.

After finishing, Nettie and I prayed again before calling Papa. When he stepped into the room we left, shutting the door behind us. But his weeping rose beyond what walls could contain, traveling throughout the house like some nightmare's echo. Another first, for well you know, Big Jim rarely cries. How very ironic that the last time he did was at their anniversary celebration.

After thirty minutes, the door opened. I know it's not possible, but in that moment, Papa appeared smaller and older. He gave us tender hugs before fetching Willie and Percy. Lavender and ash remained in the hallway. I'll never be able to smell that herb without the memory of my mother connected.

Papa returned carrying Percy in one arm, while his other hand rested on Willie's shoulder. Their little faces looked too old to be those of small boys, but I saw bravery in their eyes as well, reflecting Mama's lasting legacy. They hung back in the doorway...a small pause, then their little backs straightened after Papa bent and spoke something. I had to turn away from the sorrow of it. Nettie and I chose to stay outside, rather than view our little brothers' grief up close.

We were there when Ephraim brought our children for their turn to say good-bye. I wanted to spare them the hurt, but Ephraim convinced me they deserved the chance to see their grandmother one last time. The fact Lulu won't remember Mama pierces my heart, but the boys loved their "Nana" fiercely and I'm hoping her memory will never fade from them.

D.J and Jacob each kissed her cheeks, and Lulu waved good-bye when carried from the room. But when she got to the hall, she fussed until Ephraim put her down. Then those chubby little legs ran back inside and up to the side of the bed. Standing on her tippy toes, she blew her Nana one last kiss.

And then I nearly fainted. Lulu spoke!

"Ba ba, " she said.

Through scalding tears, Ephraim and I both looked at our remarkable child in awe. Lulu had said "bye-bye." My girl spoke those first words for her Nana. How incredible that Mama never got to hear it.

I ran down the stairs and crashed open the back door for some air. The sadness was near more than I could bear, and I prayed to make it through the pain. When I looked up, the road in front of our place was filled with people coming to mourn beside us. Many were on foot since losing all their livestock in the burn. These families had lost treasured possessions and, worse, loved ones. Still they were willing to take the time to share our burden.

The first to greet me was Mrs. Wilcoxson. She met Mama when they both arrived in the valley near the same time. They were instant sisters. She grabbed me in a bear hug, only able to sob on my shoulder. No words were spoken between us. None needed. I pressed one of Mama's hankies into her hand, knowing she'd treasure it forever. She used it to wipe away tears that wouldn't quit. Those tears carried the comfort she could not declare. Oh, how I understood those tears.

After all had bid Mama their respects, we shared a bountiful feast from poor larders, stretched to the limit by other wakes. Those whose homes still stand have opened up their parlors, living rooms, and bedrooms for others to lay out their loved ones if they wish. Some have no bodies to bury, so the church has become a memorial place of sorts, where pastor can give a measure of comfort and closure for those remaining. Many have no strength for a funeral.

Pastor said wonderful things about Mama, but I could see that grief was taking its toll on him, though I believe his faith is stronger than his mortal flesh. Said the Holy Spirit was keeping him full of the necessary energy until he's able to stop each day. Ephraim has offered to help him in whatever way needed, making me proud.

Since everyone's energies are stressed to the hilt, Papa made a decision to bury Mama right after the layin' out and visitation. After we wrapped her body in the bedclothes, the same men carried her back downstairs and into our buckboard for her final ride to the cemetery. It was the longest walk of my life.

The ash is thick and deep, like a January snowstorm. Everyone had handkerchiefs tied over noses and mouths, or we couldn't have made it. Old Blue struggled himself, but loyal as always, he was a trooper. Our boys walked side by side with Will and Percy, While Ephraim carried Lulu, and Little Dove held my hand. Our dire procession was completely silent except for the coughing.

Some precious saint had already dug Mama's grave, right next to little James, a task that must have taken monumental persistence. I wondered to myself if it had been Papa, but Ephraim said he'd seen Shepard McFarlane with a shovel. Pastor struggled to say something, but was plumb worn out. It seemed we all were spent with emotion.

Finally Papa came forward and stood looking down on her wrapped body. (There were no coffins left anywhere in the county.) He pulled the cloth from his face and cleared his throat.

"My Louise was a good woman...a good friend. She loved her children...all of them. She even loved me, a stubborn, strong-willed Scotsman."

I saw Nettie lean into Cal until he pulled her close.

Papa continued, "But I know that she'd most want to be remembered as a Christian woman. One who trusted God in good times and bad. A woman who found joy in the simplest gifts of life...her children's shenanigans, and their God-given-talents." He swallowed hard, his face contorted with misery. "She gave the best of her for the best of us. When grandchildren came, Louise said she was given three extra gifts from Heaven. Everything they did made her laugh. She was ours for a season, but now God has her for eternity."

He bowed his head, and put his hat back on, raining gray ash around his face.

I could hear Aunt Etta crying, and the voice of someone comforting her.

Pastor walked over and gave Papa a great big hug and shook his hand. Then it was Pastor's turn to weep...he couldn't stop.

Mrs. Wilcoxson started to sing "Amazing Grace." For the second time that day, Nettie and I joined in. It was the last verse that meant the most to me, and I didn't cry once.

"When we've been there ten thousand years
Bright shining as the sun
We've no less days to sing God's praise
Than when we first begun."

A thousand years are as a day to God...we will have all eternity with Mama...all eternity.

After we said good-bye to the faithful, some came back to our place to wait for news of loved ones, and to live the best they can in temporary shelters that have gone up. A hundred families have lost their homes, so we struggle to put up as many as possible.

I know all of this will be hard for you to accept, little sister, but it's hard on us all. I'm exhausted with the telling. I love you.

Eva Jo

September
Dear Gracie,

I've scarcely have time to sit down, but writing helps me process things. I've no idea how long our letters will take to connect with one another, since the fire has disrupted everything.

Our place continues to be a holding station of sorts with friends and strangers alike on the property. We've set up several stoves out of doors, so families can cook for themselves and divide the work some.

Stories continue to drift into town, each one sadder than the previous. When Sarah Johnson went back into her burning house to get her prized Singer sewing machine, the whole place exploded into flames. LaVern was already in the wagon. He looked back just as his home collapsed. The horses bolted off and he survived. But later when the ground had cooled, he went back to the very spot where his wife had died, and killed himself. They'd been married for forty-two years.

Do you remember the Foleys? The mister had a thick Irish accent, and orange hair with freckles all over. All five of his children bore the same heritage. Despite the smoke, on the 11th, he took the entire family, including his mother visiting from Ireland, towards St. Helen's, for a picnic. There was evidence that they'd tried to out-run the blaze, but every one of them ended up nothing more than cinders. Two things survived: a wagon wheel melted into a peculiar sculpture, and a nugget of metal from a horse halter.

Help has poured in quickly from all over Oregon, California, and Seattle—every bit of it needed and appreciated. Of course all the crops not destroyed by the burn are buried in ash, though a few things in our garden survived.

Canned goods by the wagonloads have trailed into the valley, so it looks like we'll have enough food for winter. A committee has been appointed by the mayor to set up fair distribution, but many who survived have left to distance themselves from any more danger. Some, like Papa, are determined to rebuild regardless. With Ephraim, Cal, and Shepherd helping, he'll succeed.

The hotel is full with survivors, but without income, half are being allowed to live there free of charge.

A couple of rascals from up north came in selling supplies attached with inflated prices, but they were run out of town, like the dogs they were.

Some Indians have gone great distances to healthy waters, bringing back fish to can and smoke. I feel good about how far this valley has come in a few short weeks.

I'm so, so, sorry, Grace. I'm sorry you didn't get to say good-bye to Mama. I'm sorry this only adds to the many burdens you already carry.

But know this: she loved you. She loved you no less for your leaving. Please believe me. I know it to be true. Her love for you never wavered. Never.

Yours in sorrow,
Eva Jo

P.S. Mama would want you to have this note. I found it in her Bible.

The sunrise is a serenade of sight instead of sound. Color weaves its melody in and around the clouds and sky, coaxing the rising sun from its rest. With a crescendo, the promised light appears and I, an audience of one, applaud appropriately. My Lord invites me to partake of the new day—His gift—His promise of fellowship and leadership for the tasks ahead. His love is wrapped in and around each finger of light. Somehow, my Lord, the Creator of the Universe and every sunrise since, invites me to partake. Delighting in the benefit of His light gift, I am grateful.
Louise Rose McLeod, May 30, 1896

Prayer Journal
Eva Jo

September

Dear Lord,

This earth is not Heaven. My mama is home. I know she'd not want to return, yet my heart breaks for Willie, Percy...for the many who've been blessed by her. Papa is strong, and we are leaning on him heavily, but her sons seem smaller now. I'm asking for courage and wisdom to comfort them.

Thank You for Ephraim, who always knows the right things to say to me. He's a man after Your own heart Lord, his pure faith pours out into our family daily.

Everywhere I turn I see my mama. I hear her voice as I write. "Eva Jo, life is hard, but God is good. Don't try to figure it all out, Missy, you'll not succeed." Every day of my life, she's been a reflection of You. No daughter could ask for more. I don't believe I could bear the pain if that were not so.

Father, I ask for Your continued mercies on this valley; many families have lost more than ours.

Wasn't it only recently that this journal contained wondrous praise at the miracle of Your deliverance of Nathaniel Bottemiller? And now, O Lord, I scarce can write the words, so heavy are they...all dead. Can those from the grave praise You? You know how faithful they were to give You the glory for Nathaniel's recovery. Sometimes this little heart cannot understand the peculiar ways of Your plans. It's all sad. So sad.

We wonder why the Bottemillers hid in the root cellar, when they would have been safe in the river. Maybe they ran out of time. Ephraim says we'll never know, but there are times when the thinking of it keeps my mind restless with pain.

Ephraim needs Your help, Lord, to erase the picture of what he saw when he found them. All huddled together...a family complete, even in death. Nathaniel would have been with Nettie in the classroom, but he was still being home-taught. At first Ephraim thought they could be helped with fresh air, but that was not to be. No one in Yacolt had any idea how to contact family, and we never heard from a soul.

Ephraim wrapped each one in blankets sent from Vancouver for burial purposes.

Though most families have laid their kinfolk in the town cemetery, we believe the Boettemillers would have wanted to be buried by Miracle Creek, so that's what we did, far enough away to be out of the flood plain. Ephraim spoke little, but I'll never read Psalm 121 again, and not think of the Bottemillers.

> *"I will lift up mine eyes unto the hills,*
> *from whence shall come my help?*
> *My help comes from the Lord, which made heaven and earth.*
> *He will not suffer thy foot to be moved:*
> *He that keepeth thee will not slumber.*
> *Behold, He that keepeth Israel shall neither slumber nor sleep.*
> *The sun shall not smite thee by day, nor the moon by night.*
> *The Lord shall preserve thee from all evil.*
> *He shall preserve thy soul.*
> *The Lord shall preserve thy going out and thy coming in*
> *from this time forth, and even for evermore."*

Ephraim continued. "Lord, Your word says You preserve Your children from evil. The fire looks mighty bad, but we choose to stand and believe that this young family did not just happen to die. It was their time, and we take comfort in knowing their souls live on with You, even for evermore. Amen."

Cal, Nettie and Papa came to help with the burial. It wasn't easy. Every step in the acrid ash caused it to fly everywhere, clinging to body and clothing. None of us escaped the filth. Yet standing there in the nightmare of calamity, we had the gift of peace.

Nettie began to sing:

> *"Fearest sometimes that thy Father hath forgot?*
> *When clouds around thee gather—doubt Him not!"*

Her voice carried crystal clear, cutting through smoke, ash, and sorrow. I joined in.

"Always hath the daylight broken—
Always hath He comfort spoken—
Better hath He been for years, than thy fears."

Up till then the entire countryside's sounds had been muffled by dense ash, creating eerie silence, except for the small trickle of Miracle Creek. But when the singing finished, we heard birds. First one, but soon a chorus of many...from one side of the creek, then the other... calling back and forth. Did our hymn bid their return? I truly believe You brought them back, Lord. Or, maybe you just cleared our heads enough to listen. Regardless, it was a gift.

Please bless Marvin Bauer for his dedication in making their grave markers, for the effort was birthed with a multitude of his tears.

Thank You for Your constant direction, because I'm unable to make one more decision. Sometimes I think I'm in the middle of a horrible nightmare, only I've yet to wake up.

EJ

Dear Gracie,

Remember Miss Jacquelyn and Miss Ovie, from church? They came by today, bringing a huge basket, overflowing with love gifts from their kitchen. That's not all they brought. Each of them had remembrances of Mama they wanted to share, so we laughed and cried together all afternoon. Maybe I shouldn't have taken the time, but it was just the tonic I needed.

I especially loved the story of Mama's accidentally putting salt in an apple pie instead of sugar. Miss Ovie said Mama's face turned the color of beets when she realized what had happened. Because guess who took the first piece?

It was Pastor Bill...at the church picnic. After trying several times to swallow, he gave up his valiant effort, abruptly jumping up from the table. Well, in his hurried escape he tripped and fell....right into Aunt Etta's lap. This sent her into a tizzy, causing her to tumble over backward with both legs extended in the air in a very unladylike manner, her face completely covered with yards and yards of fabric from her skirt and petticoats. Pastor, by then, was now lying soundly on top of her entire body. Eventually the whole congregation caught onto the ruckus, erupting into laughter. Since this was Mama and Papa's first social gathering after joining the church, Miss Jacquelyn said Mama couldn't look Pastor in the eye for months. Miss Ovie added that Aunt Etta never spoke of the incident, her dignity having been so compromised and all.

"Weep with those who weep," the Bible says, and I thought I understood what that meant. Now I see the truth of this in a new light. As people came by and cried with us, their tears poured into our grief and God's love was extended. Each tear contained His compassions. Weeping is a wordless ministry that goes to the heart of how we're called to love one another.

Miss Ovie and Miss Jacquelyn are amazing in their love journey. You'd never know they were both in their 80s...even drove themselves over here in their ancient buckboard, pulled by a cow. Called him Hercules, I think. When they left, some of their love lingered like a sweet morning's fragrance, easing the burden of my day.

My, it's late.
All my love to you,
Eva Jo

GRACE'S DIARY

September
Dear Diary,

I want to scream, to run and not stop. My mama's dead! She's gone, and I never told her I was sorry. Sorry for leaving and breaking her heart. I have no hope. I'm not able to sleep as memories of our final conversation assail me in the night.

It was Christmas Eve, and Mama had whispered out of earshot of the boys to meet in her room. I got there first, and looked around,

156

mentally saying good-bye, since I knew I'd be sneaking out later. Sounding a little breathless, Mama entered.

"Oh Gracie, good, you're here. You look a little flushed." She walked over to put her cheek next to my forehead. "I certainly hope you're not coming down with something on Christmas Eve."

"I'm fine, Mama." My heart trembled with the knowledge of what I was planning. I'd never been so deceitful. "I'm just excited about Christmas."

"And that's why I asked you here. I've something special for you and wanted to give it to you with a little privacy. You know the boys. If they saw you get a present early, they'd want one too."

Now the guilt was laying heavy on me. Mama walked over to the highboy, opened the top drawer, and lifted out a small package.

"I was going to wait for your wedding day to pass this on, but I changed my mind. Here." She reached out and handed me the gift, just brushing my hand with hers. How warm and tender those hands had always been towards me. My eyes filled, even before I opened her special surprise. She didn't know my tears were for the deed I'd planned for later. Oh, if I'd just listened to my conscience then, I would have never given in to the sinful lust of my willfulness.

Mama was beaming while she watched me open my present...my inheritance as it turned out. Her locket! My hand trembled so much, she had to fasten it.

"Grace, you look lovely. Somehow, I've always known it was for you. My own mother gave it to me, and there's quite a story surrounding it. But, goodness, there's no time for telling it tonight." We embraced, lingering in a special mother/daughter moment I'd give anything for now. Before leaving the room, she turned, one hand on the door. "I love you, Gracie...all the stars."

"All the stars?" We always said that to one another.

"All the stars, Gracie, never forget. Promise?" She put a finger to her lips, a silent request for my being quiet over her early surprise.

"Promise!" She shut the door, and that's the last time I ever saw her. *Mama. I'm sorry.* I want to see her again. I know the only way to do that is to believe in the God she called Father. I'm sure she's alive in Heaven with Him right now. But I don't know if I can believe God loves me anymore. How could He, after all I've done? Mama would say he could, but I feel as though a weight is pulling me down to the bottom of the sea. How can I live knowing I was Mama's biggest disappointment?

This poem seems to be calling me.

When lovely woman stoops to folly
And finds too late that men betray,—
What charm can soothe her melancholy,
What art can wash her guilt away?
The only art her guilt to cover,
To hide her shame from every eye,
To give repentance to her lover
And wring his bosom, is—to die.
  —O. Goldsmith

September
Dear Gracie,

Goodness continues to rise from the ashes of our sorrow. We've had a most special visitor, one of Mama's favorite. Hulda Klager came from over near the Columbia, loaded down with gifts. She and Mama used to spend long hours together, building up our orchard. Do you remember her? When we were kids, I thought her to be the most focused person I'd ever met.

Mama was a devoted follower of Mrs. Klager's garden advice, but I'd forgotten that our favorite apples come from Hulda's cross breeding. She took the mild "Wolf River" and combined it with a sour, juicy "Wild Bismarck." It's why Mama's pies were always everyone's favorites at church picnics, weddings, or baby dedications. As I recall, it was yours too.

Every time Mama prepared those fragrant beauties she'd tell me the story of Hulda's determination to grow a bigger apple. To her, time was precious, and small apples absolutely took too long to peel. Hulda's talent for growing things, and her generosity for sharing, is the reason our little orchard became a stand-out in the valley. Mama loved her.

Seems Hulda's green thumb extended beyond growing apples. Her wagon was filled with an incredible variety of healthy plant starts. They came with tears of condolences for our loss, and hers. All the plants were those she knew Mama would love. Of course they look a might puny right now, but Hulda brought pictures of promise. Each photograph held magic images of lush lilac trees...I could almost smell them. And of course there's the apple starts...dozens...all labeled.

When Ephraim began to unload the wagon, Hulda shooed him away, and told us she was actually headed out to the old homestead. We convinced her that with all the leftover tree snags, it wasn't safe to continue, so we unloaded everything, and promised we'd get the planting done ourselves.

The more I see what others have lost, the more I appreciate all that Ephraim and I have. Before Hulda left, she shared some secrets for making new plants. Now I'm excited that I might share some of our bounty with those in the hills who've lost their food trees. It's a way to come together for something other than grief.

More to you later,
Love, Eva Jo

September 25, 1902
Dear Gracie,

We've not heard a word from you, sister. Please don't despair. We're praying for a way to get you home. Even though these days have been bleak, we live with hope. I know it's been a spell since I've written, but you can imagine the chaos surrounding us. Despite the turmoil, every day brings more of God's grace, poured in our direction.

When the fire mowed down homes of nearly a hundred people living outside town, it destroyed the animals' dwellings as well. There are varmints out and about that we've never seen, except at night. At first they made me nervous, but if you can believe it, we're actually getting used to some. Others have gotten too close for comfort.

We had to shoot a couple of aggressive half-grown bear cubs last week. They most likely belonged to that big mama sow I wrote you about, though we've not spotted her anywhere near. They were spooked beyond sense with hunger and distress, losing all fear of man. That done, their fate was sealed.

They came right into our barn looking for food, one of them climbing up my Trixie's stall. That sweet little cow was dancing around for all she was worth, out of her mind with the horror of her forthcoming demise. Her bellowing got Ephraim there in the nick of time. Clearly he had no choice, though he made an effort. First he reasoned he might scare them off, but both stood their ground. Even if he'd been able to chase them away, some other farm would have fallen victim later. He took the first one down with one shot, same with the other. Though they had fat left, Papa said they wouldn't have made it through winter in their stripped-down territory. Might even been eaten by a bigger bear, he said.

Winnowett skinned them, while we watched in amazement at how skillful she was with a knife. She had both animals strung up and butchered in three shakes of a lamb's tail. We saved most of the meat to smoke, but had a delicious pot of stew for several meals. With the extra mouths we feed, it was one more example of the Lord's provision out of what could have been a disaster.

Several days later

Mama told me once about a small, long-tailed bird she'd read about from Africa. A widowbird. Have you ever heard this before? She said folks named it after the black garments women wear when their husbands die. Mama said that even though she understood perfectly why black was worn for the dead, she believed that for a Christian, such a forlorn color gives a dismal impression.

"Leaving this earth for Heaven is sad for the ones left behind. Yet, how not true for the believer who's departed," she'd said. "They're part of the Maker's glorious celebration." She thought we should wear a joyous color, like yellow or green...the colors of new life in spring. I remember laughing when she told me this because she wore a smile from ear to ear, like she was seeing into a corner of Heaven.

"Mama," Papa scolded, "what would people say?"

"I'm not sure," she piped up, "but can't you see Aunt Etta's face burning bright with the improperness of it?"

Remembering that conversation is what prompted me to do what I did the first regular Sunday church service after the burn.

Ephraim said nothing when he saw what I'd put on myself. He didn't have to—the look on his face said it all. His wife, who had been walkin' on a slippery edge, had gone over...all the way to madness. Perhaps he was right, but being Louise's daughter, I'd be expected to remember what she'd shared with such passion about everything, but especially in my mind, about the widowbird. No doubt.

I would have worn my wedding dress...if it still fit. Instead, I chose my green taffeta with the hat to match. It was the one I made for Ida May's wedding. Mama said it always brought out the color of my eyes. I don't know about that, but it sure brought out plenty of clucking tongues.

Ephraim spoke not a word the entire walk to service. We were the last family to be seated and, wouldn't you know, the only pew left was the one right in front. So there we were marching down the aisle like some kind of Ehlers' family parade, and of course Little Dove. I slowly unbuttoned my winter coat, dusted off the clinging ash and placed it behind me. You could hear every woman in the place take a big, deep breath all at the same time. Like a choir right before it begins. Ephraim deliberately avoided making eye contact with a soul. It all made me set my jaw tighter while settling the children between us. Tears I couldn't hold back rolled down my cheeks at will. It didn't matter. I was being true to my mama.

When Pastor Bill ended the service with a final hymn, he came right over to where we were sitting and greeted Ephraim and the children. He took my hands, drawing me to my feet. In a booming voice he says to me, "Eva Jo, you look lovely. I remember how much your mama loved you in that dress...said it brought out the color of your eyes. I declare, you favor her more every day." Next he squeezed me tight.

You could have heard a pin drop, the place got that quiet. Then in a rush, all the ladies came up to greet me. They finally understood. Ida May thinks I might have started something. I doubt it, but time will tell.

Trying to move forward, I'm forever Eva Jo, stubborn daughter of Louise McLeod

Ten

Dear Sisters,

I've struggled with writing for weeks, at a loss for words to express my heart. I feel unworthy to declare my love for our mama, because I walked away from her so willingly. I know I've let you down, and Papa...every one. Most of all, I'm sorry that I wasn't there, because I know I might have done something to save her. I would have done anything, you must believe me. I should be there right now, sharing the burden of this deep sorrow. The weight on my soul is unbearable because I know she loved me to the end. I was selfish, and now I'm being punished for my dark sins. I did love her with all my heart and soul. I cannot forgive myself. I pawned Mama's locket. I traded my inheritance for money. I'm so ashamed.

I value every detail of your letters, even though the tragic news is unbearable. Poor little brothers! Their suffering is heartrending, but they have you dear ones and a strong, strong, Papa to guide them. Family will be everything for them.

Mrs. White is generous with her comfort, a true reflection of loyal friendship, though I'm hardly worth it. It's difficult to think about the future, especially without my mama. Regardless, this baby will be here soon, so Mrs. White is putting together a layette, including a colorful quilt. I've helped with the piecing, but my skills pale in comparison to the expertise she bestows on every stitch. I should be giving more time to the preparation, but I'm not always here. The days seem to slip away after long nights with friends. They've been the distraction needed to cope with losing Mama, even if nothing dulls the steady pain for long. I yearn for peace, but it's allusive, like the scarlet tanager I wrote you about. Sometimes, in the quietness of early dawn, I imagine his haunting song...his freedom song.

This letter is short, but I promise to write again soon. If Papa will receive it, give him my love, and kiss Will and Percy. Please don't worry about me; save your energies for your own grief. Stay close to each other, dear sisters, and know that I love you all with a deep resolve to see you again.

Your sorrowful sister, G-

Prayer Journal
Eva Jo

October

Dear Lord,

I can't find me! I don't feel like me, look like me, or talk like me. I'm different, completely changed by grief. If hope is a patient waiting, help me to wait. Scripture says, *They that wait upon the Lord shall renew their strength. They shall mount up with wings as eagles. They shall run and not be weary, they shall walk and not faint.*

My heart hurts. Day after day I'm pushed by a force that seems bigger than life. The pain is intense. At times, I'm convinced I'll not bear up under the weight. How do I explain this to others? Is the pressure boulder-sized? No, more mountain-sized, like St. Helens.

I have no words, either, for what it felt like to see my mother lying in the back of a dirty, ash-filled wagon. May I only remember the vibrant person she was. Better yet, help me to see what she's like in Your Heavenly home, Lord. I'm grateful Nettie and I had the chance to dress her out, for that memory lingers well in my mind and heart. There was a deep connection with my mother, I didn't even know existed. Regardless of how close we were, now that our earthly tie is broken, I feel adrift, my dreams full of huge, crashing ocean waves.

You're my anchor, Lord. I'd be like a sailor lost at sea if this were not true. Keep me close to You always.

EJ, Your willing captive

Prayer Journal
Eva Jo

October 12th
Dear Lord,

Help me to bear bravely and with honor. May I not fail You. I'm so grateful I don't have to apologize for my tears. I will get better. I will BE better, though I'm not able to pull myself together. At first I was thinking that a weakness, but I'm just admitting I can do nothing without Your help. I realize, more than ever, I've no control over circumstance. I so want to be better, not bitter.

Help me to trust you more,

To give myself over as before.

I want to dance again!

I want to sing again!

I want to trust and be fearless…again!

Thank you that I'm known as Louise McLeod's daughter. Most of all, I thank you that I will be known eternally as YOUR daughter.

Lovingly, Eva Jo

October
Dear Gracie,

I love you so much. We need you here…not just for your sake, but for ours. It feels as though the world is falling apart, first the fire and then Mama. I still cannot believe she's gone. Sometimes I wonder if God is mad at us.

Yesterday, I took time for a walk to Miracle Creek. There's no privacy at the house, and my patience had worn thin, emotions ready to boil over. I needed some quiet. Beside the creek, tears forced me to my knees. Drained of prayer, I let my emotions go.

When I was nearly exhausted, I felt a gentle touch on my back. Shepard had walked up behind me.

Turns out, he's a great listener. I guess sometimes it's good to talk with someone other than family. Of course, I have Cal, but he's been so busy since the fire. It seemed like I talked a long time, before Shepard asked about you, Gracie. Please don't be upset, but I told him everything...even about your baby. His jaw went rigid and those brown eyes flashed like lightning before excusing himself. It was baffling, to say the least.

A little later I came back to the house and saw he was having an animated discussion with Papa. When they finished, Papa stepped closer, put his arm around Shep's shoulder. It looked like they were praying. I had to get back to helping Eva Jo in the kitchen. I never did find out what went on. Try not to be angry with me because I talked with Shepard. He's a real friend.

Ephraim and Eva Jo have been wonderful at making Will, Percy, and I feel at home, but we miss Papa. Many nights he spends at the old place, mostly because he's just too tired to leave. Sometimes it feels as though we've lost Mama and Papa.

At night when I tuck the boys into bed, I like to snuggle next to them until they fall to sleep. It helps with the lonely feeling in my heart, and they don't complain about it at all. I'm glad they take comfort from me being there. We miss Mama's kisses, and the way her hair would tickle, when she leaned down to tuck us in. One night after prayers the three of us had a touching conversation about some things we missed about Mama.

"Guess what I miss?" asked Will, his voice soft with sadness.

"What?" I whispered, pulling him closer.

"Her smell." He put his head on my shoulder and cried like a newborn.

"Me too," wailed Percy. Overwhelmed with their sorrow and mine, I started bawling. I guess Eva Jo heard the ruckus, because she walked in on a pitiful heap in the middle of the bed. She spoke sweet words to us and prayed a simple prayer. She left, promising to return. In a few minutes she was back cradling a bottle. Mama's favorite shampoo! We'd had some leftover from her laying out. Will, Percy and I took turns sniffing deep from the memory bottle.

"I know how to make this," Eva Jo said. "Mama gave me the recipe and I have some dried lavender on the porch. It will be awhile, though, because of all the extra work right now. But I'll let you use what's left in this bottle until then. Will that work?"

The three of us said yes at the same time, and reached up to give hugs. One minute we were a pile of grief, the next we were laughing for joy...all over a promise of sweet-smelling shampoo. It felt good to laugh. The boys transformed into a couple of jumping monkeys.

She kissed us all and this time we clung to her neck an extra long time. Suddenly the door flew open and DJ and Lucas joined our family circus. Those four boys nearly broke the bed before Eva Jo and I got them settled. They begged to sleep together, and of course we gave in because it's hard to resist a room full of charming little men.

Lately, I've been wondering if your child will be a girl or a boy. We haven't told any of the children about you having a baby yet, but you know how much Will and Percy love being uncles. And if you could see the gentle way DJ and Lucas treat Lulu, you'd realize how they'd be with a new baby cousin. I love being an auntie, Grace. I'll always love your baby exactly the way I love you.

Oh Gracie, how I wish you would come home. It's all been heart-wrenching, but Eva Jo and I have each other and family. You are alone, and that just isn't right. Take care of yourself and listen to Mrs. White. She seems to really care about your well-being.

Write soon, Annette

P.S. Cal and I are going ahead with our wedding. Last Tuesday morning I got up before the house was awake to have a few minutes with the Lord. The sun came splashing over the hills with yellows and pinks lighting the entire horizon. Cal joined me on the swing to enjoy the display with me. That's when he told me he'd asked Papa about going through with our wedding plans. See, Cal thought it might not be appropriate to celebrate a marriage right now, but Papa said we should go ahead. It's what Mama would have wanted. I'd just assumed we'd postpone everything. But maybe it's exactly what everyone needs...something to focus on besides our broken hearts.

Isn't my future husband wonderful?? I gave him a big old hug just for being him. Honestly, I don't know what I'd do without him. He's been a great friend to me and a big help to Papa. Sometimes, when Will and Percy are being cantankerous, he will gently step in and take over while I do chores. Winnowett is here now too. All the children love her quiet ways. She's strong, yet something deep within keeps her a long way off. It truly isn't rudeness. I think she just doesn't know how to reach out. Maybe it's all the sadness she's had to bear. I more appreciate her losses, since Mama died. Winnowett is quite beautiful—Little Dove favors her.

October
Dear Gracie,

I pray things in your life are tolerable, little sister. I'm feeling completely helpless because I can't be with you. I'm asking God to help you trust Mrs. White for sharing confidences. With Mama's death and you being pregnant, it can't be healthy to keep it all bottled inside.

Nettie is full of bravery. Has she told you? She's made the decision to go on with her wedding as planned. For sure, I do not have that kind of courage. She's grown up to be a young woman with many traits I could use myself. Having her here is a blessing. When she puts her arms around me, her grief matches my own, and somehow the burden of it is lifted a little.

Mama was working on Nettie's wedding dress, but of course it's in ashes, so I'm piecing up another. It gives me a chance to stitch some of Mama into it, even though she's gone. Seems every pull of the thread brings to mind something more of her, like drawing water from a well.

Aunt Etta's been here often to help, but she chose to stay at the hotel. I have to say that I'm actually enjoying her presence. The kinder, gentler version of her is remarkable. Since we've been working side by side, barriers have come down, and Aunt Etta has revealed things our Mama never shared. I never knew she was in love once—her true love, she said. Though I'm pressed for time, you'll want to know this.

When Grandma and Aunt Etta were girls, they worked for a wealthy family in Portland, who owned a huge house overlooking the Columbia River. Aunt Etta said it was surrounded by roses, and had so many wonderful things growing, they had a full-time gardener. Grandma's job was in the kitchen doing most of the cooking for the family of six children, five of whom were still at home, much younger than the oldest son, who was away at college.

The mother became ill and unable to cope with family needs, so Aunt Etta was hired to help with the children. It was spring when she began, and she never met the oldest, Robert, until several months later when he arrived home for summer. Immediately, she thought him the most handsome man she'd ever met.

She was flattered when he asked to be called "Robbie." Since Etta was living at the home, they saw each other every day. She ate with the children, and frequently their big brother joined them, making those meal times delightful.

They all adored him. He had a way of speaking to each one as if they were the most important person in the world. Aunt Etta said at first, when he spoke to her, she was flustered and said little. But another of Robbie's gifts was building up a person's confidence, and soon Etta was chattering away like one of the children. He'd often compliment her appearance, noticing the littlest things. This set her heart aflutter in unfamiliar response.

One evening while strolling in the garden after the children were tucked into bed, she came upon Robbie praying in the moonlight. She stood silent, mesmerized, not wanting to interrupt. When he realized her presence, he extended an invitation to stay and talk. Her heart pounded. Could he hear it? But the entire conversation centered on Etta's life. No one had ever asked so many personal questions before. She was not only flattered, but grateful for the attention and time. They lingered in that spot for hours, until the moon moved far across the night sky. When she became cold, he removed his jacket and wrapped it around her shoulders. Feeling those warm hands against her chilled skin caused a completely new sensation. Breathing was difficult.

When they stood to go, he expressed sincere gratitude for the evening. Though barely sixteen, from that moment on, she was hopelessly in love with this gentle, kind, young man. In her heart she knew that God had brought Robbie to be her one true love. No doubt they would spend the rest of their lives together, maybe even in this very house. Their children would play in the charming nursery, run through the exact gardens where Robbie had romped as a child. Surrounded by love and family, Etta Jane and Robbie would grow old with grace. Only days later did she learn the reality of a young girl's dreams.

Robbie was leaving. But not back to school. Something bigger was taking him away, having been called by God to serve on the mission fields. Dear Robbie was going to leave for a place so far away it would take him a month or more to get there. Not that he'd shared the information with her directly, because that was not the case.

Etta had been coming down to the kitchen to fetch something for the children, and passed by the main dining room. Robbie was taking breakfast with his father. His mother was there too, having recovered enough to do so.

"When will you leave, son?" the mother asked.

"In a few days."

"So soon!" The mister got up from his chair to embrace his oldest child.

"It may seem that way to you, but I've been ready for at least a year. It's just taken this long to arrange it all with the mission society."

Etta's breath left as reality set in. Robbie was leaving! Surely he would take her. There certainly wouldn't be much time for her to prepare to leave all that was familiar to her.

"I imagine communication from China is agonizingly slow, Rob, especially for a mother's inquiries."

He was going to China! Etta's mind exploded, thoughts colliding like ocean waves. She left her listening post and headed for the kitchen to talk with Grandma.

When she shared her heart and the conversation overheard in the dining room, Grandma took her aside. "Etta, what are you talking about? Are you daft? If you think Mr. Robert is going to take a sixteen-year-old girl to China with him, you've got a mighty colorful imagination."

"We're in love."

"What?"

"He loves me."

"He's said this to you, Etta Jane?" Grandma had her by the shoulders.

"Well, no, he has not said this, but...I know he does, Mary."

"You can read minds now, little sister? Really, Etta!"

Grandma's lack of belief stung, but Etta wasn't worried. She only had to wait for darling Robbie's declaration of undying love. Then she'd pronounce all the many thoughts she had for him—their life together, their future. Even if she had to go to the ends of the earth with him, so be it. All that really mattered was that their lives would be intertwined. Two separate vines growing as one, like the glowing yellow roses climbing over the garden arches she loved.

Poor Aunt Etta, she only got part of the rose vision. Thorns.

That evening, Robbie knocked on the nursery door. When Etta saw who it was, she could scarcely speak. The children grabbed him at once, nearly knocking the poor man over. He hugged them all, then bid each to leave him alone with Etta, who now trembled with anticipation. Dreams were about to come true.

He took her hand in his—cleared his throat. "Etta, I have some news."

"Yes, Robbie?"

"I'm leaving."

Eyes fixed on his perfect face, Etta hoped he'd see the love and devotion contained within a faithful heart.

"I'm leaving," he repeated, "for the China mission fields. God has been calling me since I entered college. Now the time is right." He laughed lightly.

She blushed.

"Etta, you've become a dear friend, and well, I've come to ask you something."

Her heart stopped.

"I'd like you to...

"Yes?" She interrupted with a gasp.

"Well...friend, would you write while I'm gone? I mean, pray for me foremost, of course. But truly, I value our friendship and would appreciate a letter from you often."

Her ears began to ring, and Etta thought she'd faint with the reality of his words. *Friend!* He thought of her as a friend. Suddenly she was filled with shame and something more. Anger. So much for trusting God. What a cruel and spiteful thing to allow. She nearly choked before speech returned.

"I'm very busy here," she stammered. "I...I...have the children." She walked to the window so he couldn't see the humiliation of her heart splintering like fine glass. Was it audible? Her forehead rested against a cool pane, while she followed a raindrop's path with an index finger.

"Oh, I know, dear Etta, you're a treasure. Your presence in this house has eased the burden of my entire family. But now that mother is nearly back to perfect health, you're free to move on. A vibrant young girl like you must have many dreams. Am I right?"

Looking down into the garden. Etta spoke but two words. "I'll write."

"Oh, thank you. I shall look forward to every word. Thank you, friend." He walked over, turned her around, and took both hands. He put them to his lips as a parting gesture, just as the children came bounding back.

Without a word, she ran out the door and down the hall to take the rear stairs into the garden. How could she have been so dim? Her sister had been right; she was young, out of her mind with foolishness. Never would such stupidity befall her again. What has never made you happy can never make you cry.

Etta never saw Robbie again. Two days later, he left by train for San Francisco. She kept the promise to write, but he never wrote back. He died. He'd contracted malaria aboard the ship to China and passed away one month later. His parents were at peace, they said, because their firstborn was doing what he was called to do.

It made no sense to Etta. She'd been totally wrong about Robbie, which meant for sure she'd been wrong about God. When Robbie died, so did her innocence. But her heart was not left empty. Instead it filled with anger and bitterness.

She spent years taking care of her ailing parents after Grandma married. But when the folks died, loneliness nearly consumed her. By then Mama was five or six, with two younger brothers. Aunt Etta moved in with Grandma and Granddad, to help with the children. For some reason, Mama became her favorite. Etta was a protective mother hen, often causing conflict in Granddad's territory. Seems the older Aunt Etta got, the sharper her tongue became.

I'm telling you, the fire burned more than timber and grass. It's had a purifying effect on all of us, but especially our great-aunt.

When Nettie and I were laying out Mama, Aunt Etta told me she'd come up to the bedroom to help, but couldn't bear coming in. Instead she listened from the hall. Hearing our singing, she was overcome with emotion. In that moment, something lifted from her spirit. While Nettie and I raised our voices in song and submission, years of anguish began to leave Aunt Etta. Standing in that place of unspeakable grief, for the first time in fifty years, Etta released her will to God. When *Not my will but Yours,* escaped from her mind, healing followed.

Now, I don't want to use the word *miracle* lightly, but I'm thinking that's exactly what happened. God brought beauty from ashes, exactly like he promised.

I've gone on way too long. Please receive this, Gracie...what God has done for Aunt Etta, He'll do for you.

Your big sister, Eva Jo

P.S. Papa would not have been able to start rebuilding so soon, if it had not been for Cal and Shepard McFarlane. Shep is on the quiet side, but he's proven himself to be reliable to this family in ways we couldn't do without. Papa told me Shepard has suffered deeply, but it's not made him bitter. I'm sure that's because of the Lord. He also told me that Shep had been saving money for his own spread, but it was all in cash, stored underneath the bunkhouse floor. Of course, it's all gone. Shep said he'd just start over...money was only money...and it all belonged to God anyway. Please don't be angry that Nettie shared with him about your situation. Later—Eva Jo

Prayer Journal
Nettie

October/Wedding Night
O, Lord,

I am blessed! Tonight I laid nestled in Cal's arms, my head on his chest, desiring to soak in all I could of the moment. I pray it will remain in my forever memory...his sweet smell, the feel of his heartbeat, and the warmth of his body next to mine. Who am I, Lord, that You would bless me so? He is beautiful. How perfect is Your plan for a husband and wife. We are one. Jesus, I am humbled to be part of such loveliness. Thank You for the best day of my life.

Mrs. Calvin R. Stewart

The next eve.

Dear Lord,

Bless Eva Jo and Ephraim for giving up their room for Cal and I. Eva Jo's bedding smells of lavender and strong sunshine.

How well I remember Mama telling me that there are only two things in life that matter in the end...my relationship with Jesus, and the people He gives me to love. I understand what she meant more clearly now. I'd love to have one more minute with my mama, to share this happiness with her. I miss her laugh, her singing, her...everything.

Sitting here, watching my husband sleep, the moon moves across the autumn sky. I realize how small I am. Yet I know, Lord, Your eye is on even the tiniest bird. Grace is just like a bird that wanders from its nest. Lord Jesus, I pray for your covering, Your robe of righteousness to be upon her unborn child. Protect both from all evil, and please bring them back to us...safe and sound.

In Jesus' name,

Nettie

October

Dear Gracie,

I'm sure you're wanting to know everything of our little sister's wedding. Nettie wants to be the one to tell the details, but just let me say...it was perfect. Well, almost. Of course, if Mama had been there, it would have been complete. She would have been proud as punch of her little girl.

I've never been to a wedding with so many people. Since the fire, there seems to be a deep need in folks to celebrate anything that's good. I think Nettie knew this all along when she chose to go through with her plans. Anyway the church was full, with guests standing at the back and all around the sides.

I promised I wouldn't tell anything about the ceremony, so I'll get right to the reception. The only way I know exactly what happened is because I was behind a curtain in the church basement, nursing Lulu. I would have felt like some kind of sneaky creature, if I'd jumped up in the middle of things. Besides Lulu had fallen asleep in my arms, so I remained. What an earful.

Aunt Etta was sitting on a chair, balancing wedding cake and a cup of tea, when a strong man's voice interrupted.

"Excuse me, ma'am. Would you be Etta Jane Baker?"

I heard her swallow, and clear her throat. "And who might you be?"

"Oh, beg your pardon, I thought you might remember me."

"You thought wrong, mister. Who'd you say you were?"

"Brewster, uh, Voyle Brewster."

I heard feet shuffle.

"Vee Brewster!" Well, land sakes. Why didn't you say so?"

"Well...I just di..."

"Where have you been all these years? My goodness, how long has it been?"

"Well, you might recall, I left for California right after the folks died. Made a good life for myself there, too."

Aunt Etta's voice sounded kind of queer. I wondered from my hiding—uh nursing—place, what this Mr. Brewster looked like. But I never made a move.

"Then, tell me, Vee." Her voice went all buttery. "Why did you come back?"

"The fire, Etta Jane. The fire's what brought me back. Too much tragedy. Just seemed like I might could help a bit. You know, do some good, what's I was thinking."

"Funny, I've not seen you in town at all."

"No ma'am, haven't made it there much. Been towards Fargher Lake, helpin' my nephew rebuild his place."

More feet shuffling.

"Don't call me ma'am, Vee. For Pete's sake, sit down. My neck's got a crick from looking up at you."

"Thank you, Etta Jane. Mighty nice of you."

Now I heard chairs scooting, and they made more small talk, before getting into a history lesson of sorts. Seems Mr. Brewster had been sweet on Aunt Etta when they were kids. She'd had nothing to do with him, but he was mighty persistent for a season or two. When he went to California, he'd met and married a woman whose father was a Mexican land baron. They had a whole passel of kids, but

174

they'd taken off to build their own lives. Voyle sold off the land he'd inherited from his father-in-law, making him a rich man. Said he wants to use some of it for good before he dies. They spent a half hour catching up with each other before LuLu woke and gave away our listening spot.

Polite as I could, I made my getaway, though I kept an eye on them from a distance. Aunt Etta turned into quite the flirty Gertie, if you know what I mean. She was fanning herself with a napkin, obviously enjoying the company of a fine gentleman.

Mr. Brewster is medium tall, with hair the color of winter's moon. Makes for a striking contrast to his very tanned face. He's handsome... in fine shape too. I know this, because when the fiddles started, he danced nearly every dance...with Aunt Etta. What a surprise! Who knew she had that much energy. Maybe when she received her soul healing, her body got a whole new power as well.

The two of them got nearly as much attention as the bride and groom. Not that those newlyweds minded. They were oblivious to anything or anyone, except each other, as it should be.

Ephraim and I had to leave when the children began nodding off, but I heard from Ida May, that the dancing lasted long after the bride and groom left, and Aunt Etta and her Mr. Brewster were the ones who locked the church doors. Can you believe it?

Since then, every evening after supper he comes courting. More goodness from God, since Mr. Brewster is a devout Bible believer. He's a quiet man, but I count that as strength. It's probably a good thing he's more on the downside, conversation wise, since Aunt Etta's such a talker and all. Yes, her talking is still the same monumental, one-sided conversation as usual. But the one huge difference is that she pauses...a lot.... Then she throws back her head and laughs, especially when she's talking with Mr. Brewster. Once she laughed so loud, I truly believe LuLu heard her. He stares at her like she's a fine piece of china to be cherished and admired. Love is wonderful. More beauty out of the ashes.

Voyle's soon to leave for California and settle up some business before coming back here...for good. He still has family land at the east end of the valley and wants to raise workhorses for the loggers. Wouldn't it be wonderful if he asks Aunt Etta to marry him? I cannot wait to see what will be.

Mama would love what's happening. Oh, I miss her. Every day

something unfolds, and I make a note in my mind to share it. Then I remember...she's gone!

Again, I could just squeeze that Nettie for having her wedding this way. I can tell the difference in people at church as well. The day marked something of renewal on the inside of everyone.

I already feel like Cal is our brother. His girls are the sweetest things. They really perk up around my brood. Fit right in. All of them had some adjusting to do, of course. But children have a magical way to go about that...especially Lulu.

At first, Cal's girls were holding back around Louisa Ann, not knowing what to expect from a child who can't hear. But Lulu can win over anyone God puts in her path, that one. She's the most charming human I believe I've ever met. Those girls are wrapped around her little finger like Christmas ribbon.

Now, I really do have to go. Love to you always, EJ

October
Dear Gracie,

I'm a married woman! I'm sure there's never been a wedding more beautiful than mine...thanks to Eva Jo and Aunt Etta. My dress looked like it came right out of some fine catalogue, with delicate lace around the neck and a flowing train made from Eva Jo's wedding dress. Aunt Etta spent hours sewing hundreds of tiny little beads along my veil; and right before leaving the house, Eva Jo curled my hair and even put color on my lips. Oh my goodness, Gracie, when I looked into the mirror, I couldn't believe my eyes. There, looking back, was a princess, just like we pretended when we were little.

Cal got dressed at church, making sure we wouldn't see each other before the ceremony. I don't know about him, but I was shaking in my boots, nervous, right up to the moment I took Papa's arm to walk down the aisle. With the first step, sweet peace swept over me. Some of it was due to Papa's reassuring words.

"Annette Louise, you look just like your mama. If she were here, she'd be proud as the day you were born."

"How do you know, Papa?" I said, trying not to cry and ruin my princess face.

"Because I am." He gave my arm a pat, and we were on our way. Every step brought me closer to the day I'd imagined for so long. (Except for you not being there, of course.) All my attention was now given over to Cal.

He looked more handsome than ever, his eyes fastened on mine with that silly crooked grin of his. When it came time for Papa to give my hand to my soon-to-be-husband, they both were misty eyed. Of course, that got everyone sniffling.

When Cal and I exchanged vows, I was looking into his eyes the entire time, even when he put the wedding band on my hand. The instant I looked, I nearly fainted. It was Mama's! Seems Papa had saved it for me. What a blessing! I heard Sissy and Cassie giggling at my surprise, their laughter, music in the background. Pastor Bill called them forward. How beautiful they both looked, despite the obvious missing teeth. They're each a gift to me, unique and precious, directly from God.

"Girls," Pastor Bill said, sounding very solemn, "this is your special day too. Not only has Nettie promised to be your papa's wife, she's promised to be your new mama as well."

"Oh, we know that," Cassie offered, serious as can be.

"We want her bad." Sissy's hand went over her mouth, trying to keep from laughing out loud. But it didn't work, and the entire church jumped into her joy.

Pastor had us form a circle, joining hands while he prayed. Cal caught my eye and winked. Oh Gracie, I can't begin to give words to my heart's happiness, and at that moment I realized something profound. Despite the fire, Mama's death, and all the other bad things gone on in our valley, God's faithfulness had won out.

The entire party afterward is kind of a busy blur, but I laughed so much, my cheeks hurt for days.

Aunt Etta gave up her room at the hotel so Cal and I could be alone. We only stayed one night, though, because we couldn't spare time away from work.

By December we should have Papa's new barn set up for winter living, if the weather holds good. It will be a little rustic, but we will be okay. There's a wood stove for heat and cooking, and heavy canvas will be hung to divide up living spaces. It's going to be a long time before we'll have our own place, yet Cal says our barn space will make us snug as bugs in a rug. Eva Jo and Ephraim have been more than generous, but it's time to give them back their home. Hopefully all the others will have moved on too.

School will start again in a week, though our enrollment is down with many families having left Yacolt. People seem to have forgotten a good deal of the prejudice that was swirling about earlier before the burn. Good thing, but time will tell for sure.

I'm under obligation to stay on teaching, even if some frown on a married woman working. Will, Percy, and the girls, will be with me daily, making me think it will work out. I'll still have time to clean up the school room, and get all of us home in time to fix supper.

Well, dear heart, there's lots to do. It's washday, and Eva Jo needs all the help she can get. Papa has hired some men from town to work on the barn, since Shepard is gone. He might be on a buying trip to Portland, but I'm not sure. Papa's never said.

All my love,

Mrs. Calvin R. Stewart

P.S. I know Eva Jo told you all about the wedding reception...and Aunt Etta's new beau. Maybe there will be another wedding soon. Oh my!

Eleven

PRAYER JOURNAL
EVA JO

D ear Lord,
Beautiful fresh morning. The breeze blows clean, thanks to autumn rains. I can actually smell something besides the ash. Thank You Lord, that You're the dawn, the Light of the world, and Light of my life. *As a deer panteth for the water, so my soul longeth after Thee.* And, *If you slay me, yet will I praise Thee.* You, and You only, give meaning to life…and to death.

Thank You for my children, Lord. I see my mama in their sweet faces. I wouldn't have them if not for her, which is comforting and sorrowful at the same time. I'm beginning to think all of life is like that. Both the bitter and the sweet make up the days.

Love, Eva Jo

November/California
Dear Mr. McLeod, Miss Nettie, and Miss Eva Jo,
As you know, Miss Gracie's been staying with me for a spell. I've afraid there's some harsh news from here. She's in the hospital…in safe hands. For sure the good Lord is looking out for her.

Last Friday evening she didn't come home from visiting her so-called friends. Of course, right away I got worried and went to lookin' in her usual haunts. Most of them in those places were too far gone from John Barley Corn to make any sense, but one gent said he'd seen her leave hours before. I looked and looked but had no success. I finally gave up. Goin' back home, I prayed all the way, because it's always been my belief that when I can't do something, God can.

Imagine my surprise to find a complete stranger a-sittin' on my doorstep. "Well, I declare," I said, "you might be the answer to my prayers!" (Something about his serious face told me he was there for Miss Grace.) He stood and introduced himself as Shepard McFarlane, and well you know him up there in Washington. I told him about how Gracie had not come home, and how it'd been hours since anyone had seen her last. By this time it was pitch dark with a blanket of fog laying in damp and clammy.

Mr. McFarlane is a man of action and was gone in a flash. When he returned in the middle of the night, he had Gracie with him, and ho! what an hysterical state she was in! We took her to the hospital right off, and that's where she's stayed, now these three days. Mr. McFarlane's not left her bedside the entire time. They talk until the nurses hush him out so Grace can sleep. When I was there yesterday, he had her outside in the garden in a wheelchair, just lookin' and yakkin'. She's been a sad, sad, bit of a girl. Despite everything, her little one is still alive and kickin'.

He told me he found her on the pier over the ocean. There she was, still as a statue, staring into space. A crowd had gathered, but she wasn't speaking a word to any of 'um. Not until Shepard came along. She recognized him, you see. He was the only one who was not a stranger. They were all shoutin' at her about not jumping. No doubt, the fall would've been sure to kill her and the baby. I don't know what he said to talk her off that bridge, but all's well that ends well, and I believe our dear Lord had much to do with this ending.

That's a good man, that Shepard, and he's done her a world of good already. Try not to worry; she's promised to write you herself. I think you'll be able to tell our little Grace has changed, I'm sure of it.

Yours truly, Flossie White

Prayer Journal
Grace

November

Dear Heavenly Father,

I'm a little shaky today, but they say they're going to let me go home soon. I told them I have no home. But the nurse said they would let me go with Mrs. White and Shepard McFarlane.

It has been so very, very long since I've addressed You. This is a feeble beginning, but I thank You for sparing my life, wretched though it's been.

Slowly, I'm remembering what happened, like watching a hazy dream. I couldn't find You anywhere in all that swirling mist. I climbed on the railing of the bridge over the Los Angeles River. It was quite a drop! I felt dizzy every time I looked down. I thought about Mama, mostly, and how I'd disappointed her. First I pawned the locket, and then I lost her forever. Standing there, I wondered what her last thoughts were.

I was not scared at all in that place. I knew I had to end my life. I could not have a baby by myself, far from home, knowing I'd never see Mama again. And knowing my papa would never accept me back home, after doing so many bad things, was certain. How could he? Of course there was Jake! Jake never loved me. He just used me, leaving me like dirty garbage. Who was I? Where did I belong? Where were You, God?

Then I saw a man's face through the fog. It was a familiar one, from home. He spoke my name, "Grace McLeod," clear as day. The haze lifted a moment.

"Shepard McFarlane?" I whispered.

He came closer, sliding over the railing himself, one hand extended towards me. I refused the offer. I looked down...to jump. I could no longer bear the label of *cheap tramp*. It was time to be finished with the voices in my head.

Without hesitation, he said. "Grace, come away. Don't do this. Your papa loves you and wants you to come home."

"Not true," I said. "Mama's dead. Papa will never forgive me for all that's happened."

"He already has."

"But he doesn't know about…"

"He does, Grace. He knows about your baby. He loves you…."

"No, it's impossible…"

"Grace, he sent me. Let me help you." He stepped closer, eyes pleading with my reason. His arm gripped me around the shoulder. I clutched the railing with one hand, and let go with the other.

"I have to do this, Shepard. It's too late!"

The swirling vapors swallowed him and he vanished into the darkness that enveloped everything. My hair whipped around my face in the wind, and I could feel cold rain pelting my entire body. I took my other hand from the railing and fell.

But Shepard's strong arms caught me, because the next thing I knew I was in a crisp white bed with light streaming in through a window. I turned my groggy head and saw him in a chair next to me. He said nothing, but took my hand and gave it a hearty squeeze. I wanted to say something, but I was too ashamed. Just then the nurse brought soup. Weak though I was, it tasted so good after not eating for two days. The fog was gone.

Shepard told me everything would be fine, and I believed him. He said he would not leave my side, and he hasn't. I told him I was sorry, and thank you, and that I owed him more than I could ever repay. He said I owed him nothing, but to get well.

I am mystified that of all the men in Yacolt, Shepard McFarlane would come down here to fetch me back. Does he really care for me? How could he when I'm pregnant with another man's child? Maybe he only came because he's Papa's hired man.

Regardless, I believe You guided him, Father. How else could he have found me? At least I have more confidence to live. No, *confidence* is the wrong word. For the first time since I left home, I have hope. Please don't let my baby suffer because of my foolishness.

G-

The next day

Dear sisters,

I know that Mrs. White has written you and you've been informed of my foolishness. I'm sorry to be so much worry to you all. Please forgive me. Shepard has been a good friend. He would not want me to call him heroic, but literally, he saved my life. Positive things are happening now, for the first time since I left home, though some of it is strange. Strange indeed.

I'm still in the hospital, growing stronger daily, my dears, but here I'll stay for a few more days. The doctors inform me that my baby's heartbeat is strong, and I can testify to the strength of its kicking.

Yesterday afternoon I was napping. At first I thought I was only dreaming, still half asleep, when I sensed someone standing over me. Shepard? I opened my eyes slowly, expecting his stocky figure, but it was a woman. A nurse perhaps? No, she wasn't wearing white. Who then...?

"Miss McLeod, you don't know me, but I know of you."

"I've seen you before," I said. "Who are you?"

"Someone who wants to help you." She was dark, striking, and spoke with a slight Spanish accent.

"But why?" I was confused.

"I care about what happens to you...and your child."

"But how can that be?"

"You're carrying my grandchild."

"What?" I tried to sit up, but my head spun with the effort. "You're Jake's mother?"

"Yes." She extended her hand. "I'm Sylvania Ortega Hudson." I was stunned. "Please call me Sylvia."

Her eyes—they were Jake's, large and deep mahogany in color. She was the woman I'd seen twice before on the street.

"But I thought you were...were..."

"Dead?"

"Yes, I assumed so."

"I'm not dead, Grace. May I call you Grace?"

"Gracie."

"Gracie, Emory Hudson wanted me out of his life forever. But most of all, he wanted me out of Jacob's life."

"Why did you leave him behind? I mean, how could you

abandon your child?"

"I believed I had no choice." Her eyes closed until a shudder passed. After composing herself on a chair near the bed, she asked, "Do you want to hear the truth?"

"I'm not going anywhere, Mrs. Hudson...Sylvia."

She cleared her throat and began her story. "I met Emory here in Los Angeles, when I was sixteen. My family was very poor and had sent me from Mexico with two of my older sisters. We were to work for my Uncle Carlos, who was married to our father's sister.

"They ran a cantina near the docks where the three of us toiled long hours for no pay. We had food to eat and a place to sleep, but our uncle was wicked. In the beginning, we had no idea the high price we'd pay for his evil "charity." She paused. "He began making physical advances towards my oldest sister, threatening her life if she told my aunt. His brutality went on for months, until finally Elaina, my sister, walked into the ocean, and drowned herself. She was not even twenty years old."

I shivered when she told me that. I could tell it had been a long time since she'd shared this story. Taking her hand seemed to bring comfort, and she continued.

"Maria and I were frightened out of our minds. Exhausted from work, we had little energy for grieving Elaina. We lived in a deep, dark pit, with no hope for escape. With our sister gone, Uncle Carlos came after Maria, who was one year older than myself. He beat her and ravished her body, often locking her in the cellar below the cantina. Our sleeping room was above the kitchen and I'd sneak her food if I could. But if he caught me, he'd whip me with a leather strap."

"It was in the middle of one of those beatings that Emory Hudson stepped in. He was a regular customer, meeting there with clients or friends. Emory was at least six inches taller than my uncle, and strong as an ox. With me cowering on the floor, Carlos' hand raised to strike, Emory grabbed him from behind. There was no struggle. My uncle was forced to give in to the younger, stronger man."

"'Only cowards beat women and children,' Emory spoke with authority, in Spanish. My uncle was furious, but not stupid. He knew he'd met his match.

"Emory gave me a hand up from the floor and helped me get

Maria out of the cellar. We were beyond grateful, thanking him over and over for his intervention. For days afterward, Uncle Carlos kept his distance, although he still barked out orders like we were slaves. Whenever Emory came into the place, Carlos avoided him, and for a short time Maria and I were spared. But things did not stay good for us.

"Carlos made us get up before dawn every morning, but one day Maria left me behind when I complained about the early hour. 'You stay a while longer, *mi hermana pequena*. I'll tell Carlos you are not well.' She kissed me on the forehead and left. It was the last time I would ever see her face.

Sylvania was crying now. "I'm so sorry, Gracie. Even after all these years, the pain goes deep. Forgive me."

"Please," I begged. "What happened to your sister?"

"After a few hours, I felt guilty about not getting up. Maria would have all her work and mine as well. I dressed and went to join her. She wasn't anywhere in the cantina. I asked all the helpers. They were silent, as was my aunt. All day Uncle Carlos seemed jubilant, but he drank himself into a stupor and passed out in the back of the kitchen by nightfall. I knew he'd gotten rid of my sister, and I knew something else. He'd get me next.

"Before going to bed that night, I slipped a kitchen knife from a drawer and hid it under my pillow. I couldn't let myself fall asleep, because I knew the devil would rise from his lair and come for me. I was right.

"I heard his steps creaking up the stairs, closer and closer. I wanted to run, but there was nowhere for me to go, so I waited. He opened the door, his heavy breathing getting nearer to where I feigned sleep. I was his prey. My hand clutched the knife exactly the moment he reached for me. He must have known what I had planned, because he grabbed my wrist and jerked it from under the pillow. He spat on me, and swore under his breath. I jumped up from the bed and ran for door. The knife got there first. He'd thrown it at my back, but it missed and stuck in the doorframe instead. He laughed before lunging at me again. Still drunk, he was not sure on his feet, which gave me chance for escape.

"Taking the steps two at a time to the kitchen, I ran before stumbling over something large in front of the cellar door. Landing flat on my face left me stunned for a second or two. When my eyes adjusted to the darkness, I could make out the form before me. A large stained rug was rolled and tied with rope. My hands flew to my mouth to keep from screaming in horror. It was red with blood."

Sylvia could not go on. Her hands covered her face. "It is still so difficult, Gracie. I've told one other person this entire story. Emory Hudson is the only soul who knows the truth about what happened to Maria, and Uncle Carlos."

A nurse interrupted Sylvia's story to inquire about my state of health. After assurances of my well-being, the nurse left and Sylvia went on.

"I knew, beyond anything real, that my beautiful sister was wrapped in the filthy carpet, and that Uncle Carlos had killed her. I scrambled to my feet like a wild animal, but in my panic fell back to the floor, panting for breath. Carlos was now on the last step, about to strike again. I scooted to a spot under a counter, and waited.

"'Come out, come out, wherever you are, my darling niece. Come to Uncle Carlos.'

"He was close enough for me to smell the stench of sweat and tequila. I held my breath. I could not let out a cry, could not scream, yet my mind went wild with fear, and I bolted for the back door. He had me before I could turn the knob, pulling me backwards, knocking me against something solid...the butcher block. Carlos was laughing like the demon he was, completely given over to the lust that drove him.

"'Now, now, my little Sylvie, you could do much better than your sisters, eh? Let me make you the woman you were meant to be.'

"Gracie, at that moment, I was staring death in the face. Out loud I prayed, 'Lord Jesus, help me.'

"'Not even Jesus Cristo can help you now, Sylvie dear.'

"He spoke in a raspy whisper, making his move. I was quicker and reached for another knife. He lunged and knocked it from my hand. It landed with a clang on the other side of the kitchen. But he still had one, waving it in front of me. Moonlight from the window glinted off the blade, shocking me into another try for freedom. This time, Carlos grabbed my arm and threw me against the door. I kicked at him with all the strength I had. One foot landed in the middle of his body and he spun around, hit the butcher block, and fell to the floor with a grunt. I waited in absolute terror for his next move. It was then I saw a red stain oozing from beneath his wretched form. Gracie, he was dead. He'd fallen on his own weapon and accidentally killed himself.

"Hysterical beyond reason and scarcely able to think, I knew my aunt would be no help. She'd stand by her husband against me for sure. I had only one friend in all of Los Angeles."

"Emory Hudson." I interrupted.

"Yes. I ran all the way to his home in the dark, barefoot and nearly naked. When I got to his estate, I was too frightened to ring the door, so I hid in the garden house until morning, praying he'd believe my story.

"Exhausted, I slept until a groundskeeper poked me awake with his shovel handle. I spoke little English, but my dire state was obvious, so he took me to Emory. Immediately, the master ordered a maid to draw bath water and find me some clothing.

"Later, I managed to get out the entire story of what happened, and what Carlos had done to Maria. Emory believed every word, and told me not to worry, that he'd take care of everything. He was kind and gentle...then.

"He went into town and didn't come back until late afternoon. Talk there was Uncle Carlos had been murdered by his youngest niece, since she was now missing. The police were looking all around the docks for the 'killer.' When I asked him about my Maria, Emory said no one mentioned another body. Only my aunt could have manipulated the truth to maintain Carlos' innocence. She was willing to send me to the gallows in order to preserve her dignity as the grieving widow.

"'Never mind, Emory said. He had money and power, and he'd protect me because he knew the truth and could make it work out. And he did...but there were strings attached. Strings he could manipulate at will."

"Sylvia, I know about those strings," I said. She got up and walked to the window and rested her forehead against a pane.

"There's more, and I do want to share it all, Gracie. But in your sensitive state, it could be burdensome."

"Please," I begged, "tell me the rest. I'm stronger than I look." She came back to the seat by the bed, folded delicate hands in her lap, and went on.

"None of Emory's servants would dare speak of the runaway he was protecting, so I felt safe while he made plans for me. Elaborate plans beyond my comprehension, as it turned out. He booked passage on a ship bound for Europe and took me with him, disguised as one of the many staff that served him aboard the ocean liner.

"When we arrived in Europe, we traveled from place to place in a style that I'd never dreamed. But I was exceedingly homesick for my native land. No one except Emory spoke Spanish, so he became everything to me—teacher, parent, and friend. However, he had grander schemes.

"When we arrived in Spain, things looked up for me. There I could talk with others and enjoy my own culture. Emory left me in a convent for six months while he returned here for business.

"I had much healing during that time, thanks to the dear sisters who cared for me daily. Although austere, love abided there, and I thrived. Nearly eighteen when Emory returned, I realized I loved him deeply. When I inquired about my uncle's death, he assured me everything was taken care of and I was not to worry.

"We returned to California, where he told people we'd met in Spain. A quiet wedding ceremony followed our brief engagement. I was happy to be Mrs. Emory Hudson, but my husband was away on business a great deal and loneliness was a constant companion. When I became pregnant with Jacob, I was the most blessed woman in the world. My pregnancy went well, his delivery too, but only hours afterwards I was over come with an infection that nearly took my life. Emory was solicitous and full of compassion, while I hovered between this world and the next. I believed it was his strength and my intense maternal love that pulled me through.

"Jacob was beautiful, full of laughter, and every day being his mother brought my deepest joy. He grew so quickly that I soon longed for another child to join our family. Emory agreed, because I was not the only one enamored with Jacob. This smaller version of himself became Emory's obsession; the ' moon and the stars,' he called him. When he was in the house, Jacob received all of his affections. I wasn't jealous because I understood the magnitude of that kind of love.

"Jacob was around two when I discovered that Emory's time away was not spent on business only. By now, my English was perfect, and I overheard the servants gossiping about Mr. Hudson's escapades...in great detail. I was heartsick because I truly loved him. I waited to confront him with what I'd heard.

"He denied nothing, saying if I didn't like the truth, I shouldn't eavesdrop on things that were none of my business. Furthermore, he said I could always go back to Mexico if life in California as Mrs. Hudson was too burdensome. My heart was broken, but there was always Jacob to attend to. His total well-being became my entire focus, for Emory had no desire to change. And so our lives continued.

"Because I was still Emory's wife, I denied him nothing. Truthfully, I believed another child might bring us together as before. Jacob was well beyond three when doctors assured me that I'd never conceive another child because of the intense infection I'd suffered after his birth. I was devastated. Emory was furious.

"His ranting went on for days, and well beyond reason. He blamed me and punished me in cruel ways. He would take Jacob away from home, staying for days, and sometimes weeks, at a time. I'd be frantic, of course, but he'd only laugh at my 'emotional outbursts.'

"The more time Jacob spent with Emory, the more he seemed to evolve into his father. Once, after a particular long absence, I caught him being cruel to one of the house cats. He had him trapped in a bucket of water, forcing the poor creature's head under. I admonished him, as a mother would, but he promptly retorted that I should mind my own business, and leave him to his play. Frantic with fear over the loss of my child's innocence, I approached Emory. Something had to be done. To my surprise he agreed..

"' You're right, Sylvania,' he said. 'Something must be done, and I have a plan.'

"I was relieved and touched his arm in tender response. He grabbed my hand, crushing it in his grip."

"'However, my plan, dear wife, concerns you...not Jacob.'

"'Emory,' I protested, 'what concerns our son will always concern me.' By now, I was shaking.

"'No, my dear, what concerns my son from now on will solely be my responsibility.'

"'Where will you take him?' I wondered out loud.

"'I'm not taking Jacob anywhere, Sylvania. You'll be the one leaving.'

"'Never!' I was ready to charge him. There was no way I'd leave.

Never.

"'Very well then, I'll give you a choice. You may take Jacob, and leave.'

"My ears heard the words, but my mind knew there was more.

"Emory continued: 'Take him, Sylvania.' He gestured to the outside. 'Take him away from here, and I'll not give you a penny.' He walked closer, and stood over me for the purpose of intimidation. 'And don't forget, my sweet wife, there's the little matter of your Uncle's death.'

"My knees buckled. 'Emory, you told me you had taken care of it all.'

"'Indeed,' he replied, 'and believe me when I tell you, Sylvania, that I'm willing to take care of it...until it's finished. Do you understand what I'm saying?' He didn't wait for my reply.

"'The police would be most interested in bringing to justice the person who killed Carlos Mendoza, prominent business proprietor. Such a tragic death...should be vindicated. Wouldn't you agree, dear?'

"'Emory,' I pleaded, 'you know the truth. Carlos fell on his own knife, after...after killing Maria.' I was in anguish. Somehow, Emory was going to win. He would see to it that I'd be hung for the crime of murder, and then my son would have to live forever with the scandal of his mother's legacy. Emory knew I'd never allow Jacob to suffer in that manner.

"But Sylvia," I interrupted, "surely there must have been someone to help?"

"Gracie, you know the man Jacob became. He only mirrors his father. Emory had me completely at his mercy, offering what he knew I couldn't refuse in order to survive. Money. I couldn't go back to Mexico, the authorities would find me there. I was void of any help from locals because of Emory's powerful influences. I was trapped, held captive by evil once again. If my son was going to survive at all, it would have to be without me. Only later did I realize the horrible mistake I made. God is always on the side of goodness, and then, Jacob was still good. If I'd taken him away, somehow we could have survived, but I didn't believe that then.

"Emory stole Jacob away again, the next day. When they returned, I was gone. I agonized for years at what my sweet little boy was told by his father, wondering what went through his young mind when he ran through the house calling, and couldn't find his Mamasita. Did he cry for me at night when I wasn't there to sing our lullaby?

"I took the money Emory gave me and went to San Francisco. A man like Emory Hudson makes many enemies. It took some time, but over the years I made a friend from nearly every one of them. Well, allies, if not friends. From them, I acquired information. Information that, today, has made me a wealthy woman. Have you heard of Rosa Garcia?"

"The famous socialite?"

She leaned back in her chair and sighed deeply.

"You are Rosa Garcia. I can't believe it! How have you been able to avoid Mr. Hudson?"

"Emory is not the only one who found power in money, Grace. I have many ways to remain hidden behind the persona of Rosa Garcia."

"I'm so sorry for your suffering, Sylvia."

"No Gracie, it's you who deserves my sympathies. I must take partial responsibility for Jacob's wretchedness. That's why I've come...to make amends...to..."

"No," I interrupted, "I left home of my own free will. I knew it was wrong to run off, but I did it anyway. Everything that happened to me has been my fault."

Sylvia stood and took both my hands in her own, then sat on the edge of the bed. "Gracie, you're young; everyone makes mistakes. But you did not deserve Jacob's wickedness. Now, no one can go back and undo what's been done. It is possible to move forward, but sometimes we need assistance. I am here to help you...and your child. It's too late for me to rescue Jacob, but I can offer aid to you, if you'll let me."

I was still groggy from my ordeal, and I wasn't sure what she meant. "I'm very touched by your offer."

"I have a lot of money, Gracie. It affords me the ability to support many worthwhile charities, and institutions. I've been able to help my family in Mexico as well. But you are carrying the future...for both of us."

"Mr. Hudson doesn't believe this baby belongs to Jacob."

"I do," she said. And I could tell by the look in her eyes, she did. By this time, I was falling asleep. She excused herself, saying she'd pray for me. Sylvia bent to kiss my forehead before leaving. *"El adios mi pajaro pequeno."*

"Good-bye," I whispered. "Good-bye, and thank you."

It was dark when I woke again. For a minute I thought perhaps I'd dreamt the entire afternoon, but then I saw a large white envelope addressed to me, on the bed table. My name was hand-written, but the inside papers were typed. And there was more. Cash. A large amount of it. My head muddled with the find.

When Shepard returned, I told him the entire story. He was as stunned as I, especially when we discovered what else the envelope contained.

My Dearest Gracie,

Meeting you has given me hope, and a peace I've not had since the day I left Jacob so many years before. I sense within you a depth of character that you do not realize. I believe that you will be a strong, loving mother to your child, though unspeakable things were done to you. The God of Heaven can heal anything. He alone knows the river of tears you've shed because of my son. Comfort in this, Gracie…He's saved every one, because they are precious to Him, as are you. And of course, you are not alone on this earth, with family and friends who love you. If you're wondering how I know these things; money makes information accessible, lovely girl.

Please take what I'm offering, and use it for you and your little one. There are no strings attached to any of it. There's enough to protect you from Emory Hudson, and if by chance you ever need, or want, to get in touch with me, I've left a way to be contacted.

My daily prayers will always contain intercession for you and my grandchild.

I remain faithfully yours,
Sylvania Ortega Hudson/Rosa Garcia

I was speechless. The entire time I was feeling hopeless, wanting to end my life, God was at work. The legal papers lay out a trust fund for the baby and me. It all seems very complicated, but sisters, the provision is beyond generous. And there's more. This you will not believe.

Besides the legal forms, something else remained in the envelope, wrapped in fine tissue. Gingerly, I shook it onto the bed before opening it. Overwhelmed, I scarce could believe what I was seeing. Light from the bed lamp bounced off Mama's locket...shiny and mine once more.

"Oh, Shepard," I whispered, "how can this be?" He only shrugged at my question. "I sold this months ago. It was all I had of my mama. Look!" I held it out to him in wonder.

"Open it," he said. There, inside, was Mama's wedding picture, none the worse for wear. Oh, how beautiful that face. I traced it with a finger. "How did Sylvia find this?"

"No matter the way it came back to you, Gracie, God is responsible."

Shepard was right, sisters. I'll never take it off again—unless I have a daughter—then it will be hers someday.

Remembering there was a second compartment behind the first, I looked in to find this engraved inscription. *"Like a bird wandereth from her nest, so is a man who wandereth from his home. Prov. 27."* The sweet small bird on the back reminds me of the scarlet tanager I saw months ago.

Oh, sisters, I'm the one who left like...a bird wanders. How blind I've been. My sweethearts...I do love you both. Thank you for your unwavering faith.

Oh my, how quickly things have changed. I'm grateful to be alive, glad to have another chance. I see now how blessed I am. Especially to have my family and, of course, Shepard. Please pray that my baby will be spared the consequences of my foolishness.

I'm very, very tired. Shep has promised to mail this long letter immediately.

Your grateful sister,
Grace

November 1902
My sweet Gracie,

How thankful I am for your survival, grateful for God's divine intervention. If the Lord God of the Universe spared your life, little sister, I believe He'll spare your child. All those who love you are praying for your delivery time, and many women at church have worked hard to put a handsome layette together. Nettie and I have been working on a special gift. Much to our surprise, Winnowett has asked to help, and now Little Dove is involved.

Shepard is right about Mama's locket. God brought it back to you, and God will bring you back to us. I never cease to be amazed at the mighty power of His ways. Things are looking up, my Grace. Things are looking up. You left here yearning for riches and such, but it was when you had nothing that God intervened. You have a future and a hope, thanks to Him. All these years God has been working in Sylvania's life and now she's blessed you with the fruits of it all. Amazing! Isn't it just amazing??

The last of our tent dwellers left as of Wednesday. They're headed for Seattle, hoping to make Bellingham by spring. It's been hard to say good-bye to those brought close by the fire, but it's good to be moving forward. Of course, our place is far from empty.

I want to get this in the mail right off. I'm your forever sister.
Love to you,
Eva Jo

P.S. The burden I've felt for you all these many months has been lifted. I have more hope than ever that the heaviness of grief will lift as well. Please tell Shepard "thanks" from all of us.

PRAYER JOURNAL
EVA JO

Dearest Lord,

My grateful heart contains one big prayer. Thank You for sparing my sister's life. Thank You for Shepard's willingness to go the distance searching for Gracie. I'm overcome with emotion when I think how close my sister came to ending her own life. You've had her in the palm of Your hand the whole time, and now, I believe she knows it. I've my own suspicions as to how Gracie ended up pregnant, and I'm sure it was not by her choice. Such evil scares me, Lord. When Gracie lost her innocence, so did I. This valley was once a safe place of refuge. But now

I see that You are the only true safe haven, our strong tower.

Your most grateful servant,

Eva Jo

TELEGRAM
DATED NOVEMBER 17TH
LOS ANGELES, CALIFORNIA
MCLEOD FAMILY STOP GRACIE's BABY GIRL BORN STOP MOTHER AND
CHILD DOING FINE STOP WE'LL LEAVE WHEN ABLE STOP SHEPARD
MCFARLANE

Prayer Journal
Nettie

Dear Father God,

My sister is safe in your loving arms. And now she's a mother! I'm an auntie again, and I can hardly believe it. Oh, how my mama would love to know she's got another granddaughter. But I'm believing she does know.

It's so hard to wait here for their return. But since we've waited this long for Gracie to come home, I'm thinking a few more weeks won't be that bad. It will go quickly, since I'm busy from morning to dusk. And now that winter seems close, the days are not long enough.

Getting up extra early to get all the darlings ready for school has become quite routine, thanks to Eva Jo's stern hand. You know what a pushover I am with all those little ones. Good thing she's been in the schoolroom these last two months, else I'd have been a pushover for the entire class.

Things have settled a lot since the fire. I want to believe that the fire has taken most of the meanness out of this valley. At least for now, prejudice against the Indians seems to be on the back burner. And for

195

that, I breathe a big sigh of relief. With Thanksgiving just around the corner, and with so many people still living together, Eva Jo will have be at home instead of with me, so please make me strong. Strong in You.

Cal and I have been getting up extra, extra early so we can have prayer time together. It's bringing us even closer. I have a wonderful husband. Every time I realize that, I remember that Gracie doesn't have one. Lord, prepare the way for her homecoming. Please soften the hearts of those who might judge her. Give us all wisdom to help her adjust to who she is now. She left a girl, and now she's coming home a woman…with a child. My, now that I think about it, there's not one of us whose stayed the same. We've all changed. What a year! What a God!

Your loving daughter,
Annette

November 1902
Day after Thanksgiving
Dearest Grace,

Oh what a difference a year brings, our Thanksgiving table incomplete with you and Mama missing. Of course, Cal's girls are pure sunshine, thanks to their papa's winning ways, and the three of them complimented the day, as well as Mr. Brewster.

We had another new guest as well, one who sought control over the entire day, though silent. Not one of us addressed the intruder, yet the house could barely hold its presence. You see, sorrow came and never left. Oh for sure, the children and others brought comfort and distraction, but the unseen, unwanted guest claimed our attentions nonetheless.

Papa's usual robust thanksgiving prayer was short (and he asked God's blessings on you and the baby), but he did remind those present that we serve a God who is faithful, trustworthy, and loving. Our quiet "amens" sounded a bit weak, but in truth we agreed. Well, I shouldn't speak for everyone, because I'm not sure that is true with Winnowet. I did, however, hear Little Dove utter a soft ending. When

I looked up, she caught my eye, and I saw understanding, proof to me that the Lord is drawing her to Himself.

I need to back up a little here. Somehow the task of preparing the turkey fell to me this year. I just couldn't ask Papa to do what Mama usually took care of, and Nettie, the girls, and Cal, were all working on the rebuilding. So I sharpened the ax and went to the coop, determined to be brave in the killing of my first bird.

I confess, I've never seen a turkey the size of the one Papa had been fattening since the fire. It had near the bulk of a small pony (minus a saddle), with two legs instead of four. Of course he only needed two since the spurs on each leg were at least three inches long. His wingspread matched those big osprey nesting on the Lewis River, and he flapped them heartily, charging the fence where I stood. There I was, walking around the outside, sizing up our dinner, while he paraded on the inside, daring me to enter. Finally getting up enough courage, I approached the gate, cracking it but a few inches.

The instant he realized it was open, he struck with lightning speed, powerful like a mule's kick. I flew off my feet, back whacking against the coop hard enough to knock the wind out of me. Thankfully the gate was between me and him, otherwise I'd still be wearing scars from those leg spurs. Using the gate for a weapon, I began screaming at the top of my lungs. The only one who heard me was Little Dove, and she came running onto the porch.

"Get Ephraim's rifle," I yelled. I'd already figured my little ax wasn't going to work.

In a minute she was back. Circling around the backside of the chicken yard, she couldn't reach me without attracting the tom's attention to herself.

I yelled again, inquiring as loud as I could if she'd ever fired a gun. She'd never even held one.

By this time the bird was making so much noise I had to scream louder. "Fire."

"Noooo." Her voice shook with fear.

"Fire over your head, Little Dove."

A deafening explosion split the air. At first I thought she'd actually hit him because he stopped his flappin' and yappin', standing still as death. Then, lickity-split, he took off for the woods, quick as any fox, though not near as graceful.

I ran to Little Dove, praising her for the bravery. But when I saw tears of fear spilling out of those doe eyes, I could only hug her tight. What a girl!

When the shaking quit, we began laughing and couldn't stop. Since Dovie rarely laughs with such abandon, I was given over to the enjoyment. I understood more dearly that, *"A merry heart doeth good like a medicine."*

It wasn't until we headed back arm in arm toward the house that I realized our holiday dinner was merrily on its way to Idaho.

We sat together on the porch steps awhile, reliving the experience, wondering what Papa's reaction would be to the escaping of his Thanksgiving delight, when Dovie suddenly asked to borrow a horse. I said yes, but had no idea what she was up to.

I'd been back inside, struggling to make Mama's holiday favorites the best I could when I heard Little Dove return. She was shouting something in Chinookan with great excitement.

Bent with effort, she staggered into the house carrying a bundle nearly as long as herself.

My curiosity was bubbling. Had she gone after the turkey?

After dropping her treasure onto the table, she proudly unwrapped the biggest fish I'd ever seen. "Salmon," she declared. "From my mother. For your dinner."

Winnowett had been gone for a few days, helping her sister at the Reverend's in town.

I was moved to tears by the generous offering. No doubt this magnificent creature would have been dried for winter, giving many more meals than just one.

Little Dove was beaming, the front of her dress stained with evidence of her fine gift.

"Will you tell your mother thank you for me?" I asked.

"Your tilixaN," she said. That means "friend!" Winnowett considers me a friend! I've admired her many strengths from afar, never knowing her opinion of me.

Thanksgiving Day she was here to show me how to prepare salmon the Chinookan way. She even brought wild onions and a wonderful pungent herb found by Fargher Lake.

Despite having sorrow for a guest, we had a feast thanks to friends. Winnowett, her sister Mawnee, and Little Dove spoke few words, yet contentment showed on their faces, even if they avoided some of the foods I'd prepared.

It took a bite or two for everyone to get over missing the traditional turkey and all, but the fish was delicious. Aunt Etta was the first one to comment, and it was all positive. The Lord and Mr. Brewster have had a profound influence on our dear Etta.

She still wears "the hat," and Lulu had her eyes on it most of the day. When Aunt Etta took a nap she never lost a feather; however it was listing to one side when she woke.

Something good is coming, I feel it. All day Mama's name went unspoken until Papa mentioned Nettie's apple pie was just as good as hers. It was like a dam broke loose with everyone chiming in his or her comments. Most had some story to share about past Thanksgivings. All in all it was healing. Especially when Papa came up to me before bed.

"Just think, Eva Jo, next year there'll be two more at the table." When I looked a might perplexed, he hugged me tight, and said, "Gracie and the baby will be here."

He patted me, thanked me for all the work, and went off to bed.

See, Grace...Papa is ready for your return. I'm just hoping it will be for Christmas.

Love to you, Eva Jo

PRAYER JOURNAL
EVA JO

Day after Thanksgiving
Dear Lord,

I'm full up with thanks right now, grateful for many things. Your steadfast love never ends.

The laughter of the children goes on—what healing this brings. I'm fairly certain that the joy of another's voice will be added to our family next summer. Is it true, Lord? Guess I'll know soon. Keep my faith strong, so I don't worry about having another child who lacks hearing. I wouldn't trade Louisa Ann for anything, but You know the hidden things of my heart. I'll pick just the right time to tell Ephraim when I'm sure.

Yesterday Papa seemed younger for a time…really let himself put work aside. He wrestled with his boys and grandchildren like the old days, but he needs Your help, Lord. Always a man of few words, I've seen him working out his grief through labor on the new place. He's exhausted when he finishes the day, yet Will and Percy need more of him. Ephraim's noticed the lacking himself, and tries to give them some time.

Having them here continues to draw us closer and closer, and I thank You for that too. They're more like brothers to my children than uncles. Their gentle way with Lulu is sweet, and the effort they've made to learn sign language makes them heroes in my eyes. She piles on first one and then another, looking for a "horsy" ride. She's never bored.

I know they miss our mama, because even though they always return my hugs and kisses, I sometimes see tears. They match my own. I must thank You for the interest Winnowett has shown them. Just yesterday, when Percy got a sliver in his thumb, he ran to her to take it out. She was saying something low and comforting to him the entire time. Before going back to play, he gave her an endearing hug around the waist. I'm not sure, but I think she wiped away a tear or two.

Lord, thank You for this woman's presence in our life. Help me to be faithful to treat her with the love of Jesus. What a hard worker she is, give me insight into her heart, to reach her tender spots.

Love to You, EJ

All my dear family,

My baby has been born…a daughter. Oh, dear ones, my heart is overwhelmed. How great is our God! He shows me that He is my Father. He takes care of this child through every storm. He will be this baby's Father, even though Jake abandoned her. A tragic beginning will not stop she and I from following God now. He must be our all in all.

I've never been so exhausted, yet I know what it means to have a family now. How very much it means. My pains lasted through the night, but the joyful arrival of my baby girl in the morning made it worthwhile. Flossie White never left my side, and Shepard remained out of the house, "a'pacin' a pathway," as Flossie put it.

When Flossie laid her on my breast, I never wanted to let her go. She weighed in at 7 pounds and about 5 ounces on Flossie's postal meter. We laughed about that together. "Sent special delivery from the Lord!" my friend said. My little muffin is lying in a dresser drawer (made up into a crib) so I can sleep. She's all I can think about. When I remember the selfish girl I've been, I want to weep. But I have a chance to be the kind of mother Mama was to me, and that brings me peace.

I know my bundle of joy needs a name, but right now I'm just calling her Muffin. I thought of naming her after Flossie, but that seems a bit old-fashioned. She has dark hair and eyes, and definitely inherited my chin. She's already won over Shepard completely; he holds her like a precious doll. Just this morning he was humming a song, and when he bent down to kiss her, he called her his "wee little Bonnie." Her temperament is as sweet as they come, crying only when hungry. My, how babies eat and eat!

Oh, I wish Mama could have been here to hold this baby. But I do have you, my sisters, and Papa, if he'll even see us. I think he will love my dark girl in spite of himself.

As soon as my strength returns, Shepard says he'll bring us home. I'm longing to come home...I'll be there soon. God goes with me.

Love, Gracie

Later...

After thinking about Shepard calling my baby "a wee little Bonnie," I've decided she will be called by that name. Do you like it? My Bonnie. Perfect!

Twelve

My dear daughter Gracie,

I must start this long, overdue letter by saying I love you. No matter what's happened or what choices you've made, my feelings haven't changed. True, I was angry, but never have I stopped loving you.

The first time I held you, a fierce protective emotion came over me. I wanted to create a perfect world for my beautiful Grace. When you ran off, my desire to protect you, to make every day of your life happy, was stolen from me. You jumped right out of my hands...out of my protection.

Immediately, I believed that man Jake was not someone I would have given a blessing to. He lacked respect for Mama and I by not making his introductions, proper like. It was all a game to cause a young innocent girl to fall for him, and then snatch her away like a thief in the night. He knew we would see right through him; I suspect you thought so too, Gracie.

All of that is in the past, my girl. You'll be home soon, back into the lives of this entire family. There are some facts I want to make sure you understand before you arrive.

God's blessed me with three girls, and each of you is special. Eva Jo is a lot like me, drawn to things out of doors. Little Nettie is a whole lot like your mama. I am blessed every time I look at her, especially now. She's a reminder of when Mama was young.

Then there's you, Gracie...a bit of both of us. But, in thinking this all through, you are more like my own mama, rest her soul. She too loved adventure and experienced quite a bit of it through her love of reading. Just like you! If you'd known her, I believe the two of you would have been inseparable.

I'm asking for your forgiveness, Gracie. I should have done a better job at steering your adventuresome spirit. Although you left by choice, I believe I could have helped you more if I'd a took the time.

Well, the past is the past, and now we can live with what's ahead. It's what your Mama would want, because that's what the Bible teaches. You'll have a home with me for as long as you need. A home and my covering. There will be those who oppose us, but believe me when I say, God is on our side. He's given life to your child and now He's bringing the two of you back. Thank Shepard for me. He's a good man.

Your Papa

P.S. I have been reading your mama's journal that survived the fire. I think you would find it a blessing to know she prayed for you daily. I'm sending you a page to read.

Prayer Journal
Louise

December 25, 1901
Dear Lord,

It is hard to write, I'm trembling all over. My baby is gone!

The last time I saw Gracie was in this very room. I'd given her my locket, and she seemed delighted and surprised. Now I remember more. She was nervous. I thought it was just Christmas excitement. When we said our good nights, I had no idea she would leave. Where is she? Where could she have gone in the middle of the night? At first, when I found her bed empty, I thought she was probably in Nettie's room. Her running off was the furthest thing from my mind.

Lord, I love my children more than life itself. Every time I hear a door close, I think it might be Gracie, returning. Please bring her home, Father. I will wait, and wait, and wait for her in prayer. Somehow I believe she WILL return. Just give me faith to endure until that day happens

Your praying servant,
Louise

December 10th, 1902
Dear Gracie,

I'm not sure if you are on your way home or still in California. Hopefully all is well with you and my little niece. I have the utmost confidence in Shepard, and his commitment to the two of you. We love the name Bonnie! But, of course, Aunt Etta was wanting her name to be used!

I'm needing to share with someone my yet unresolved grief. Always I've had you or Mama to talk with. Oh, it's not that Nettie wouldn't listen, but she has her new life and is struggling with moving on herself. The grief work in this valley has been exhausting labor. Getting ready to celebrate Christmas is a welcome distraction...but not pleasurable as it should be. Or once was.

I've been cleaning house madly, working off some of the sorrow that clings to me like stale ashes from the fire's aftermath. I was dusting a forgotten ledge, long neglected by my eye, when I found a small piece of paper with words of encouragement Mama had written me when Ephraim and I married. I clutched it to my breast in hopes of feeling some of her on its surface. I rubbed it on my cheek. It was not to be. Nothing. Suddenly deep sorrow crashed over me like gigantic ocean waves, its magnitude pounding me to my knees. I scarce could breathe for the weight of it.

Imagine my surprise at finding an ocean right in my own house? How strange that something so large could be contained, and then remain in a small, hidden place. "This is your heart," whispered the Lord, "a deep, precious place, created for love, but you've filled it with grief...pushing out the love."

Tears fell at this profound revelation, before confessing the holding on. Then more tears came for not giving it over sooner. Flowing grief can only pass on by my willful letting go. I'm sure waters of grief will lap at my ankles perhaps, but now I know I'll not drown. My heart was made for the permanence of love, not grief. Oh, sadness will always be a part of life. But for sure, it does not...cannot...define me. I will not be known as "Eva Jo, sad person," instead I will be a person who sometimes experiences sadness. I'm standing on the promises of God for this, Grace.

After the fire, I became hard as nails. I guess I was trying to protect myself from any more sorrow. I see now I've shut out friends and, worst of all, I know I've not let Ephraim into my hurts like I need to, even though he's made great effort. The whole house has been hurting and I've kept them at a distance.

God did not spare me the pain of losing my mother, for the privilege of being called her daughter. God is faithful, Gracie. He wants us whole and healed. I sense that you have more grief in your life than just losing Mama. I'm hoping I'm wrong on this account. But if not, please know that He will never leave you, nor forsake you, little sister. He's a God of wonder—a wonderful God, faithful to us on our journey.

How I'm longing for Heaven right now. Mama always said that we should want to go to Heaven to be with Jesus, but I think God understands that because she's there, I believe it to be an even sweeter place. I'm reminded daily that earth is NOT Heaven. I for one am glad that I'm just passing through.

Love to you, Eva Jo

P.S. All of us cannot wait to meet your little darling. Goodness, I can barely contain my curiosity. Do you think she'll have red hair?

December 1902
Dear Papa, Nettie, Eva Jo, Percy and Will,

I'm coming home! Home to see all of my faithful family. I can't wait to meet Little Dove, and Aunt Etta's beau, Vee Brewster.

Of course, I wouldn't be able to make the trip if not for Shep. His help has been invaluable. His and Mrs. White's. What dear people God has surrounded me with. More than I deserve. I still struggle with the past, but Shepard and Flossie pray with me daily, and I'm finding strength to believe all God's promises are for me.

Me, Gracie! God saw me helpless and saved me. What a good God!

Even yet, I tire easily, but I am beginning to feel like myself again. I had been persuaded to veer from the narrow pathway our parents had taught us to follow. I'm on that road again, and oh so happy and pleased. Knowing you forgive me my sins of this year, gives me courage to face anything now.

God is showing me how to be true to TRUTH. I'm not to follow left or right off the path where He has set me, created for me since time began. Shep has helped me see that I am valuable to God, and that if I were the only one on earth, Jesus would have died just for me. Now I actually believe it, because I'm leaning on what the Bible says is true...about me and about God. I'm drawn to His Word like never before, seeing things I've never seen. In the past, I lived from the outside in, now I'm living from the inside out... from my soul, and a heart given over to obedience.

You were right, Nettie, Shepherd is a wonderful listener. The best I've ever known. He says I could talk the ears off a donkey, so he must be! Although Shepard is a man who says little, he is a man of giant deeds of which I will someday tell you. In my letters, dear sister, I cannot reveal to you all that I have gone through, but it is my hope that when I see you face-to-face, I can confide my secrets.

We've had time to go over the papers that Jacob's mother left. There is a wonderful trust fund for my daughter when she turns twenty-one. Until then she and I will have a monthly stipend that is generous to be sure. And then there is the cash, twenty-five thousand dollars! My mind struggles to comprehend this kind of generosity. I'll be needing some financial counsel from Papa, so that I can use it properly. I'm very young to have this much responsibility, but for the first time in months, I have complete peace about the future...mine and my little blessing.

I will be sending details on our journey home, though the exact date of our leaving is not certain. Even if I'm not sure of the time, I am sure I'm ready.

Until then, I'm forever yours,
Gracie

December 1902
Dear Grace,

The most incredible thing happened today, and I'm setting it down on paper so as not to forget the impact.

It snowed last night. Of course you know that's not unusual, but the remarkable part is this. All the ugliness of the fire's aftermath is gone, hidden this morning in a blanket of purity. God is so good to let me see this. I've been waiting and waiting, sensing something good was coming. This is it. Oh, not the snow or its beauty, but the realization that He is able to bring beauty from ashes. It's exactly what grace is about, covering all my sins, transgressions and just plain ugliness. All the blackness of it is covered in white...the color of the pure white Lamb who died. Of course, in a few days the snow will melt, but that's not grace...grace keeps coming and coming, never ending.

There's a new hymn we learned at church, from the book of Isaiah.

White as snow, white as snow.
Though my sins were as scarlet,
Lord I know, Lord I know, that I'm clean and forgiven.

Clean, clean, clean! How I've longed for the countryside to be wiped clean of the scars from the fire. Now everywhere, for all to see, is evidence of God's promises.

Truthfully I don't know if everyone in the valley feels like me, but Ephraim and I rejoiced together. We bundled up the children and joined them outside to play until we near froze.

How good it felt to laugh with the boys and Lulu, them thinking their parents a little daft. Of course Little Dove couldn't resist the frolic, taking the opportunity to teach her prize student the sign for snow, and snowman.

Nettie, Cal, and the girls were over at Papa's place and got snowed in. Mama would be so proud of Nettie and how she's taken on all these grown-up responsibilities with determination and joy. Despite her young age, Nettie's role as mother is inspiring. Cassie and Sissy adore her. I thought maybe Willie and Percy might be jealous having to share their sister with an instant family, but that's not been the case.

Nettie's lighthearted ways have won over even the very serious Winnowett. I've caught her putting her hand over her mouth to guard a smile when Nettie breaks into one of her spontaneous outbursts.

Yesterday, she was mimicking some of Papa's stern ways, when he walked in behind her. All of us but Nettie saw him. So there was your little sister doing her best dramatic impression, when he quietly laid a huge hand on her shoulder. She froze, instantly recognizing the touch.

"Papa?" she squeaked.

"Nettie?" came his stern reply.

"Want some coffee?" she asked, ever so meekly.

"Yes, and I'll have it with some of your humble pie."

We'd all been holding our breath to that point, but broke out with laughter. Nettie's face went red like winter long johns, but she laughed too.

"Oh Papa, I love you."

He gave her a big hug, then left. I happened to glance at Winnowett, whose hand was at her throat, that beautiful face bearing an unfamiliar expression, looking right at Papa. Was it admiration, or something more? I didn't have time to figure it out since we had supper to put on the table, but when she saw I was looking her way, her face blushed crimson.

Even though Little Dove says her mother calls me friend, Winnowett is a tough nut to crack. Part of it is our language situation, though we manage some communication between her English, signs, and a scant bit of Chinookan I've learned from Little Dove. Still she seems awkward around me, and never speaks unless spoken to. I feel inadequate, too, because of my lingering ignorance surrounding her culture.

Things are mightily different between her and Louisa Ann. Lulu adores her, and the admiration is returned in great abundance. I've often seen Winnowett pick up my daughter, spinning round and round, until Lulu squeals in delight. Winnowett's whole countenance changes when this happens and she looks like a young girl. I'm certain she's close to my age, since the Chinook marry so young and all.

Having this many people living under one roof has been interesting, for sure giving us opportunity to live out our faith before

Winnowett. I believe she is seeing Christians in a way she's not experienced. Her younger sister, Mawnee, has been boarding at the parsonage to help out Pastor Bill and Betty, but she's smitten with a man she met after the fire...Charlie Smith, and it's looking like they'll wed. He was one of those who came from California with the Levi Straus Company tents for those burnt out of the hills. He's older and a widower with no children who stayed on with Pastor. Been a righthand asset, too. Ephraim thinks Mawnee and him will do well together, but there's a lot of prejudice left around here towards mixed marriages and I worry some.

Ephraim's been helping Papa daily in the rebuilding of the home place, which makes for long days because of his own work load. My husband's capacity to give unconditionally is a remarkable thing since he's willing to sacrifice his own needs for others without complaint, or hesitation. What a Godly example for his children...and wife. Me? I complain too much. Good thing God sees my faults and loves me anyway.

More soon, EJ

December 1902
Dear Grace,

I'm hoping you'll get this letter before you leave, because I'm enclosing a copy of Grandma Osmond's Christmas tale. Finding this helped put me into a much better frame of mind for the Christmas season...hope it does the same for you. It seems like a lifetime ago, when she'd give into our pleadings to hear it over and over. Remember how she never changed a word? Though, as I recall, I wanted her to make the little shepherd boy a shepherd girl...named after me. Then the wrangling spread to Nettie, then you, arguing back and forth to be the main character. Grandma never gave in, did she? It's written in Mama's hand, which makes the memory even more dear. I've found a few more things I thought you'd like, set aside for your return.

I have some wonderful news. Even though sadness remains in this place, I believe Mama would want us to celebrate the Lord's birthday with as much enthusiasm as she'd be given. I'm walking in obedience to Him, because I have to admit I'm not feeling like celebrating anything.

Years past, Ephraim and I liked to start early with Christmas because it gives us more time to remind the children why we celebrate in the first place. Even though the house is filled to overflowing with others, we were pressed to continue these traditions.

We read Grandma's story, then Ephraim reads the Bible's account as well. Last evening after putting Lulu to bed, we had all four boys together, ready and waiting. We'd invited Winnowett and little Dove to join us, but they declined the offer and were in their sleeping quarters. Ephraim was just about to begin, when D.J. spotted Dovie on the stairs, huddled in the shadows.

He called for her to join us at the table, and reluctantly she left the stairs to sit beside me shyly.

I love the sound of my husband's voice when he's reading from the Word, so I was totally absorbed, and not paying real attention to the children.

Suddenly Little Dove began to weep, loud sobs shaking her entire body.

"Little Dove, what's the matter?" Lucas asked sympathetically.

Looking into her soulful eyes, I saw deep sadness, fearing she might bolt any moment.

"I...I...", she stammered, but couldn't get out what she was feeling.

"Dovie." Ephraim's voice went all gentle. "Dovie, why are you crying?"

She tried again, sitting up a little straighter, sniffed, and said, "Little baby was sleeping with animals. Right?"

Ephraim nodded yes, his eyes still on hers.

She continued. "Cold, not good for baby to be there. I was thinking of LuLu sleeping in the barn and, and, my heart hurts bad for this baby." She began to sob again.

Lucas rushed around the table to comfort her. "Tell her, Papa. Tell her why baby Jesus came and slept in that old barn. Tell Little Dove the good news." His face glowed like candles on a Christmas tree.

Dovie looked up at Ephraim, her eyes still welled up.

"Wait until you hear this part, Little Dove. You'll be happier."

D.J.'s enthusiasm was inspiring.

Ephraim got down on one knee beside her chair, drying her tears with one of his big red handkerchiefs before speaking. "Dovie, Jesus came down from Heaven for just one reason...became a little baby for one reason. Want to know what it is?"

She blew her nose hard in the hankie, then nodded yes.

"For love, and for you, little Dove. Jesus came to earth just for you, because He loves you."

Ignoring the look of disbelief on her face, he continued. "It's true, little girl. You know Eva Jo and I would never lie to you. To be sure, He came for every man, woman, and child ever born. See, that's all of us, and for certain that's you."

Little Dove began to smile, ever so slightly, then cleared her throat before speaking. "This baby Jesus, same Jesus who died on cross when He was big man?"

"Yes," I said. Remember all the times we've talked about how Jesus loved us so much that He died for us? I told you he came to earth, died, then in a miracle came alive again. Well, first he was born, just like you. He had a mother named Mary."

I tell you the truth, I could see her mind working on all she'd heard. For certain God's Spirit was at work because all of a sudden she clapped her hands.

"My mind has it now. No," she corrected herself, then pointed to her chest. "My heart has it now." She reached up and hugged Ephraim's neck. The boys came around the table and she squeezed them tight, then left her chair to stand before me.

"Evie, Little Dove thinks you don't lie. This makes my heart happy. Evie, *Nayka qat mayka.*"

Suddenly, me, the one person who is never speechless was silenced by emotion. I pulled her little body close to mine. You see, Gracie, she told me she loved me in her own language. What a moment...I'll never forget it. But there's more.

I quick told her "Thank you."

Then she looked up at me with those amazing brown eyes and said, "I love Jesus too. I love the baby and the man. What man from Heaven would sleep in a barn? What man would die on big cross?"

Ephraim came to where we were, pulled his chair beside me, and took both Little Dove's hands into his giant ones. "Little Dove, that baby Jesus...the man who grew up and died for us, is God. The only God, who made the salmon your people smoke, the elk we eat, and all the land around us. The mountain rumbles when He says, and deer have babies in the spring because that's how He's made them."

Dovie's face was glowing. She stood perfectly still, listening to every syllable Ephraim spoke. I could see she understood it all. My mind was praising God and praying all at the same time.

"Now here's the most wonderful part, Dovie," Ephraim continued. "He wants to live in your heart."

She put her hand on her chest again, a puzzled look on her face. "He wants to live here? Jesus wants to live in this place?"

"Yes he does." Ephraim's voice was soft and reassuring.

"How does this happen?"

"Well, you pray and ask Him."

"Only ask?"

"Yes," Ephraim said.

"I do this now." Her face radiated with the truth.

Ephraim prayed first, and she repeated it.

DJ, Lucas, Willie, and even Percy were jumping around like barn cats when they finished, rushing over to grab Little Dove's hands. They twirled her round and round.

D.J. spoke first. "I told you it was good news. Didn't I? Now, Dovie, you'll never have to be afraid because Jesus says he'll never leave you....never, ever. Right Papa?" Ephraim nodded.

"Little Dove, your papa prayed this prayer before he died, and now he lives with Jesus," I said.

She began to cry again, and came to lay her head on my shoulder, then whispered, "Little Dove happy."

Ephraim went on to explain what the Bible says about baptism. When Dovie heard the part about being dunked, she shivered, but I explained it was all right to wait for warmer weather.

I'm not sure what Winnowette will have to say about her daughter's conversion, but I'm praying we'll have the chance to explain it to her understanding.

This might be my last letter before you'll be home. Sitting here in the glow of the fire, I'm thinking home is the best place to be. Even with the many changes the valley, and this family have gone through in one short year, our remembrances remain, somehow, holy.

Love to you, Eva Jo

"What Do You Say to a King?"
A Christmas Tale
By Grandma Osmond

A long time ago in the hills of Judea, there lived a small shepherd boy named Jeremiah. Although very young, his older brothers would sometimes let him spend the night with them in the fields with glittering stars for company. This made Jeremiah very happy.

It was winter and his brothers had built a huge fire to scare away wild animals from the sheep and also to keep themselves warm. They worshiped the God of Abraham, Isaac, and Joseph, their ancestors, and loved to sit around the flames talking of the promises the Lord had made to all the people of Israel. Jeremiah wanted to talk, but he was too shy.

"Someday God will send us a King," Jeremiah's oldest brother David shared.

"He will be our Messiah," Micah, another brother, added.

Jeremiah had never met a King, but knew that Messiah would be mighty and powerful.

When Jeremiah began to get tired, he wrapped himself tightly in the blanket his mother had sent and snuggled close to David's side. His eyes became heavier and heavier, until he was sound asleep.

Jeremiah woke suddenly to find the sky ablaze with the most brilliant light he'd ever seen. His mouth dropped open with wonder and he was filled with fear. Right in the center of the dazzling display was a Heavenly being who took up the entire night. An angel? Jeremiah's little body began to shake. What was happening? His brothers were on their feet now with other shepherds in the fields. All were shouting, pointing to what their eyes could not believe. Jeremiah was speechless.

Then the angel said to them. "Do not be afraid, for behold, I bring you good tidings of great joy which will be to all people. For there is born to you this day in the city of David, a Savior, who is Christ the

Lord. And this will be the sign to you: You will find a Babe wrapped in swaddling cloths, lying in a manger."

The Angel's voice rolled like thunder across the hills. Only now there was no storm overhead...only more angels. Suddenly they were surrounded by a multitude of the heavenly host praising God and saying:

"Glory to God in the highest, and on earth peace, goodwill toward men!"

As quickly as they came, they vanished, with the sounds of their praise still echoing off the hillsides, fading away into velvet darkness.

David spoke first. "We have seen the Heavens open up and speak to us. What do you make of this, my brothers?" They were all filled with excitement and began to talk at once. "Glory to God! We join with the angels and say: Glory to God in the highest."

"And you, Jeremiah, what do you have to say?"

Jeremiah stood first on one foot and then the other, still wrapped in his blanket. He wanted to answer. He wanted to praise God with the others but when he tried, nothing came out. He'd been so afraid, his voice had left him. His brothers patted him on the head to tease, which made him feel even worse. *Glory, glory, glory,* he practiced in his mind. Yet...no sound.

"Don't worry, Jeremiah, you've seen a miraculous thing tonight, your voice will return. But it's not over, come, I'll carry you and we'll go to Bethlehem, just as the angel said. A baby King should be quite a sight."

After putting Jeremiah onto his back, David and the others set off to see the Infant of promise.

Though the littlest shepherd felt safe with his brothers, secretly he hoped they'd not see another Heavenly being for a long time. Jeremiah swallowed hard, trying one more time to speak a word of praise for all he'd seen. Nothing.

He'd nearly fallen back to sleep, despite the bumpy ride, when they arrived at Bethlehem. The manger wasn't hard to find, since a bright, shiny star gleamed and twinkled directly above the spot. David woke Jeremiah, then put him on the ground, rushing ahead to enter an animal shelter carved into the hillside. Jeremiah stayed behind, feeling very small, and unsure that a real King would live in cave.

Jeremiah's heart skipped a beat when he saw a small beam of light near the entrance begin to grow and grow until an angel almost like the one he'd seen earlier appeared. He wanted to run in fear, but the angel motioned for him to enter. With his heart still pounding he moved closer.

Once inside, he walked to a bed overflowing with straw. It held the tiniest human being Jeremiah had ever seen. He was confused. Was this the King? Just then the baby woke, stretched his little arms, then turned His head to look right into Jeremiah's face. Jeremiah reached out and touched the infant King's very small hand. When the baby took hold of one of his fingers, all fear left the shepherd boy and he felt the most wonderful joy spread over him like warm honey.

He laughed out loud. His voice...he'd gotten his voice back!

"Jeremiah," David asked, "what do you say to a King?"

A huge smile spread across Jeremiah's face as he leaned down and put his mouth right next to the baby's tiny ear.

"Glory" he whispered, "Glory to God in the highest."

PRAYER JOURNAL
EVA JO

December

O, Lord,

My heart overflows with gratitude for Your grace and truth. Thank You for touching Little Dove's heart with understanding to receive Your salvation. I'm convicted to thank You once more for the miracle that is Christmas, as well. Tonight the tears falling on this journal are from joy instead of grief. Beauty from ashes, beauty from ashes. Only You could do this thing.

I'm imagining Mama's first Christmas with You. Aren't you proud of Your daughter? She served you well, and though I shall miss her the rest of my days, I have peace because of Your promises now fulfilled in her destiny.

We've news that Gracie's had her baby. A girl! I'm an "auntie." What a wonderful Christmas present. Keep them safe on the long travel, please, Lord.

I'm not sure I've ever understood the meaning of "irony" until this very moment. While one of us has gone to their eternal home, another completes her painful prodigal journey. I struggle still with Gracie's reasonings, but I'm willing to forgive anything You are.

I'm a little confused as to where Shepard fits in to all of this...his actions are admirable, but puzzling as well. Though I'm thinking he must love Grace. Why else would he travel over a thousand miles to bring her home?

Love to you, Eva Jo

December 25th, 1902
My Dearest Lord,

She's home! My sister is home. Oh, thank You for Gracie's return. I can scarce see the paper for these tears of joy. Only You know the real journey she's experienced, but all that is behind us now as she sleeps beneath my roof. Although lacking healthy meat on her bones, underneath there's a spark of newness...a fresh glow of something intense, beyond appearance. Hope. It's hope. That could only come from You.

The deep love she has for her daughter is apparent. She's so small, yet her lusty cries are strong. Our little Bonnie. I didn't say it out loud, but something of Mama is reflected in the perfection of her face, especially the dimpled chin we all got from her. I believe Papa saw it as well, for he wells up each time he holds her.

I'm wondering. Does Mama know her prodigal has returned? There are many mysteries in my understanding of Heaven, Lord.

Forever perfect in my memory will be the first glimpse of Grace and our reunion.

Every person in church last night knew we were at a threshold in our grief. Though we'd suffered much in the last few months, here we were...living testimonies to You, Lord, and the one thing the fire could not steal from us...our faith. Sorrow had the opportunity to turn into rejoicing, beauty begged to come out of the ashes. Not that any of us had actual words for the expression of it, but for sure we felt the changing.

When Nettie and I took our places upfront to sing our annual solo, we looked at each other only briefly, both knowing the other was missing Gracie. We waited while Ida May walked to the organ, gave a few good pumps, then played the introduction. We began.

"O holy night, the stars are brightly shining.
It is the night of our dear Saviour's birth.
Long lay the world in sin and error pining,
till He appeared and the soul felt its worth.
thrill of hope, the weary world rejoices
For yonder breaks a new and glorious morn.
Fall on your knees, O hear the angel voices.
O night Divine, O night. When Christ was born
O night divine, O night, O night divine.

The two of us slipped right into old harmonies. With each note, something good and familiar grew in my heart. True worship. I closed my eyes in the sweet comfort of the experience.

We were about to start the second verse when a strong gust of wind from the front door blew its way to where we stood, just as a third voice joined our duet. Gracie!

There she was, cheeks flushed, walking towards us, her alto voice strong and rich as always. I ran to kiss on her face. Could I have been dreaming? When we touched, joy flooded over as the three of us embraced. Suddenly the entire congregation broke into applause. Not one eye remained dry as they rose to their feet.

We all had much to say, but that would have to wait. Other voices lifted to join in until we were one body, celebrating You. Celebrating Your faithfulness to each of us, but especially Your one little prodigal who'd come back from her wandering. Your own special bird is all the way home. Thanks be to You.

Your Eva Jo

Prayer Journal
Nettie

December 25, 1902
Dearest Lord,

My heart was not faithful in remembering Gracie's beauty. After the house became still following our grand celebration, I grabbed the Christmas quilt Eva Jo had made, and stole down to the parlor...just to watch Grace and Bonnie sleep. What a miracle...both of them.

I keep replaying the events of Christmas Eve over in my mind. What a night!

Whenever I sing "O Holy Night," I know I will remember looking down the church aisle and seeing the door slowly open, revealing Papa, beaming the brightest smile he's ever worn. I turned my eyes away to focus on the song, for I was about to lose my place. I struggled, because I wondered what had suddenly caused him so much obvious happiness.

Before service, our family and others had huddled together for comfort. We were all suffering because of the empty spaces beside us. Papa had stayed outside, unable to come in and hear Eva Jo and I sing Mama's favorite song. So I was quite surprised to see him enter the church right in the middle of it.

It was when I glanced up the second time that I thought I saw a Christmas angel. A familiar and precious face was walking toward us. Gracie!

We completely abandoned our solo to run and greet my sister. We couldn't stop crying and kissing. I wanted that moment to last forever. She looked different. No, she *was* different. In a new and wonderful way, I mean. She'd been changed all right, but with my own eyes, I could tell it was for the good. I thought I knew the depth of my love for Grace. Not true, though. For it was only when I held her again, that I realized how much I had missed her. I just wanted to hang on...forever.

And of course, there was Bonnie, our new precious bundle. My, she is a beauty. There is no other as beautiful.

It's been a whole twenty-four hours, yet I can hardly believe she's back home with us. And with Shepard at that! I will never forget this Christmas.

Lord, You have not only restored our family, You've added to us. Thank You.

Also thank You for the secret Cal and I have not spoken of yet. I cannot keep it to myself now that Gracie's here. I've always shared everything with her. Bonnie is going to have another cousin! It is the most wonderful news for Cal and I to share together.

Merry Christmas to us. Merry Christmas to You, dear Lord. I love you,

Annette

December 25, 1902
Dear Flossie,

To be safe here with my family is a blessing beyond belief. I have been a wanderer and now I am home. Much has happened to me that was unfair, but I know that through it all, God was watching over me, and I survived for a reason.

Christmas Day is over now, but oh, what a Christmas it was! I want to capture my memories on paper, lest I ever forget one thing of God's faithfulness. And of course, I wanted you to share in it all because of your abiding friendship.

When I first saw the Columbia River after my year-long absence, a small familiar terror rose in my throat, and I choked back a sob. What would the valley be like without my mama there? Another level of reality struck, knowing I'd never see her again. Everything and everyone was now completely different. Where would Bonnie and I fit in...her with no father and me without a husband?

Shepard's eyes were on me. He has a way of calming me without saying a word. He knew how fragile I was. I pretended to fuss with the baby's things for distraction. The train pulled into the new Yacolt station at 8:00 pm. The very station that Jake Hudson had been here to build. The night was dark and threatening, without stars. Shepard borrowed a wagon from Mr. Buckley, the station master, who was glad to lend it. I ate a leftover biscuit from the train and fed Bonnie in the back room of the tiny railroad station while Shep harnessed the horses.

"They're all at church for Christmas Eve service, in case you don't know," Mr. Buckley said to Shepard, after he'd come inside.

"Then we'll go there," he answered.

That old companion, shame, crept over my being. I wasn't sure I was ready to go into that church. I really wanted to hide out somewhere, but my house, the one I'd lived in with Mama and Papa, was burned up. Maybe at Eva Jo's I could be alone with my baby.

"Your sisters and father are there, Grace," said Shepard softly. "Don't believe the enemy's backtalk again."

I nodded, burping the baby over my shoulder, rubbing her tiny back. "Shepard, you can't know how I feel..." I hesitated. "I can't go into that church. Not after what I've done."

"You can go anywhere, Grace, with your head held high, because the Lord receives you and forgives you."

I could accept that God forgave me. But at times I still doubted He loved me.

We rode in silence, while snowflakes began to swirl. I covered Bonnie's little pink face with her blanket. Despite the dread I was experiencing, I had a strange longing to be at the church with all the town's survivors.

"Whoa."

Shepard's voice startled me. We were under the oak tree, just outside of Yacolt Church.

"Grace—" his breath hung in the cold air—"don't trouble yourself about what people think. After the fire and losing so many, it's a joy to have you and this little one back home."

I looked into his honest face. Shepard McFarlane loved me. I knew that he'd loved me a long time; fool that I'd been. A lump rose in my throat, but I could not—would not cry. I gulped for air. "Do you think Papa meant all the things he said in his letter?"

"I know your father loves you."

Warm yellow light reflected on the snowy ground surrounding us. Music, drifting from the windows through the weather, seemed to call me.

Shepard lifted me down, rearranged Bonnie in my arms, and

then jumped back into the wagon.

"Shepard, aren't you coming with me?" I asked, the wind carrying my question away.

"I'm returning Buckley's wagon. I'll be back as soon as I'm through."

"But I don't want to…" I watched Shepard's broad back disappear into the white slate distance.

I struggled with going in alone. Yet I heard a song, sung in clear voices that beckoned me again. I recognized those voices, drawing me closer. At that moment, I knelt down in the icy mud, moving Bonnie to a shoulder. I prayed: "Jesus, if you truly love me after all I've done, please show me."

And He did. No sooner had I breathed that prayer than a light wind stirred my hair. It became stronger, but not cold. It was warm and friendly, an all-embracing wind that surrounded me in sun warmed tenderness. Then heat, hot as fire consumed me from head to foot, and anointed, as with oil, the top of my head.

I felt, in that instant, so loved by Jesus, overwhelmed by His kindness. For the first time in my life, I was aware of a Presence so large that it took my breath away. I couldn't move.

"That was you!" I whispered, as snowflakes melted on my forehead.

I stepped closer to the church, my shoes sliding on the pathway. I had never felt more alive than I did then. It was as though God had breathed His own breath into me, and I was a new person. Inside, I was made pure white like the ground beneath my feet. And He'd shown me He loved me. I could feel hot tears on my cheeks. I'd never doubt again! I looked down at my Bonnie's sleeping face, snug in the crook of my arm. A lone drop fell on her blanket. "We're going to be fine," I whispered.

The church steps looked slippery, and I gripped Bonnie tighter. When I glanced up before making the ascent, I saw an outline of someone standing at the top. Just then the figure stepped out of the shadows. Papa? "Gracie, Gracie," he was saying. His arms were stretched out and he was coming down to greet me. I fell into his embrace. "I'm home!" was all I could say. Papa held me at arm's length, his gaze moving from me to Bonnie and back again. Then he gave me a bear hug, careful not to squeeze the baby.

"I love you, Gracie."

"I know," I whispered. "I know." He took my elbow and walked me up the stairs and into the crowded sanctuary.

It was as though angels shared the candlelight. Eva Jo and Nettie were singing, "O Holy Night." Every word pierced my being.

"O Holy Night,
The stars are brightly shining,
It is the night of our dear Savior's birth.
Long lay the world, in sin and error pining,
Till He appeared and the soul felt its worth."

It was a long way to the front where Nettie and Eva Jo stood, but I joined my voice with theirs. Nettie, when she saw me, gave a little shriek, and forgetting herself, came running toward us. Eva Jo, startled, looked to Heaven with a joyful smile, before joining us in greeting. We were all crying. There I stood, surrounded by love: Nettie's, Eva Jo's, and Papa's. And, oh how they loved my baby, passing her back and forth, with "oohs and aahs" over her sweetness.

Suddenly the entire congregation was on its feet with applause before they gathered around with warm hugs and kisses for Bonnie. Aunt Etta, looking lovely, made her way through the lively group, just to say how glad she was to see me back. Nettie and Eva Jo had been right about the changes in her life. Before me was a woman in love.

The songs of Christmas brought unspeakable joy that I did not know was possible to possess on earth. God's almighty power to forgive, and the feeling it carried, was just as my sisters had described in their precious letters. They were right all along. There is no path for me other than following God's plan. Even without my Mama there, my soul was full.

I don't remember how long it was before Shepard came into the back, snow making his hair appear white. Papa went to greet him just as the bells pealed a Christmas greeting in the steeple. I could barely hear amidst the din, but I think he said something like, "Well done, Shep, you've brought her home for Christmas." Shepard only smiled and stood staring at me, his cheeks flushed with weather.

Christmas dinner at Eva Jo's was pandemonium of the most delicious kind. For some reason, everything was brighter—gayer than ever. Colors appeared more vibrant, and the food tasted beyond good. Love poured forth, and at times, I cried at the drop of a hat. I wasn't the only one.

But now, in the ebb of day, there is quiet, and I can write it all down. I'm a weary lass, but a happy one. Bonnie's long been asleep, and I'm going to bed, too.

Good-night dear Flossie, God is with us. God is with me.

Your forever-grateful friend,

Grace McLeod

P.S. I've finally met Little Dove and Winnowette, her mother. I'm charmed, for lack of better expression. Everything Eva Jo has said about them is true. I feel blessed to have each one in our lives. What a future we all have...together.

Thirteen

Tender winter light forced itself into the attic, falling across the last letter Julia held against her chest. Howling winds matched her emotions. Never had she been so moved. How was she supposed to process all she'd read, all that had been revealed in the letters that now lay scattered at her feet?

She stood to stretch, wrapped the blanket tighter, then fell back into the chair. She sighed heavily.

"Gran, I never knew you." Emotions washed over her. "Not the real you." Confusion overran her thoughts.

She leaned to grab a tissue, her gaze returning to the letters. Now that the trunk was empty, the bottom exposed, Julia spotted something in a dark corner. She reached in, fingers brushing against a small bundle of silk cloth. Julia picked it up with expectation, and turned down all four corners. A locket. No, "the" locket! Gran's, to be sure. Nestled in the palm of Julia's hand was the wondrous treasure she'd just read about. Its delicate nature had not been compromised over the years; rather, the patina glowed in the richness of its inheritance—vibrant with meaning and memory. With awe, she turned it over and over, admiring the small bird on the back. Would the tiny latch still work? She pushed on it. Obediently it opened partway. She lifted it.

Time stood still in black and white. There was Gran's Mama, resting while she waited to be found. Julia shook her head in wonder. She used a fingernail to pry up an edge. There it was, the Scripture Grace had found, written in the most delicate script Julia had ever seen.

She touched the lettering while profound word pictures ran

224

through her mind. Childhood flashes mingled with what she'd just read...like a movie.

Each remembrance of her great-grandmother was still good. Her hands trembled as she smoothed out the locket's lavender ribbon, then tied it around her neck.

"Everything that happens to us, by choice or circumstance, God will use for good, if we let Him." It was Grace's voice, strong and clear, lingering about her like heady perfume. Julia recalled the very conversation. It was after Papa Shep's death, and they were suffering with loss.

"How could something good come from death?" Julia had wailed.

"Well, Missy, the ultimate good came out of Jesus' death. Salvation for any person who chooses Him."

"That's different," had been Julia's reply. "Jesus was God."

"But it was human flesh that got nailed to the cross. And all of it done while we were still sinners. Your Papa Shep believed that, and had no fear when he breathed his last. Remember this, Julia...when my time comes, I won't be afraid either...rest assured."

"Rest assured." That's what Julia craved now, rest. And not for her body alone. She wanted something, no needed something, to calm the restlessness in her spirit.

She stood again, knowing what she would do. Going downstairs quietly, she put on a heavy coat, boots, and a woolen scarf of her mother's.

A thought pushed at the back of her mind while she finished dressing for the Christmas Eve weather. Every incident from Grace's past had made her the woman Julia knew and loved...strong, never shaken in faith. Gran had been able to move forward from the past despite the pain, despite the bad choices she'd made that had caused herself and others so much grief. Her very last gift to Julia had been to put her own reputation at risk in order to share the letters that had held the unspoken all these years. Her hand went to the memory gift resting on her chest.

"Thank you, Gran." She was outside now, undeterred by threatening storm clouds.

Jake Hudson's influence had been strong enough to lure Gran away from all that she'd known as good. The letters revealed he had nearly destroyed her life. It happened when Gran had stopped listening to the still, small voice of conscience. She gave into temptations she knew were wrong in order to have her own way.

Julia spoke to the wind. "Look where it got her."

She stopped dead in her tracks, reaching into her pocket for the crumpled note.

Julia, the lion will destroy you.

Gran hadn't the strength or time to tell the entire story, so she did what she could. Julia knew who the lion was. Grace had nearly been destroyed by Satan's temptations and was warning Julia of his power in those last cryptic words.

Michael.

Gran had gone to California with Jake Hudson, and Julia had plans to do the same with Michael. The intensity of the reality of where she was headed with Michael Hanson drew a familiar longing from its resting place.

"Come home."

There it was again, that unrelenting, strong voice.

Julia tied the scarf tighter, pulling it over her nose for warmth. Head down, she walked into the wind with determined steps. Even though damp air pushed back, the cold cleared her head. What revelations she'd found...on Christmas Eve of all times. Never had she felt closer to Gran. Waning bits of energy were spent arranging things so that Julia might be warned and rescued from her own willfulness.

A barking dog startled her contemplations. She looked up to see the cemetery directly ahead. Julia hadn't been here since Papa Shep died, when she'd been ten, or maybe eleven.

The iron-gate was still intact, with the same carved sign: Yacolt Cemetery. Smiling, she remembered the scolding she'd received the day of his funeral, having been caught swinging back and forth, aging rusty hinges protesting the rowdy treatment.

"Horses are for riding, Julia, not gates," her mother had reminded.

Even though she was processing all she'd read, the fact that Papa

Shep wasn't her real grandfather was disturbing.

But then, she reasoned, had her heart ever known the difference? It was his encouragement that kept her on the back of her first horse. She was afraid every time she got on, but Papa Shep never gave up on the praise—or the girl. Once she'd come into the house in a meltdown over lack of ability, but Papa had led her outside again, put her back on the huge white horse. "Julia girl, you can do it. Show him whose boss...he'll respect you for it. Now wipe those tears."

She'd practiced diligently going round and round the barn, each turn building confidence. Within the month, she was galloping through surrounding pastures, wind whipping her hair. Often she saw him watching. She was proud of her success because he was proud of her.

It was his heart love, poured out into her life, that made him the man she remembered. What was the measure of a man? An old Sunday school verse brushed against her mind. Something about the heart containing what defines a person. Papa Shep's heart must have been full of all that was good because even now Julia's memory warmed with the recollection.

She wondered if Bonnie ever knew the "truth" surrounding her biological history. Biology was one thing, heart truth another. No man ever put more devotion into raising a child than Shepherd McFarlane. She was sure.

Despite the discoveries made the night before, she tenaciously believed in the steadfastness of the love they shared as a family. Albeit not perfect, they belonged to one another regardless, quirks and all. Along with her red hair, she admitted to inheriting a personality full of them.

Touching the gate's graceful curves with a gloved hand brought her back to the present and with it, recognitions of sadness. She shivered.

"I came all the way out here just to freeze."

Walking through she stopped abruptly...she wasn't alone. Two people were standing at the "McFarlane" headstone. Since their backs were turned, she couldn't tell who it might be. As one of them bent over, placing something on the ground, Julia recognized her great-Aunt Eva Jo. Nettie accompanied her.

Eva Jo paused for a minute more, lightly putting a hand to her lips before touching the stone. Arm in arm they walked away to the other side of the cemetery, stepping through the back gate. Who was supporting whom? Julia couldn't tell.

Embarrassed that she hadn't come forward sooner, Julia walked over to the McLeod/McFarlane's plot.

Drawn first to a lichen-covered statue resting on a simple headstone, a sigh passed her lips. Louise Osmond McLeod's name was barely visible. The figure was a sweet-faced child…a boy, still intact though weathered. Was it supposed to be James, Louise's and Big Jim's firstborn? Surely. His head full of curly hair, was slightly turned, bent towards his right hand. Julia stepped closer and saw a small, carved bird nestled in his palm. A thought stirred in her mind.

She tore at the neck scarf to get to the necklace, took it off, and held it next to the bird carving. They were strikingly the same. Puzzle pieces floated together. This bird and the one on the locket were linked with the Scripture, "Like a bird wanders…" Julia made a mental note to ask Eva Jo, and Aunt Nettie who had placed the statue atop their mother's tombstone, and if her hunches about the symbolism of the bird were right. If so, then she surmised that it was probably a scarlet tanager, like the one Grannie Grace had seen so long ago in that California garden.

The wind picked up and Julia rewrapped the scarf, dropped the locket into her jacket, and walked to the other side of the plot. She stood before a large stone with bold carving.

Shepard Jeremiah McFarlane
Born: 1875
Died: 1954
Loving husband, father, grandfather; follower of God and not man.
"Welcome home, good and faithful servant."

On the bottom half, Grace's name and date of birth had already been engraved.

Gracie was the first of the "sisters" to die, and Julia could only imagine what that must mean to the other two. They were as close in

228

their later years as they'd been in their youth. Living within walking and talking distance made them inseparable in different ways. Most visits were centered on fond recollections of the past they'd shared over the years, but pictures of grandchildren and others kept each home full of wonderful current family news as well.

Julia sighed, recalling the vibrant "discussions" that occurred over afternoon tea. Since each of the sisters was vocally opinionated, with widely different outlooks on life, they might have been debating about plant preferences, current events, or the new preacher's long hair. If ever one of them happened to doze off, they were surely teased...in sisterly fashion of course. But they could always laugh at themselves. Like the time someone walked into Nettie's living room and found all three sleeping soundly, balancing delicate teacups precariously on snoozing laps. Even the cat was snoring! They'd laughed themselves into tears over that one.

Death's realization washed over Julia, and she crumpled to the ground. "My heart will never be the same."

Removing her gloves to get a tissue from a pocket, she noticed the envelope propped in front: *For Julia.*

The handwriting exactly matched Aunt Eva Jo's, but when she opened it, the letter was from Aunt Nettie, addressed to Grace. Pushing up from the ground, Julia brushed off some leaves, ignoring the dampness on her pants. This couldn't wait for the comfort of home, so she found a small bench nearby. Despite the cold, she had to finish this monumental journey. Somehow this letter held more. But what? Pressing beyond her fragile emotional state...and the cold, Julia opened the envelope again.

December 24, 1966
My dearest sister Gracie,

I'm sitting here on a cold, lonely bench, desperately avoiding my heart's last good-bye. My handwriting is a little bit shakier than normal because I realize how final this letter is. Final until we meet in Heaven.

"My dearest sister." How many times have I written those words? How many times have I spoken your name and looked into your sparkling eyes. Eyes so full of eagerness for the life ahead. I can only imagine what your eyes are taking in now in the presence of our Lord.

I'm staring at a plot of ground that tells me it's over for you down here, yet that's not really true. You will live on in the countless fruits yet to be seen through the life you lived for our Lord and Savior.

He used you mightily, my sister, while you were with us. I know that as I turn from this place, I'll be able to see you in places you've been and people you've spoken to. Wherever you walked ended up a better place because you left the footprints of Jesus.

It's ironic that you've gone home so close to Christmas when those many years ago you returned to us on that day. Now you are with Him and those who've gone before. Is it really beautiful, Gracie? Are you able to stand, or are you bowed down in worship in the presence of His perfect love? Have you found Mama and Papa? Oh well, you have eternity and you've only just arrived. No more tears for you.

I envy you. Your walk is completed. I know, I know, I have work left to do.

Your last desire is finished, my dearest. I've left the letters for her to read. If only she would hear His voice and know His love...and come back home to walk with Jesus. She's just like you, you know. Filled with passion and loyalty, no matter what direction she's taken. I know it was your prayer that her passion be used for God and His kingdom. When I see the legacy you've left her, I can't imagine that it won't happen soon.

I have to stop writing...my hands are nearly frozen, yet I don't want to break this connection. When next we meet, it will be on the threshold of eternity.

I love you, and will see you as soon as MY work is finished.

Your sister forever,

Nettie Louise

Oh Gran, my Gran. Emotion flowing down Julia's face fell onto the stationery, creating delicate watermarks as they spread. "Lord, you waited for my Gran, just as You've waited for me. Even though I

230

haven't left for Los Angeles yet, I've been absent from your side, living behind Your back for too long. Thank You for your faithfulness. I've heard Your tender voice. I'm grateful You still want me. The Lord God of the Universe wants all of me. Praise You, sweet Jesus...and thank You too for my family's faithful prayers, and constant love. Forgive me, Father. Help me get back on track, so I might be the woman You want me to be. Please take my small faith and make it bigger. Amen."

She looked up. Something had fallen onto one cheek. It wasn't her tears this time. Snow. It was snowing...on Christmas Eve. Jumping up she lifted her hands, wanting to embrace it all. Turning in a slow circle, she stuck out her tongue to taste the feathery flakes. Falling harder now, snow began drifting in pillow fashion, creating an instant Christmas card.

"Gran, can you see me? Do you know your little prodigal bird has returned? I do still love you. I love you...all the stars."

Stuffing the letters in a pocket, Julia glanced at the headstone again before walking briskly out the gate, letting it bang behind her.

She stopped to dance round and round again in the silent, velvet snowfall, grateful arms once more raised to Heaven. "I'm home."

The moment a Christian wanders away from his place—that is, from the simplicity of his faith in Jesus—that moment he departs from his safe shelter in the solid rock.

What Christ did, what Christ is, what Christ has promised we cling to as the home of our faith. The sinner that seeks solace elsewhere, that moment he is like a bird that wanders from her nest. The bird away from her nest has no comfort; the instincts of nature make her feel during her incubation that the nest is her proper place…. Like Noah's dove…we may search the world around, and fly over the great waste of waters, but there never shall be found rest anywhere but at the cross.

Oh, Christian! do not leave your nest…Let the joy we have had in Christ constrain us still to cling to Him.

—"STAY CLOSE TO THE NEST"
CHARLES H. SPURGEON (1834-1892)

Authors' Notes

Before the infamous 9/11/01, there was another 9/11 in Yacolt, Washington, nestled at the foot of Mt. St. Helen's. In the southwest corner of the Evergreen state, prior to the mountain's famous volcanic eruption in 1980, the valley was well known for a huge forest fire that brought death and destruction on September 11, 1902.

"The Yacolt Burn" spared nothing in its path, killing thirty-eight people, and consuming a hundred family homes in the hills. Miraculously, just as the nightmare blaze threatened to destroy the entire contents of Yacolt proper, the devilish winds shifted, leaving all fifty-five buildings intact.

In our fictional story, we've included places, people, and events that were actual in 1902, and some that were not. To our knowledge, there never was a McLeod family in the valley, but we discovered the first name of Shepard on a tombstone in the Yacolt cemetery. There is a Basket Flats...not quite in Yacolt, but close. You'll never wade through Miracle Creek or climb Roan Mountain, but Farger/Fargher Lake exists, now minus any water. Today the Chalatchie Prairie lumber mill sits silent, a ghostly testament to the once- thriving lumber industry of bygone years.

Hulda Klager's apple hybrid story is true, and a lilac garden in Woodland, Washington, bears her name, paying homage to her pioneering gardening expertise. Although we have no way to know if she ever helped any "Burn" survivors, her well-known generosity makes the trip plausible. "Good Hope School" once thrived in Salmon Creek, outside Vancouver, WA, and the "Clamshell Railroad" provided a pleasant ride down the Long Beach, Washington Peninsula, in 1902. We've also enjoyed including some special names from our own lives, past and present.

Coming Soon...

Old Sins, Long Shadows

BOOK TWO
The MacLeod Family Saga

Sharon Bernash Smith

"Shadows have sounds, but they are not all the same," she said. "Shadows, cast by trees in summer are cool, like the water's song as it flows over stones in the Lewis. But...shadows from old sins carry a moaning voice...long, low and very, very sad."
—Winnowette

It's one thing to suffer the consequences of one's own sin, but quite another to deal with the aftermath of someone else's past.

Long shadows from Gracie's past threaten the peace that she and Shepard have established in the five years since their marriage. There was never a good time to explain to Bonnie about her birth father, Jake Hudson. But when his mother, Sylvania, pleads with Grace for mercy, she is forced to make the most difficult decision of her life.

Calvin Stewart is a hard-working, devoted father and husband...except for one thing. For many years he's concealed a secret that will shake not only the foundation of his life, but Nettie's and their children's. When a shadow from his past steps in—one full of evil intent and deadly consequence—everything Calvin values will be threatened....

For more information:
sites.google.com/site/sharonbernashsmith/
www.oaktara.com

A Sneak Peek

Old Sins, Long Shadows

"Cal," Nettie interrupted, "how can you even say the word *truth* to me?" Her entire body shook, every word a struggle to spit out. "All these years you've let me believe a lie bigger than life. Bigger than our life." She looked at the man standing before her. He was a stranger she didn't know—not her faithful, loving husband.

Cal was pierced to his soul, watching grief contort Nettie's face. He turned away, unable to bear the guilt.

"Look at me, Cal," she demanded. A sobbed ripped from her throat. "Look at me!"

He faced her. "Nettie?" he pleaded.

Despite the pain, her heart tore with empathy. But anger's pull won out, causing her hands to tremble. Both knees buckled, and she gripped a chair for support. "I cannot even begin to process this with you here. I...I...need you to leave."

Starting towards her, he stopped in midstride when her hand went up in protest. "Go to my father," she said, her voice now a wisp. "You tell him what you've done. If he can forgive you, I might be able to consider it."

Cal's face drained of color. He swayed with a deep sigh, looked in Nettie's direction, and left. The door latch caught with finality.

From a window, she watched him mount up and ride hard toward Papa's. Within minutes, he melted into the horizon. Gone.

Her head rested against the pane. It was cool but did nothing to clear her throbbing head.

They'd survived gut-wrenching life: Gracie's prodigal detour, the devastating burn, and Mama's death. But this? This intimate betrayal rocked the foundation of her soul....ached beyond the limits of experience and comprehension. It felt worse than death because she still loved him. Truth was: in all the world, he was the only man she'd be able to love.

But how could a liar ever be trusted again? He'd deceived them all, including his own children.

The children! Eva Jo would be bringing them home soon. The boys were too young to understand, but how would this kind of news affect her girls?

Nettie walked away from the window. No matter who gave them breath, she was their mother. Love and devotion left no doubts. She'd fed them, made their clothes, laughed when they laughed, and cried when they suffered.

Right there in the kitchen, the weight of grief dropped her to the floor. "Lord God, Help! Save me...save us! I've nowhere to go, but to You. Please." Her body shook with sobbing until her teeth rattled.

While still on the floor, she slowly became aware of an all-encompassing warmth. Her head lifted with the initial nuance. She wanted more. It brought comfort and contained power. Releasing herself to God, a sunrise of healing rose from within, bringing a remarkable peace. She couldn't move, only receive out of the abundance.

"Lord, thank You," she whispered out loud. "I believe I will survive, but what about my marriage?"

Then another thought struck her hard. *What if Cal and I aren't legally married?*...

⧉⧉

Old Sins, Long Shadows
boldly demonstrates the power of forgiveness
in restoring broken, contrite hearts.

About the Authors

Sharon Bernash Smith, Rosanne Croft, and Linda Reinhardt formed their creative team in 2002. Having written for church and Crisis Pregnancy Center newsletters, AMG Publishers' *Prayers for Troubled Times,* Multnomah Publishers' *What Would Jesus Do Today?*, they've also composed Christian plays, worked on children's Bible curriculum, and have been featured conference speakers.

Writing this book opened a treasure chest from heaven for each author, allowing friendships to be born in the sweetness of the Lord. It was Him that wove words together through the three authors, who each indeed found healing in different areas of their own lives. What an incredible experience!

Married and raising two sons in rural Washington state, SHARON BERNASH SMITH wore many hats, including preschool teacher, midwife's assistant in home birth deliveries, and a Pregnancy Resource Center volunteer. Now, as an author/speaker, Sharon desires to touch lives for Christ through the written word and her own life experiences. "REALITY FICTION™ is my commitment to direct my writing toward the human struggles we all face," Sharon says. "Because there are no 'pat' answers in life, you won't find them in my books. However, God is faithful, and all my works will reflect Him as just."

Sharon's Christmas story, "What Do You Say to a King?" was first published by Focus on the Family. She's also been published through AMG's *Prayers for Toubled Times* and is currently an editor for a Pregnancy Resource Center newsletter. She serves in women's ministry as a Bible study leader, and contributes to daily devotions and children's curriculum at her church in Washington. Sharon loves to watercolor and enjoys "landsailing" in the Columbia River Gorge near her home. Spending time with friends and family, especially her two granddaughters, fills her life with joy.

For more information:
sites.google.com/site/sharonbernashsmith/
www.oaktara.com

 ROSANNE CROFT has backpacked through Europe, worked on an archaeological dig, served bagels and lox at a local synagogue, hiked Wyoming's Wind River Range, and acquired a BA in European History from the University of Minnesota.

She is always happiest when surrounded by books, so work at a library for ten years was a gift to her. Her fourth-grade teacher is the one who inspired her to write. Rosanne's writing credits include contributions to *What Would Jesus Do Today? A One-Year Devotional*, by Helen Haidle (Gold 'n' Honey Books, Multnomah Publishers, Inc.). Rosanne lives near Salt Lake City, Utah, with her husband and daughter, a cat, a dog, and a hamster.

You may write the author at **rosannecroft@gmail.com.**

For more information:
www.oaktara.com

Raised in beautiful Washington State, since age eight, **LINDA REINHARDT** has always enjoyed writing a poem, song or story. She has contributed to church newsletters, a puppet ministry curriculum, and wrote/directed a Christmas play. Linda wrote a song performed at her wedding, which has now become a lullaby to her daughter before bed. On the top of the list of favorite past times is spending time with family, especially husband, Ben, and miracle daughter, Sarrah.

Linda is a stay-at-home mom. She is now working on several serial novels, including one about an issue she holds dear to her heart: to minister to post-abortive women.

She also enjoys sitting over a cup of coffee with a friend, sharing the details of their hearts. Involved in women's ministry, Linda is active in leading small group Bible studies: HEART (Healing and Encouragement for Abortion Related Trauma), Time to Heal, and Life Groups. An avid believer in the power of prayer, she has met for the last 5 years with a prayer group dedicated to supporting family and friends.

You may write the author at lindareinhardt@comcast.net

For more information:
www.oaktara.com

Printed in the United States
131911LV00004B/1/P

9 781602 900820